THE UNEXPECTED TALE
of the
BAD BROTHERS

For my little loves:
my nephew, Jojo, and my nieces, Ida and Flo.

First published in the UK in 2022 by Usborne Publishing Ltd., Usborne House,
83-85 Saffron Hill, London EC1N 8RT, England. usborne.com

Usborne Verlag, Usborne Publishing Ltd., Prüfeninger Str. 20, 93049 Regensburg,
Deutschland VK Nr. 17560

Text © Clare Povey, 2022.

Cover and inside illustrations, including map by Héloïse Mab ©
Usborne Publishing, 2022.

Typography by Thy Bui © Usborne Publishing, 2022.

A CIP catalogue record for this book is available from the British Library.

ISBN 9781474986502   05998/1   JFMA JJASOND/22

Printed and bound in Great Britain by CPI Group (UK) Ltd, Croydon, CR0 4YY.

MIX
Paper from
responsible sources
FSC® C171272

THE UNEXPECTED TALE
of the
BAD BROTHERS

CLARE POVEY

USBORNE

CONTENTS

1	The Good, the Bad and the Unexpected	13
2	The Reinvention of Olivier Odieux	22
3	Wicked by Name	32
4	A Night to Remember	40
5	An Unexpected Warning	50
6	An Unrestful Sunday	61
7	Meeting Mathilde	75
8	Daughter of the Enemy	84
9	Flames Along the Seine	89
10	A Story to Soothe	98
11	Printed Lies and Archive Spies	106
12	The Head Archivist	117
13	The Red Ink Society	125
14	The Return of Olivier Odieux	137
15	Paris in Protest	142
16	An Unexpected Guest	153
17	The Other Side of Madame Gentille	162
18	Escape From La Santé	176

19	Pandemonium in Paris	185
20	The Many Inventions of Theo Larouche	203
21	Under Cover of Darkness	217
22	In the Belly of the Beast	228
23	The Ancient Royal Decree	238
24	Secrets of the Throne	249
25	The Trouble with Invisible Ink	257
26	The Place Where Stories Breathe	268
27	Betrayal at the Bookshop	279
28	Into the Forest of Fontainebleau	286
29	At the Top of the Gorge	292
30	The Odieux Family Lie	299
31	Never Too Young to Make a Difference	310
32	A Little Help From Friends	317
33	Meet the Resistance	325
34	All the World Comes to Paris	332
35	The Face of Distraction	342
36	Two Against Two	346
37	The President's Speech	355
38	Bastien Rewrites the Ending	361
39	A Voyage to the Edge of the Sky	370
40	The First Edition of The Paris Patrol	378

Bastien's Glossary
Author's Note
Acknowledgements

« *Pour accomplir de grandes choses, il ne suffit pas d'agir,
il faut rêver ; il ne suffit pas de calculer, il faut croire.* »

"To accomplish great things, we must not only act,
but also dream; not only plan, but also believe."
Anatole France
(1844-1924)

BASTIEN'S MAP OF PARIS, 1923

Grand Palais

Eiffel Tower

Le Chat Curieux

Le Champ de Mars

Odieux family home

Le Malheur

Sacré-Coeur

Gare du Nord

Buttes Chaumont Park

Le Louvre

Notre-Dame

Mazarin Library

Gare de Lyon

s Catacombes

La Santé Prison

Forest of Fontainebleau

Orphanage

Le Parisien

MERCREDI, 7 MARS 1923

GUILTY, NOT GUILTY

After an intense two months of proceedings at the Palais de Justice, the trial of the Bad Brothers, Olivier and Xavier Odieux, came to an end yesterday afternoon with a shocking outcome, fitting of a novel itself.

The trial took longer than expected due to a change of judge in early February. The replacement judge, Pierre Niney, found Xavier Odieux guilty on multiple charges of kidnapping and imprisonment. A few of the kidnapped authors gave evidence about their time in the catacombs, where they were forced to write for days on end.

Xavier Odieux was also charged with the deaths of celebrated writers, Margot and Hugo Bonlivre, and the arson attack that killed them at the InterContinental Hôtel in Cannes. Their son, Bastien Bonlivre, and friends Theo Larouche and Sami Afriat, uncovered the catacomb cavern where the kidnapped writers were held against their will.

Yet, the news from the Palais de Justice was not all grim. Olivier Odieux was released on all charges due

Quotidien

PRIX:
0 FR.30

60, RUE LA FAYETTE

to insufficient evidence to place him in Cannes at the time of the fire and solid alibis for the dates the kidnappings took place. In fact, none of the kidnapped authors ever saw Olivier during their time in the catacombs. Leaving the courthouse yesterday afternoon, he spoke of his great relief.

"I find myself both saddened and relieved. I am heartbroken that my brother will spend the rest of his days in a prison cell. By trying to preserve our family legacy, he has disgraced himself beyond recognition.

"As for me, I am determined to show the citizens of this country that we, the Odieuxs, a long-standing and important family in France, are worthy of their respect. I shall take some personal time to process my brother's imprisonment, but I will be back to share my words once again with the world and to salvage my family's name."

Although it is not yet confirmed, sources tell this newspaper that Olivier has been offered a lucrative deal, from one of the city's largest publishers, to write his autobiography. ■

1
THE GOOD, THE BAD AND
THE UNEXPECTED

A month later…Saturday 7th April, 1923

Bastien kicked a ball of crumpled newspaper and screamed so loud that the gargoyles of Notre-Dame almost stirred from their stony slumber. A month had passed since the outcome of the Bad Brothers trial and life had returned to normal for the residents of Paris.

Bastien, however, knew that his life could never be "normal" again.

He slumped into the reading chair in the orphanage library room and stared out of the small window that looked over the Petit-Montrouge neighbourhood. His pale blue eyes were reflected in the glass, as well as the tired lines underneath them. When had he last slept through a whole night? Bastien couldn't remember. It was warm and cosy in the library and his eyelids flickered, but he pinched his cheeks. He had to stay awake for tonight.

The library had once been the private office of Xavier Odieux, the fiendish, fake director of the Orphanage for Gentils Garçons, who Bastien and the boys had been forced to call Monsieur Xavier. Now the library was their very own sanctuary and all traces of the former director were long gone.

Except, ever since the events of last winter, each time Bastien picked up a book, he found that words were no longer enough to save him. Instead, his mind wandered to Olivier Odieux, Xavier's older brother and disgraced author, who was truly responsible for the death of Bastien's parents.

Bastien looked over at the stack of newspapers in the corner of the library. From Paris to New York, the trial of the Bad Brothers had spread like a fever across the world. Bastien had followed the trial like a detective obsessively poring over clues and from January to March he'd snuck into Madame Gentille's office every evening to steal her newspapers. His blood had boiled as he'd read the lies of the Odieux brothers and he'd hoped, desperately so, that the judge would see through them as lies too.

But a month ago, when the verdict had been read outside the Palais de Justice, six words had struck fear into Bastien's heart as hard as a hammer hitting a nail.

Olivier Odieux is a free man.

Everything had started with Olivier. He had ordered his brother Xavier to start the fire that killed Margot and Hugo Bonlivre and to follow Bastien to the orphanage to steal his notebook. Last December, when Bastien had finally come face to face with Olivier, the awful author had ranted about a secret that Bastien's parents had discovered. It was a secret that Olivier was afraid would ruin him and one that he was certain was hidden in Bastien's red notebook.

But though Bastien had told the police all of this, he had no solid proof, and without it, Olivier had not been sent to jail. And despite the hours that Bastien and Theo, his best friend in the orphanage, had since spent looking through the notebook, he had found nothing. The notebook was empty. There was no hidden secret and Bastien didn't know what to do about it.

Xavier had been sentenced to life imprisonment,

but Olivier was a free man, and now Bastien's chance to uncover the secret and stay one step ahead weakened with every day that passed. Bastien knew that Olivier was not finished and that it was only a matter of time before he reappeared with another plan.

Bastien's eyes trailed over to the shelf at the top of the bookcase, where his notebook was safely stored in a hollowed-out book. The same question had haunted his dreams every night for the last month: would Olivier still come for him and his notebook?

And much as Bastien tried to bury the truth, to convince himself that Olivier would stay away, he knew that question could only ever have one answer.

Yes.

Olivier would come after him and not just for the secret. Bastien couldn't forget the burning hatred in Olivier's eyes when the police had arrested him. Olivier also wanted revenge for the destruction of his career and reputation.

This threat loomed over Bastien like a thundercloud and a new surge of anger pulsed through him. He jumped to his feet and shoved over the stack of newspapers. They spilled across the floor, and he tore into them, ripping the words into shreds. He didn't want to know how

Olivier planned to salvage the Odieux family name. Bastien simply wanted to wipe the man's poisonous name from his memory and feel free once more.

One of his silver cufflinks popped free of his shirt and rolled underneath the bookcase. Bastien groaned. If he lost a gift from Madame Gentille before the night had even started, he'd be in trouble.

Tonight, a party was being held for Bastien at his favourite bookshop, Le Chat Curieux, to celebrate the publication of his first book. Alice, his oldest friend, had been planning it for months, and she'd promised a night he would never forget. The thought both excited and scared Bastien.

Even though he was proud of the story he had created (which was all about the journey through the catacombs last winter), a party was the last thing on his mind. He couldn't stop thinking about Olivier. There were posters promoting Bastien's book party stuck on lamp posts all over the Left Bank. What if Olivier had seen them too?

A knock at the door interrupted his spiralling thoughts.

"Just a minute! Don't come in!" Bastien dropped to the floor and kicked shreds of newspaper out of his way.

He stretched under the bookcase, his arm searching for the missing cufflink.

The door swung open.

"*Euh*. What is happening? Are you looking for your next story idea down there?"

Bastien relaxed at the sound of Theo's voice. His best friend wouldn't tell him off for dirtying his suit. If anything, Theo had probably already cut a hole in the lining of his own jacket to hide his latest invention – an extendable arm, made of wooden bed slats and metal hooks, designed to pinch extra helpings of sweet treats from the top shelf in the kitchen.

Bastien's fingers brushed across something metallic, and he grabbed it, relieved to find the dusty cufflink.

"This popped off my shirt." He stood and brushed the dust from his suit jacket.

To his surprise, the rest of the boys were huddled behind Theo in the doorway. They all wore oversized dinner jackets that Madame Gentille had bought in bulk at the Saint-Ouen flea market. Clément's came with a lopsided bow tie, while Timothée's, Fred's and Felix's black trousers all ended above their ankles. Pascal and Robin wore matching blue ties, and a strand of Theo's curly hair stood up straight at the back. Like a stubborn old man, it simply refused to be combed.

"What about the snowstorm of ripped newspapers?" Pascal looked around the library.

"Leave him alone." Theo nudged Pascal in the ribs. "You can't make fun of an author on their party night."

Bastien attempted a smile. Everyone had done their best to cheer him up over the last month since the trial verdict. He was lucky to be surrounded by such kindness.

"This is for you." Theo handed him a brown envelope. "Consider it a book-birthday present."

"I drew most of it," squeaked Robin. "Madame Gentille reckons I could be an artist."

"Only took you fifty attempts," Felix sniggered. Fred clipped him on the ear and shot his twin a stormy look.

Bastien ripped open the envelope to find a handmade card. On the front was a group of boys; the one in the middle held a book to his chest. Inside were messages of congratulations, scrawled in loopy handwriting of various sizes.

"We hope you like it," Theo said.

"We know it's been a difficult month for you," Clément added, "and we wanted to put a smile on your face."

"Your stories saved us and now they'll save other people." Robin bounded forward and hugged him.

"And we're not afraid of Olivier," Timothée declared. "We've defeated him once and we'll do it again. Although I'd prefer to avoid strenuous physical activity if possible."

"I told you *not* to use the O-word tonight!" Theo's nostrils flared at Timothée.

Bastien wanted to thank them, but the words were stuck somewhere between his heart and his mouth, and so instead the boys all bundled on top of him, smothering him in one giant hug. Bastien felt better as they broke apart, as though each boy had shared a little bit of their strength with him.

He clapped his hands. "I will push him out of my mind for tonight... Let's get to this party then, shall we?"

The boys whistled and stamped their feet.

"*Dépêchez-vous!*" Madame Gentille shouted from downstairs. "You'd better not be creasing your outfits!"

Before Bastien could protest, Theo grabbed his arms and Clément swiped his feet out from under him. The boys swung him up into the air and carried him through the library door and down the east wing.

"Make way for the storyteller of the decade!" Theo shouted.

And for the first time in almost a month, as he bumped down the stairs on the shoulders of his friends, Bastien didn't have to force a smile.

It simply arrived without warning, pushed away his last lingering thought of Olivier Odieux, and lit up his entire body.

2
THE REINVENTION OF OLIVIER ODIEUX

In the suburb of Boulogne-Billancourt, on the western edge of Paris, Olivier Odieux stood on the balcony of his grandfather's house and looked out at the city that he would never leave. He was so glad to be free.

The evening was still light, and it afforded Olivier a view worthy of a king. Across the river, preparations for the Exposition Universelle were well under way on the Champ de Mars. The world fair, which the city was to host in just over a week, would bring thousands of visitors to Paris. The fair would celebrate the technological and creative achievements of the last few years, but also look forward to the future, highlighting the brilliant inventions and influential figures that would change the world for the better.

It was the perfect backdrop for the next chapter of Olivier's plan.

Olivier had spent many weeks in a holding cell at the Palais de Justice. The cell was windowless and the only sound had come from Xavier, his younger brother, talking to him from the other side of the crumbling limestone wall. Sometimes Olivier imagined how Xavier felt, holed up in La Santé prison all alone, and it made him feel something close to guilt. Almost.

Nevertheless, the sacrifice was necessary. Olivier wouldn't leave his brother to rot in a cell. Xavier would soon be free if everything he'd plotted went according to plan.

The sharp, shrill sound of the doorbell pulled Olivier back inside. As he closed the stained-glass balcony doors behind him, the rusted, ornate handle fell apart in his hands.

This house was the Odieux family home, but it had sat empty since his grandfather, Victor Odieux, an influential French politician, had passed away over thirty years ago. Although Olivier felt a pang of sorrow whenever he thought of his own house, which had burned to the ground last December, he still felt protected in this house that had sheltered generations of Odieuxs.

Still, there was much to fix. The house was dingy, a place of shadows and dust, and Olivier dreamed of restoring it to its former glory. To do that, he needed money. When he thought of money and power, and how he was now without either, his thoughts always led back to Bastien Bonlivre, the boy who had led to his downfall.

Olivier delighted in thinking of how he would take his revenge – he'd even written a note to the boy, warning him that he would pay for uncovering the writers' kidnapping ring and exposing Olivier's books as fakes. He had lost the note in amongst the chaos of his prison-release day, but no matter – Olivier had already sent another warning to the orphanage, just for Bastien. When it came to revenge and menace, he was not short of ideas.

Strangely, even though the boy still possessed the notebook and its secret, months had gone by in silence. Maybe Bastien just wasn't as cunning as his parents. Maybe the secret would stay exactly that: a secret. As the days passed and Olivier sorted through his grandfather's old belongings, a new plan stitched itself together in front of his eyes like the Bayeux Tapestry.

Olivier would reinvent himself. The money that he had made from his bestselling books had been given to the kidnapping victims as compensation. The fame that he had once enjoyed was now a different kind, where people pointed and whispered under their breath.

How could Olivier make people admire him again? How could he make the entire country hang onto his every word and grant him the respect, power and wealth he so rightfully deserved?

Currently, the answer to that question was ringing his doorbell.

"*J'arrive!*" Olivier walked down the staircase, passing the Odieux family portraits. He checked his reflection in the hallway floor-length mirror. His skin was paler than ever, but he had found an old red suit in his grandfather's wardrobe. Red suited him; it brought out the rage in his eyes.

Olivier hurried down the corridor, which was lined with suits of silver armour standing like sentries, and turned the key in the door. Waiting on his doorstep was a tall man with a full head of dark hair that burst from his middle parting, making him look as though he was in a constant state of being windswept.

"Monsieur Fitzmagnat." Olivier smiled so hard it hurt. "I am glad you came."

"Call me Charles." The man peeled off white leather gloves to reveal a gold watch on each wrist. "Besides, how could I refuse such an invite? You're the name on everyone's lips."

Olivier rolled his eyes as though he hated attention. "You flatter me. Shall I show you to the dining room?"

"Lead the way."

Olivier took them through a set of double doors. The dining room walls were gold and royal blue, and the floor was chequered with black and white marble, like one big chessboard. A long mahogany table reached from the door all the way to the cracked floor-length windows, which looked out onto an overgrown garden.

"You'll excuse the mess. I haven't quite redecorated. This used to be my grandfather's house."

Charles sat down in a wooden chair. "You've only been a free man for a month. I wouldn't expect you to spend your days scrubbing the toilet, even for me." His laugh was the sort that demanded you laughed with him; Olivier obliged.

Charles Fitzmagnat was one of the wealthiest men in France and had made his fortune in the newspaper business. His newest paper, *La Seule Voix*, promised to be *the only voice worth listening to in the country.*

"Plus," Charles added, "we are bound by our family ties. I do believe your grandfather, Victor Odieux, was a good friend of my own, Guillaume Fitzmagnat. They were both members of the same mysterious society, *non*? I always wish I'd asked my grandfather more questions about it. He said that Victor held as many secrets as he did ambitions."

Olivier gritted his teeth. What secrets did Charles Fitzmagnat mean? He couldn't know about the Odieux family secret – the very same one that the Bonlivres had uncovered – could he?

Olivier opened the lid of the globe drinks cabinet and removed a crystal decanter. It was filled with a dark liquid that smelled of spice and burnt sugar. "Their friendship convinced me to invite you tonight. I am reaching out to family friends. It is more important than ever to surround myself with people I can trust and do business with."

"Indeed. I was sorry to hear about Xavier. But I am always in the mood to talk business."

"You and I are alike." Olivier ignored the mention of his brother. "We both understand the importance

of words. How they can carry fear and demand power."
He filled their glasses and the crystal decanter clunked
against the table, disturbing the dusty surface.

Charles sat forward with clasped hands. "Tell me
what you want."

Olivier sat down and swirled his drink. "I need you
and your newspaper to reinvent me."

"To *reinvent* you?"

"I need a fresh start," Olivier explained. "I want to
shake off the crimes of my brother and salvage the
Odieux name. I can't let those mistakes derail my life
plan. I want to show this country that I am a powerful
man with a great ambition." He took a sip of his drink,
almost believing the words coming out of his own
mouth.

Charles, however, stayed silent. His expression was
empty; not even an eyebrow twitch betrayed his
thoughts.

"Now," Olivier continued, "I imagine you're
wondering what exactly my ambition is. The time I
spent in that cell taught me that life is short and that
I must focus on my lifelong dream. I see now that I was
wasting my time and talent with books. I want to
become the strong and firm leader that our citizens

deserve. I want to rule over this country like our great kings once did."

Charles slapped his hand down on the table. Was he intrigued or angry? Olivier wasn't sure. Either way, he had the tycoon's attention.

"Our society needs saving. There are people who believe that they can *do* and *be* anything they want," Olivier snarled. "We have lost sight of our traditions and forgotten that everyone has a place in society. President Millefois only does what his staff whisper to him behind closed doors. He is not fit to lead our country."

There was a moment of silence that stretched out before Olivier like an endless horizon. He held his tongue and maintained eye contact.

"What you're proposing is no small feat," Charles finally said. "It will take a lot of work to paint you as a hero. The crimes you were accused of were horrific."

"I understand—"

Charles held up his hand and silenced Olivier. "But you were found to be an innocent man, so all hope is not yet lost. Returning to Paris after my time in Rome has certainly been eye-opening. This city has lost its moral compass. It is overrun with people who don't belong here, yet we welcome them with open arms." He clenched his glass so hard it looked close to shattering. "However, I'm afraid I'm not in the business of working for nothing in return."

Olivier felt his strength returning and he welcomed it like the first drop of rain after a drought. There'd been nights in his prison cell when he'd wondered if he was truly capable of everything he believed. But tonight, Charles's words had given him belief.

"I wouldn't insult you by asking you to help for free. Your recent publication, *La Seule Voix*, thrives on scandals, does it not?"

Charles grinned, his shining white teeth large like a lion's. "Scandal sells. I have made my fortune by telling the stories other people were too afraid to touch. *La Seule Voix* is guided by the same principles. We are the *only* voice that dares to speak the truth."

"What if I could provide your newspaper with exclusive stories? The type of stories that will scare and unnerve and *sell*? If you print them, they will convince the citizens that I am the new leader they so desperately need."

"And how would you go about getting these stories, exactly?"

"I have a skill for creating chaos," Olivier replied calmly. "All I ask is for your support and money to start our new venture. You won't regret it."

Charles tapped his fingers against the table, his lips moving up and down as though in conversation with himself. The grandfather clock struck eight o'clock in the hallway.

"Your offer did surprise me." Charles stood and walked towards Olivier, his leather brogues clacking on the floor. "But it is one I can't pass up. Perhaps fate has brought me here. I imagine our grandfathers would be pleased at the thought of us working together to restore control over this country. You have my word, as well as any financial support you may need."

Olivier wanted to fling open the balcony doors and scream with delight until the ghost of his grandfather heard him in Père Lachaise cemetery. Instead, he settled for a more reserved celebration. "*Merci*. A toast to our new partnership."

Olivier raised his glass and tightened his grip around it.

He might as well have been holding the entire world in his very hands.

WICKED BY NAME

Standing on the platform of the Odéon station, Mathilde Méchante waited for the train with clenched fists. It was busy but the space around her was empty, as though other Parisians recognized that this girl was different and it would be better for them to keep their distance. Mathilde was built of fire and fierceness: each one of her fourteen years, every year more difficult than the last, had built her so.

She tapped her foot impatiently until the train announced its arrival with a screech like a banshee. The doors opened and Mathilde slipped into the busy carriage.

It was an early April evening and despite the mild

spring sunshine outside, the carriage was oppressively hot. Standing on a crowded train was enough to make anyone bad-tempered, but Mathilde was already angrier than most. Right now, as she watched a small baby screaming at the top of its lungs from the arms of a woman, she so desperately wanted to scream back. How could a small thing make such an awful noise? The sound was as bearable as sharp fingernails on a chalkboard.

"*Désolée*." The woman met Mathilde's angry gaze. "He's teething."

Mathilde shrugged.

The train slowed down as it turned the narrow bend, already fast approaching the Saint-Michel station. Mathilde stood, pulled up her baggy black trousers and made her way to the carriage doors.

"Your mother should've taught you some manners," the woman tutted.

Mathilde spun around, her copper hair swishing in the faces of other passengers. "Don't you dare talk about Maman, or it will be the last thing you do."

The woman clutched her baby even tighter. The doors juddered open, and Mathilde ran from the train. Arriving at surface level, she turned the street corner and moved through the crowd of market sellers dragging their now-empty carts back home.

Home. It had been a long time since she had felt truly at home. And the person to blame for that was Olivier Odieux.

Mathilde checked her watch. It was just gone eight o'clock. She had time to stake out Le Chat Curieux before everyone arrived. Before Bastien Bonlivre arrived.

Mathilde knew all about Bastien and how he and his friends had rescued the kidnapped writers from the cavern in the catacombs last winter. Not much impressed her, but she was curious about Bastien, like a moth drawn to a flickering flame. And that was why she had gone through so much just to get here.

Mathilde had spent the last six months living in a *maison de correction*, a reformatory school for girls on the outskirts of Paris. Police officers had caught Mathilde stealing a bag of baguettes in October. If they had cared to ask, she would have explained that they were for her unwell maman, who was unable to work and put food on the table. But they had not asked and so Mathilde was sent to the school and poor Maman to Sainte-Anne, a psychiatric hospital in the city.

Being apart from Maman was misery. The reformatory school was strict, and the only way Mathilde could keep her sadness at arm's length was by seeking escape in the school's dusty library. She had never been a great reader but now books gave her a reason to smile again.

One evening, she came across a dusty shelf at the back of the library. Mathilde picked up a book covered in cobwebs and the name on the front hit her like the cold water she washed with each morning.

A long time ago, Maman had told her about a man called Olivier Odieux and how he had betrayed her. In the school library, she now discovered a shelf full of books written by the same man. Curious, Mathilde started to read and as she devoured tales of cruel kings and crumbling cities under her blanket at night, snippets of what Maman had told her returned: about how the apparently noble Odieux family had once been as powerful as they were dangerous and how they had welcomed Maman like one of their own. Until Olivier stole everything that she had ever earned.

After discovering the library books, Mathilde secretly read the daily papers in the school staffroom, hoping that there would be news, a clue, as to what

Olivier Odieux was doing now and where he lived. And when last December had arrived, the universe finally served up an offering.

Mathilde read every single article about the trial of the Bad Brothers. The more she learned about Olivier, the fiercer her anger swirled inside, until one day she knew what she had to do. Mathilde needed to confront Olivier and reclaim the debt he owed Maman.

On an early March morning, when the wind had clawed at her window, Mathilde learned the news that Olivier was not guilty and that he would soon be free – which meant her time had come. With a spring in her step and a fire in her stomach, she'd climbed down from her window, scaled the gates and escaped into the city. Being on the run demanded smarts and slyness. The *maison de correction* alerted the police about Mathilde's disappearance and so she always remained moving, as though scared of what might happen if she stood still for too long.

When the day of Olivier's release arrived, Mathilde had stood outside the Palais de Justice, invisible in a crowd of journalists, and watched as the man she had spent months obsessing over walked out of the doors.

The crowd had moved with Olivier, but Mathilde's

eyes were fixed on what had fallen out of his pocket as he'd been rushed towards a waiting automobile. She'd crept forward, climbing the stairs two at a time, and bent down to retrieve a folded piece of paper. On the front was the name *Bastien Bonlivre* scrawled in red ink.

For once, luck was on Mathilde's side. She'd also read about Bastien in the papers; the boy who had almost defeated Olivier Odieux. If anyone could help her, it was Bastien – and now she had a way in. She would deliver this note, tell Bastien how Olivier had wronged her too, and her plan would fall into place. And thanks to the posters dotted around the Left Bank, advertising an exciting book from a new author, she knew exactly where and when to find him.

The winding streets peeled away slowly and the book-built archway of Le Chat Curieux appeared. Mathilde glanced inside the bookshop as she passed. No sign of Bastien just yet. She would wait.

She leaned against a lamp post on the other side of the street. A woman with a short red bob walked past and Mathilde felt a pang in her chest for Maman. The last six months had gone as slowly as a watched clock-hand without her. Mathilde's latest letter to Maman, addressed to the hospital, had gone unanswered.

Lucienne Méchante had been one of France's finest ballerinas, performing all around the world, but that life was another world away now.

Once Mathilde had the means for them to live a new and better life, she would free Maman from the hospital and they could continue their lives together, somewhere far away from Paris. This city burped up bad memories at every corner and they had always talked about living near the sea one day.

Excitable voices carried through the air and pulled Mathilde from her daydreams of sandy beaches. She stood on the tips of her ballet slippers to stay hidden behind the lamp post.

"Are you excited, Bastien?"

Mathilde slowly turned towards the bookshop, keeping her eyes on the group of boys now huddled outside. Her eyes scanned each one of their faces until she found Bastien: the freckle-faced boy with a brown satchel slung over his shoulder. He looked exactly like the grainy newspaper photo she had seen of him along with his friends Theo and Sami, the saviours of the catacomb writers.

A rare smile seeped from Mathilde's lips as she watched Bastien enter the bookshop. The moment had come to start a new chapter with Maman, and she simply could not fail.

The rest of her life depended on it.

4
A NIGHT TO REMEMBER

S tanding in front of Le Chat Curieux, Bastien breathed
in the promise of the night. Emerald-green ivy curled
through the bookshop sign above and the glow from the
streetlights bounced off the tall glass windows.

"Look at that!" Theo pointed to a poster hanging
from the book-built arch of the door.

CELEBRATE THE PUBLICATION OF
THE UNEXPECTED JOURNEY
by BASTIEN BONLIVRE

FEATURING:
A **LIVE READING** FROM THE AUTHOR
& A **PASTRY BUFFET**

"Pastry buffet?" Bastien's belly rumbled. "I could get used to this!"

They pressed their noses up to the window to stare at the glittering jewels on display behind the glass. The glittering jewels were, in fact, copies of Bastien's book. The purple cover had his name and the book title in gold lettering at the very top and a group of brightly illustrated children in the centre.

"There it is," Bastien said. "*Mon livre*."

It was a bizarre sensation that other people would soon read his words. *The Unexpected Journey* was the story of everything that had happened to him and his friends last winter. He'd written the story in snatched moments and now it was a real book that he could take back to the library and place on the shelf next to his parents' books. It was a strange but stupendous feeling that would take him a while to get used to.

"I wish Sami was here tonight," Bastien said, knowing Theo felt exactly the same. Their journey through the tunnels of Paris had glued the three boys together just like the bindings of a book, and not even an ocean of water could now break such a bond. Sami was back home with his family in Morocco, but they all missed him terribly.

"That just means we can have another celebration when we see him next." Theo hugged Bastien. "*Mebruk!*"

"I couldn't have done it without you."

A blast of noise washed over them both as the door opened.

"You really couldn't have," Theo laughed, his light green eyes full of excitement. "Come on, Bastien 'Born Storyteller' Bonlivre. Let's go before Pascal single-handedly eats the entire buffet!"

Stepping through the archway of Le Chat Curieux, any nerves Bastien felt instantly fell away. He looked around the bustling bookshop and grinned from ear to ear. A huge, colourful banner hung from the rafters and swirls of bright paper sprouted from every bookcase.

"Not bad." Theo whistled. "Not that I'd expect any less, but Alice has truly outdone herself tonight. Can you see her?"

Bastien looked around and spotted Alice standing at the bottom of the staircase. She wore a sky-blue blouse, and trousers as wide as a ship's sail, while under her arm was a clipboard. Her blonde hair was scooped back, wisps falling forward as she barked orders at Charlotte and Jules, her parents and owners of Le Chat Curieux bookshop. Alice was the same age as Bastien, born only a month before him, but he often felt as though she was the most grown-up twelve-year-old he'd ever met.

Charlotte and Jules held several trays of pastries and Bastien instinctively licked his lips. If being a writer meant that he could eat cake for the rest of his life, he would write each new book as quickly as his fingers would allow.

"Let's go and save them." Bastien waved in Alice's direction.

"It's the star of the evening and his entourage!" She squished them both in a hug. "Do you like it? Papa let me miss a full day of home-school lessons just so I could make it perfect. I've been planning this since Gaston LeGrand agreed to publish your book."

Bastien thought back to when he'd first met LeGrand, the owner of one of the city's most successful publishers, right here in the bookshop. "All of this is more than I ever imagined. *Merci*."

"It's not every day that my best friend writes a book." Alice grabbed a glass of fizzy strawberry water from a waiter's tray.

"*Hum*," Theo coughed.

Alice rolled her eyes. "*One* of my best friends. Anyway, is Felix with you? He was bringing fireworks."

43

"Felix has fireworks?" Bastien didn't know whether to laugh or plan an immediate evacuation of the bookshop. "What did he tell you?"

"He said he knew a man who sold them outside the Saint-Lazare station for cheap." She frowned. "The evening finale will be ruined without them!"

Laughter spilled from Bastien's mouth as he pictured Felix haggling with a dodgy fireworks dealer triple his size. "He's with Pascal and Timothée over by the door."

"With or without fireworks, you have organized the most incredible party," Theo added.

Alice's frown disappeared, replaced with a wicked grin. "I know." She vanished into the crowd and pulled Theo with her.

"Bastien!" Charlotte wiped icing sugar from her face and waved him over. Walking over to the countertop, Bastien admired the assortment of sticky, sweet treats that covered every inch of its surface.

"*Félicitations!*" Jules grinned. "I'll be back in a minute. These tarts won't bake themselves!"

Bastien bit into a pistachio macaron, the sugary, nutty cream so rich it made his toes curl in delight. "This is so incredible."

Charlotte planted a kiss on his cheek. "I'm glad you're

happy, *mon petit chou*. Alice had me baking throughout the night! Thankfully, we hired Georges last week. He was writing in the café and we got talking. I honestly don't think we would've managed without him."

Bastien followed her gaze to a young man navigating his way through the crowd while holding a stack of books.

"I told you to stop working," Charlotte called.

Georges put down the book stack and smiled; a patchy, hazelnut beard covered half of his face. "I'm following orders from your daughter and she scares me more than you."

Bastien couldn't contain his snorting laugh.

"I'm sorry for creating a monster," Charlotte replied. "A lovely monster, all the same. Georges, meet Bastien."

"It's great to meet you." Georges enthusiastically shook his hand.

"Likewise." Bastien smiled. "Are you enjoying your new job?"

"*Oui.* My father has been telling me to get a job since I was just a boy. Now, at the age of eighteen, I've finally made him proud!" Georges stroked his beard. "Apparently I have to earn my place in the family business."

"What does your father do?"

"Oh, this and that…" Georges trailed off. "But Alice doesn't stop talking about you. Well done on your book! What writing! I bet you wish your parents were here tonight."

Bastien winced at the mention of his parents. There were times when thinking of his mother and father brought blue skies and sunshine. Other times, a dense black cloud descended. He could never predict his feelings, but Georges was still a stranger and hearing him talk about his parents didn't feel right.

"*Désolé*." Georges smacked his forehead. "My father always says I should think before I speak. Then think again and keep my mouth shut."

Bastien attempted a forgiving smile, but his eyes began to water.

"Come now. This is your evening." Charlotte wiped under his eyes with her flour-dusted sleeve as Georges bowed and disappeared into the bookshop-café corridor. "I'm sorry about that."

"I'm okay. He didn't mean to upset me." Bastien sniffed. "But he's right. I would give anything for them to be here tonight. If only I could…"

Charlotte swooped him into a hug and the emotions that had risen inside him climbed even higher.

"Whenever I feel sad, I always remember what your mother used to say," Charlotte whispered, her breath tickling his ear. "She'd open her arms and say, 'Let me share the weight of your tears.' I'd usually end up soaking her blouse, but she never complained. Not once. Now it's my turn to share yours."

"*Merci* for sharing that with me." Bastien wiped his face, picturing his mother so clearly. Her words had always healed him like his own personal medicine and, through Charlotte, his mother's wise advice still lived on.

"Watch out." Charlotte released Bastien from her embrace. "The man with the largest hat collection in Paris is coming for you."

"Is that the star of the hour?" LeGrand's booming voice echoed. The tall publisher strode through the crowd, dressed in his uniform black suit and trilby hat.

"*Bonsoir.*" Bastien scratched the back of his neck where the frayed collar of his jacket itched. "I don't think I'm a star just yet."

LeGrand chuckled. "Too modest for your own good. Now I must steal you away. It's time for a story!"

Bastien turned the pages of his book, his touch as careful as though he held a Fabergé egg, remembering what his parents had told him about seeing their books for the first time.

"It's like holding a piece of your heart and head in your very hands," his mother had said.

"No matter what happens, a part of you will always exist in your book," his father had added.

Bastien exhaled and looked at the crowd. Jules had constructed a makeshift stage from a wooden pallet. Everyone had stopped what they were doing and was looking his way. Conversation had paused; Alice had somehow managed to get Fred and Felix to shut up.

Everyone was ready to listen to Bastien and the pressure of it all pushed on his throat. This wasn't like storytelling evenings in the dormitory with the rest of the boys. Standing before all of the guests, including other writers, journalists and friends of the bookshop, panic crept in. The illogical side of Bastien's brain held his thoughts hostage. What if he forgot how to read in this very moment? What if he stumbled over his own words and dropped the book on his big toe?

Overwhelmed, he closed his eyes and steadied himself, muttering one of his mother's mantras under his breath. *"To speak a silly thought out loud is to let it lose its power."*

He could do this. This was his night. Bastien opened his eyes and smiled at the crowd. "Let's begin."

Then, just like fingertips pinching out a candle flame, the bookshop plunged into complete darkness.

5
AN UNEXPECTED WARNING

Excitable voices quickly turned to panic. The bookshop was almost as dark and heavy as the catacombs and it unnerved Bastien; he could barely see his own hand in front of his face, like a blindfold had been tied around his eyes.

"No need to worry," Jules shouted. "It's probably the new generator. I'll go and look." His footsteps slapped on the stairs leading to their apartment above.

"Hold tight, Bastien," LeGrand called. "The drama only makes the wait more exciting!"

Careless chatter soon floated through the crowd, but Bastien was still on edge. The wooden pallet he stood on now felt like a towering cliff. He had no reason to be afraid here at Le Chat Curieux, among friends, but Bastien knew how evil could seep through walls and unlock doors and his mind unravelled again.

Was this Olivier's doing? He was a free man and flyers promoting Bastien's book party had been plastered all over the Left Bank. Maybe Olivier had cut the power. What if he was in the bookshop now? Would he kidnap Bastien and hold him hostage until he handed over his notebook?

Fear trickled down his face in cold beads of sweat. He wanted to move from the stage, but couldn't be certain where he was placing his feet.

Then something, or someone, brushed against the back of his jacket.

"Is that you, Theo?" No response came, but someone was definitely on the stage with him. He sensed the lightest of footsteps.

"Who's there?"

From out of the darkness, a whisper tickled his skin.

"I have something for you."

Bastien didn't recognize the voice. It was low and rough, like gravel on an unfamiliar road.

"W-who are you?"

"Someone who could be a friend or a foe. I have a note for you. It's from Olivier."

Bastien's heart plunged to the bottom of his stomach as the unknown voice confirmed his fear. Olivier's name was always enough to summon a cold dread, the kind that froze his tongue and chilled his brain. But as quickly as it had arrived, the dread melted away, and in its place came a hot anger. This was his evening and he wasn't going to let Olivier win. Not tonight. Not ever.

"Who are you?" he shouted. "Are you working for Olivier? What do you want?"

Below him, footsteps scuffled at the base of the stage. "Bastien?" Theo called. "What's going on?"

"*Aïe!*" Timothée cried. "Watch where you're going."

There was a crackling sound and the bookshop lights flickered back on.

Bastien glanced around the bookshop, scanning the guests. His eyes landed upon a girl with long, copper hair, dashing out of the door. Bastien hadn't seen her in the bookshop until now. Instinct told him to follow her.

"What just happened?" Alice asked.

"Someone was here." Bastien ran to the door and stumbled out onto the street. What had exactly happened? Who was this girl? She'd said she could be *a friend or a foe*. What did that mean?

He looked down the street and saw a cloud of copper hair running past the fountain towards the river. The girl was quick, but Bastien sprinted towards her, ignoring the shouts of Alice and Theo, who had followed him out of the bookshop.

"Did Olivier send you?" The girl could surely hear him, despite the horns of the river boats. She moved fast and Bastien tried to use his words like arrows to slow her down. "Why would you work for such an evil man? Is your heart as cold as his?" He ran to the end of the street, panting, and turned the corner after her. He was almost there; a few more metres and he would be right alongside her. From here, he saw the ballet slippers on her feet.

"What do you want?" Bastien cried.

The girl skidded to a halt. She half-turned, as though unsure. Then she spoke. "Meet me tomorrow. The grotto at Buttes Chaumont Park. Two o'clock. I'll explain everything."

"*Attends!*" Bastien's lungs burned. "What do you mean?"

But it was too late, for the girl had already disappeared

into the evening crowds. There was no way he would be able to find her now. She was gone.

His lungs and legs cursing him, Bastien collapsed onto the ground. He slumped against a streetlamp, oblivious to the strange looks from passers-by as he caught his breath.

"Why did you just run away as though you'd seen a ghost?" Alice appeared, doubling over next to him.

"I can't believe you've just made me run," Theo wheezed. His brown curls were stuck to his forehead.

"It was a girl," Bastien replied. He ripped off his jacket to cool down and his hand brushed over something crinkled in his top pocket. The note! He fished out the paper, red ink bleeding through its surface.

"She gave me this from Olivier." With shaking hands and a roaring in his ears, Bastien read the note.

Bastien,
I am a free man. I'm sure you will read about how my brother Xavier has been found guilty of the crimes you uncovered.

I have you to thank for helping me realize that I must no longer delay my true purpose in life. Stories have always been in my blood, but I am no longer satisfied with fiction. I want to make my stories a reality.

I do not want to write about kings when I have always dreamed of being one: a ruler with absolute power to control everything and everyone. It is time for me to use, finally, my family's past in order to become the future of this country. It is time to do things the proper way.

You and your friends may have got the better of me last winter, but I will be stronger this time. You haven't even uncovered the secret in the notebook, have you? Clearly, you do not possess your father's intellect nor the shrewdness of your mother. The only way you can stop me now is luck and yours has already all dried up.

There is nothing you can do this time, Bastien. This is bigger than anything your tiny childlike brain could grasp.

I shall enjoy my new-found freedom, but I'll be seeing you. Enjoy what little of your sad, pathetic life you have left.

For the end is coming.

At the bottom of the note was a familiar symbol, of a pen dipped in a red inkpot. An eerie silence passed over the three friends as the note's meaning sank in.

"He'll never leave me alone." Bastien drew a sharp breath and looked up at Theo and Alice, his best friends' expressions just as lost as his own. "He's still scheming now, wanting the power to become king! He is relentless."

"We need to tell the police." Alice crossed her arms. "This note is a threat."

Bastien shoved the note back into his pocket. "We can't do that."

Alice frowned. "Why?"

"You know as well as I do how much Olivier has got away with," he replied. "He pinned his crimes on Xavier. He's above the law."

Suspicion spread like a rash over Alice's face. "Maman and Papa talk about the trial when they think I'm asleep. Maman said that Pierre Niney, the judge who came in halfway through the trial, is a corrupt and greedy man. He might've accepted a bribe."

"Olivier doesn't have the money to bribe people. Not any more." Theo sat down next to Bastien on the pavement.

Had Olivier learned nothing from his time on trial? Everything they had been through felt like it was about to start over and Bastien couldn't let that happen. He couldn't let Olivier worm his way back into the spotlight or his own life. It was too dangerous.

"Has Louis replied to your last letter?" Theo asked.

Bastien shook his head as his thoughts turned to the oldest Odieux brother, who had helped him get his notebook back before leaving the city. The day after the trial verdict, Bastien had written a letter to Louis at his new address in London, full of questions. How had Olivier gone free, but Xavier sent to jail? And would Louis ever come back to Paris?

"I'm going to write to him again tonight," Bastien said. "This is urgent. He needs to know what's going on."

A sentence from Olivier's note replayed in his mind: *It is time for me to delve back into my family's past in order to become the future of this country.*

"What is it?" Alice nudged him. "What are you thinking?"

"If Olivier's family past is the key to his new plan, maybe Louis can help us? He's the only other Odieux who could give us information."

Bastien looked back towards the bookshop and noticed a tall figure lingering at the threshold. Was Jules looking for them?

Theo noticed his gaze and pulled him up onto his feet. "We don't have to go back if you don't want to."

"I don't want Olivier to ruin this night." Bastien attempted a smile. "Especially when there are still pastries to eat."

"But what about this girl?" Alice slipped her arm through his as the three friends walked back towards Le Chat Curieux. "Did she say anything else?"

"She told me to meet her tomorrow in the grotto at Buttes Chaumont Park. She said she will explain everything."

"Do you think she's working for him?" Alice asked. "It's strange. Why would she just give you the note and nothing else?"

Bastien shrugged. *"Je ne sais pas."*

Alice shook her head and her hair spilled from its bun. "You can't seriously be thinking about meeting a strange girl who might be working for Olivier in a dark and dingy grotto?"

"She's got a point. It doesn't seem very safe," Theo added.

"But she had ballet slippers on her feet! She wasn't exactly spy material," Bastien insisted. "I have to find out what's going on. I thought all of this was behind us.

If it is a trap, we will be prepared. The girl said she could be a friend or a foe. What if she is a friend? It's a chance worth taking because if Olivier's coming after me again, I'll need all the help I can get."

Although the Parisian evening was loud and full of colour, they fell silent. The noise of their own thoughts felt louder than any chatter or car horn. A shout, coming from the direction of the bookshop, pulled them back out of their heads.

"We'll need to be smart about it," Theo finally spoke. "And we'll need backup in case the grotto is a trap."

Alice sighed. "You two always seem to need me to save you, anyway."

Bastien's heart swelled, full of gratitude and love for his friends. After everything that they had been through together, Theo and Alice were still ready to walk head first into the unknown. With them by his side, and the support from the rest of the boys, he never felt lonely. Even with Olivier's threat and the mystery of the copper-haired girl, the impossible felt achievable if they tackled it together.

"Everything okay?" Jules called out as they reached the bookshop. "I fixed the lights, but LeGrand said you'd ran outside."

"Just a bit of stage fright," Bastien replied. He didn't want to tell Jules, Charlotte or any of the other adults about the girl and the note just yet, at least not until he had figured out what to do next.

"Even the greats struggle with that." Jules smiled.

Arm in arm, and ready to take on the world, Bastien and his two best friends headed back into Le Chat Curieux.

They would do their best to forget everything and celebrate, if only for one night.

But tomorrow they would discover who the copper-haired girl really was, what she wanted, and create a plan of their own.

6

AN UNRESTFUL SUNDAY

The next morning, Bastien woke with a stomach full of courage. He hadn't required much of it while Olivier and Xavier had been locked away in their cells during the Bad Brothers trial, but now he needed it by the bucketful. Bastien had forgotten how courage made his insides feel like they were always dancing and never resting.

The rest of the book party at Le Chat Curieux had passed by in a subdued manner. Bastien had read the first chapter of his book to much applause, beaten Fred in a profiterole-eating contest and talked some more with Georges. The new bookseller was desperately trying to be nice after his earlier foot-in-mouth moment, yet he still seemed to dodge most of Bastien's questions about what he did outside of the bookshop.

To end the night, Bastien had answered questions from journalists, but although his lips had moved to form words, his mind had been elsewhere. His thoughts were only of Olivier and his plans, and the mysterious girl.

"Venez manger!" Madame Gentille's breakfast call lifted the boys from their beds. Bastien slowly pulled on his clothes, tangling his legs in cotton shorts. He'd spent the night in a state of half-sleep and yawns escaped from his mouth as often as breaths.

After finishing his letter to Louis, Bastien gathered the others in the dormitory and told them all about the strange girl and the note from Olivier. Last winter, when Bastien and Theo had been trapped at Olivier's house, they had only survived thanks to Alice and the rest of the boys showing up just in time.

Bastien now knew they didn't have to do everything alone. There was strength in numbers, especially when their friends were some of the most loyal and kind boys in France.

"And you're planning on meeting the girl this afternoon?" Felix asked. "In some sort of cave at the park?"

Bastien nodded. "The grotto at Buttes Chaumont. I can't ignore the truth any longer. If Olivier is coming after me again, I need to face it."

"Should we tell Madame Gentille?" Robin, who had more worries than a seven-year-old boy should have, bit away at his nails. "I think we should."

"Not yet," Theo interjected.

"Not until we find out exactly what's going on," Bastien said. "If she knew, she wouldn't let us out of her sight. I have to go later. Will you help?"

Promises made, a plan was formed between them all. At breakfast, they would convince Madame Gentille to take them to Buttes Chaumont Park, where they would meet Alice and cause a distraction so that Bastien could sneak off to the grotto to meet the copper-haired girl.

In all the books that Bastien had read, the heroes of his favourite stories never did anything unless they had a full stomach. Solving mysteries and saving the day was impossible without first eating four slices of buttered baguette, all washed down with a glass of water and strawberry syrup. Such a thing had felt like a rare treat to Bastien only a few months ago, when Xavier Odieux had been in charge of the orphanage, but now the boys were met with delicious smells every morning.

Today was no different. Bastien opened the dining-room door to a feast. The new chef, Camille Choux, spooned out triple helpings from her dinner trolley, her thick black hair tied back in a fishtail plait.

Madame Gentille had hired Camille last month after she'd visited a Montparnasse café and eaten a delicious croque-monsieur oozing eight different types of cheese. She'd asked the server to introduce her to the cook immediately. Camille Choux had listened to Madame Gentille's pleas and, with the promise of a better wage and the chance to fill the bellies of the kindest and bravest children in Paris, she'd left the café and never looked back.

This morning, there were carafes of orange and grapefruit juice, plates of croissants and fresh, crunchy baguettes as long as the table itself. Bastien sat down next to Theo, who was already on his second baguette. He ate as if he was afraid someone would snatch the food out of his hand at any second, a habit from the days of Xavier ruling the orphanage.

"Finally!" Theo pushed a plate towards him. "I saved you a couple of croissants, but I wasn't sure how long they'd last. Clément has been watching them like a hawk."

"I haven't!" Clément threw a brioche bun at Theo's head. "I have self-control, unlike you."

"What did I say about throwing food?" Madame Gentille looked at Clément, who shrank sheepishly in his chair. She pointed her manicured fingers, her nails a duck-egg blue, the same colour as the velveteen waistcoat and lapel pin she always wore. "Go and pick it up, please. Camille doesn't work hard for you to treat her food like a shotput."

"*Désolé*," Clément grumbled.

Madame Gentille shook off her frown and replaced it with her usual wide grin. "It's a busy day in the city, what with the preparations for the Exposition Universelle. I imagine you are all too young to have been to a world fair before, so I shall buy us tickets! You'll get to see so many incredible new things: technology and beautiful buildings, exotic animals and amusements, and the finest musicians and painters and dancers!"

Most of the boys murmured in approval. Bastien noticed a small smile on Theo's face; his parents had met at the Exposition Universelle in 1900, twenty-three years ago. He was curious about the fair, the place where his family had begun.

"Anyway…" The director clapped her hands. "What would you like to do on this lovely Sunday?"

Bastien looked over to Robin and winked. Madame Gentille's enthusiasm was the perfect opening for laying the first breadcrumbs of their plan.

"Could we go to the park?" Robin looked over the top of his glasses, his eyes as big as marbles.

"*Oui*," Fred added. "I thought we might play pétanque or another game. What about a running race? It's been a while since we've had such nice weather for a sports day."

Bastien kept quiet for the sake of the plan, but inwardly cursed Fred for mentioning exercise. He did not want to go for a run.

"*Quelle bonne idée!*" Madame Gentille smiled. "Why don't you all get ready after breakfast and we'll head straight to the Luxembourg Gardens."

"Might we go to Buttes Chaumont instead?"

"But that's on the other side of the river." Madame

Gentille stared at Bastien. "Why would we go anywhere else when we have the finest park in all of Paris a stone's throw away?"

The boys begged together, their voices rising in a whiny crescendo.

The director cupped her hands over her ears. "I'll agree to anything that will stop you all making such a racket." Her chair squeaked against the floor as she stood. "Finish your breakfast and meet me in the courtyard once you've found your shoes. Buttes Chaumont Park it is!"

Bastien grinned; the boys had played their parts perfectly.

The others filed out of the dining hall in search of tennis shoes and balls of various sizes. Bastien swallowed his last bite of croissant; they were really going to do this.

"Bastien!" Robin ran back into the dining hall and dropped a parcel on the table. "This just arrived for you." The youngest boy hurried away again to find his shoes, while Bastien stared curiously at the parcel. It was wrapped in crimson-red paper with a large bow on its top.

"Were you expecting anything?" Theo asked.

Bastien shook his head.

"You're already a famous author who receives fan mail." Theo elbowed him playfully.

Bastien unravelled the bow and tore off the wrapping paper to reveal a book that he instantly recognized. *The King's Return* stared back up at him and he dropped it onto the table, like a hot coal. Bastien had seen this book once before in Le Chat Curieux all those months ago when he'd found out about the kidnapped writers. This was the first book that Olivier Odieux had ever written and Bastien knew, immediately, that this was another threat.

"Do you think he sent it here?" Theo asked.

Bastien nodded. "Absolutely. Olivier wants to scare me. He wants me to know that he's always watching."

With the tip of his finger, Bastien opened the book. The familiar red pen and inkpot had been stamped on the first page and underneath was a single, scribbled sentence.

GET IN MY WAY AND YOU WILL PAY

Bastien snapped the book shut and pushed it away. "You can't let him get to you," Theo said.

Bastien shivered. "But Olivier made my parents pay for trying to stop him and now he's going to do the same to me!"

Theo picked up Olivier's book and kicked it into the corner of the dining hall. "That's what I think of that pathetic threat! Come on, you're Bastien Bonlivre! You said it yourself. Don't let him frighten you. We've got to meet this girl and find out what she knows."

Bastien didn't want to think about all the ways the copper-haired girl could be leading them into a trap. If she was working for Olivier, then who knew what might await them? But he was buoyed by Theo's words; his best friend's belief restored his own.

"You're right. Let's do this."

"Are you ready?" Theo asked.

"Nowhere near ready." Bastien shrugged. "But when has that ever stopped us?"

Buttes Chaumont Park was busy by the time they arrived; the lush lawns full of people picnicking, children flying kites and readers slumped against the tree trunks with a good book in their hands. Couples strolled arm-in-arm and parents navigated the rowboats while children leaned over to look at the fish in the lake. The weather had pulled people from their homes, demanding that they felt the soft glow of the spring sun on their skin after such a harsh winter.

"*Ça va?*" Alice stood next to the rowboat hut where they had agreed to meet. As he got closer, Bastien realized she was wearing a long beige mac and a floral scarf.

"Why are you dressed like it's an autumn day?"

"You look a bit like Madame Gentille, actually," Theo added, out of earshot from the director, who was gently scolding Clément for encouraging Fred to jump into the lake.

"It's called a disguise." Alice dismissed them. "You ought to have thought of it!"

"Why would we need a disguise?" Bastien glanced at a boy sitting under an oak tree with his father, reading together. He turned away quickly, swallowing the lump in his throat. "The girl was in the bookshop last night. She probably knows what we all look like."

Alice shrugged. "It was dark, so I doubt it. Anyway, you never know who else could be watching. I'm taking this mission seriously."

"A little too seriously," Theo snorted.

"I've found a good spot over there," Madame Gentille called. "*Suivez-moi!*" She led Alice and the boys down to the edge of the lake where the water's surface rippled. The director spread a checked blanket on the grass and pulled skipping ropes, skittles and pétanque balls from her leather bag. The boys and Alice gawked in amazement at the bag's seemingly never-ending contents.

"What shall we do?" Madame Gentille took off her waistcoat and folded it neatly. "Play skittles? The winning team gets to have an extra slice of *fraisier* tonight."

Bastien looked across the lake, towards the waterfall grotto where the copper-haired girl had asked to meet. It was approaching two o'clock; he had to sneak away now.

"Actually, I think I might go and sit by the lake," he pointed vaguely. "I'm working on a new story. Alice, would you help me with some ideas?"

Alice tightened her scarf around her neck. "Of course."

"And I must find some peace and quiet to work out an equation for a new invention," Theo said.

Madame Gentille pouted. "I wanted all of us to play together."

"You must let them create!" Timothée declared.

"Plus, it's less competition for the extra slice of cake," Pascal said.

Madame Gentille gathered the wooden skittles in her arms. "The rest of you will play with me then." She marched along the grass and the others followed. They all wanted to help Bastien out, but sometimes playing skittles was the most heroic thing a person could do.

Walking towards the stone bridge, Bastien and Theo told Alice about Olivier's book that had arrived that morning with another threat inside.

"He's a crook of the highest order," Alice sneered. "It's *him* who is going to pay."

Bastien glanced over at the Temple of Sybille sitting atop the highest hill in the park, and found it slightly calmed him. It was one of his favourite views in Paris, and the scene before him looked like a painting worthy of hanging next to the finest masterpieces on the walls of the Musée d'Orsay.

Bastien knew the park well. It had been a short walk from his family's old apartment in Belleville and he had spent many summer days curled up under an oak tree, reading with his parents. His mother had also taken him inside the grotto once and told him how this ancient, rocky cave was once part of an old limestone quarry. These happy memories grew his courage again; although his parents weren't here to help him stop Olivier, they were never far from his mind.

"Where do we go from here?" Theo asked.

Bastien pointed to a path running along the shoreline of the lake on the other side of the bridge. "That path leads to the grotto entrance. We'll need to make our way inside because the waterfall is at the back. If I remember, there are stepping stones across the water."

Alice shuddered. "A grotto is so isolated and creepy. Why did she insist upon meeting here?"

"She didn't exactly give me a chance to ask." Bastien quickened his pace. "But it's the middle of the afternoon. The others know where we are going. If something's off, then we'll run out of there as fast as we can."

Theo nodded. "As fast as humanly possible."

Finally, they arrived at the grotto entrance. It looked like the mouth of a stone giant with crumbling teeth. Water streamed through the entrance from the lake.

Inside, Bastien would find the copper-haired girl. Would she be alone or had she lured him into a trap where Olivier would be waiting too? Had the note already foretold Bastien's future; was this the end for him?

He took a breath and steadied himself. He was with friends and his notebook was safely hidden in the orphanage library. He was as prepared as he could be. Although his ears drummed with the force of his own heartbeat, Bastien knew he had no choice.

He was done with letting his fear of Olivier rule his life.

7

MEETING MATHILDE

"**I**f we're not back in twenty minutes, I told Pascal to tell Madame Gentille where we are." Bastien took a step towards the grotto mouth and looked back at his best friends. "But I'd rather her not know what's going on until we find out for ourselves. So let's be quick!"

Alice nodded. "*D'accord.*"

Theo nudged him. "You first, then."

Bastien found his footing on the first stepping stone and followed the path into the grotto. The bright afternoon light quickly disappeared and everything went dark. Once his eyes had adjusted, Bastien stepped onto the next stone. He looked ahead and saw the stepping-stone path cutting through the pool of water, which led towards the waterfall spurting out of the rocky back wall.

Bastien ducked out of the way of skewer-sharp stalactites, but each stepping stone only became more slippery.

"Be careful!" he shouted, hoping that Theo and Alice could hear over the noise of the crashing water.

This grotto was truly the perfect secret meeting place. The water masked every sound. Bastien wondered if the girl wanted to make sure no one overheard their conversation. Then a darker thought emerged. Did she want to silence the footsteps of Olivier as he snuck up on Bastien?

He shook his thoughts away like drops of water and focused on his footsteps. There were only a couple of stepping stones left, leading directly through the waterfall. Bastien waited for Theo and Alice to catch up, his arm outstretched, indicating they would have to go through the falling water.

"You mocked my disguise, but look how handy it is now!" Alice wrapped the scarf around her head. "I washed my hair this morning and I'm not doing it again. I can't spend another hour combing out all of the knots."

"You look like an old lady off to the market for prune juice," Theo laughed, teetering on the stone.

"You just need a wicker basket." Bastien tried to stuff his laugh back inside his mouth, but it was too late to save himself from Alice's death stare.

"You're both going in the water if you say one more word."

A noise echoed around the grotto then, slightly muffled by the roar of the water.

"What was that?" Theo's voice turned as wobbly as his legs.

Bastien bit his lip. "I don't know. It sounded like a sob."

"Come on," Alice gently encouraged. "The sooner we get there and find out what's going on, the quicker we can get out."

Bastien hopped along the stone path, until the running waterfall blocked his next step.

"We have to jump through the water!" Carefully, he stretched his left leg through the waterfall. The icy water soaked him, but he concentrated on where to land. He pushed off with his right foot and fell forward, breaking his fall with his hands.

"Everything alright?" Alice called.

"Make sure you put your hands out when you jump. You'll slip right over if not."

"The gap between the last stone and the waterfall is too far for me!" Theo shouted.

"If you jump," Bastien replied, "I can catch you."

"No offence, but you don't have the best catching skills."

"We haven't got all day!" Alice interrupted.

The next thing Bastien heard was a scream as the waterfall spat Theo out. His arms flapped like an eagle, but it was no use. The flying boy crashed into Bastien and they both fell to the ground like skittles.

A moment later, Alice appeared on their side of the waterfall as though she was taking a leisurely stroll in the park. "*Désolée*, I should've asked you first."

"What before pushing me through a freezing waterfall?" Theo squeezed the water from the ends of his curls as Alice helped them to their feet. "A little warning would be nice next time."

Bastien brushed down his wet shorts and walked deeper into the grotto. It was empty apart from circles of stalagmites that shot up from the ground around an old stone statue.

"I'm here," Bastien called.

Something stirred in the corner of the grotto and, slowly, a figure emerged.

Bastien dug his nails into his palms. It was too dark for him to see properly, but as a beam of sunlight fought its way through a crack in the rock face, the soft pink satin of a pair of ballet slippers appeared.

"So you came," the copper-haired girl said. "And you brought friends."

Bastien took a good look at the girl as she stepped fully into the light. She moved effortlessly, as though she did not walk but glide. Her red hair was long and knotted in large clumps at its ends and her hands looked like lumps of rock from the way they curled into tight fists.

"Who are you?" Bastien spotted the dust and dirt covering her cheeks. "And where have you come from?"

"You should've come alone." The girl fidgeted. "My business is only with you."

Theo and Alice crossed their arms simultaneously.

"We're a package deal," Theo said.

Alice nodded. "Whatever it is you have to tell Bastien concerns all of us. We're not going anywhere."

The girl rolled her eyes. "My name is Mathilde Méchante and I want to destroy Olivier Odieux."

Bastien felt unsteady on his feet. He hadn't expected her to say such a thing. His eyes darted around the grotto, double-checking that Mathilde was all alone.

"I don't understand," he said. "Then why did you deliver his note to me? This is a trick, isn't it? You're working for Olivier!"

Mathilde's mouth dropped open and her fists fell to her sides. "I would never work for that man."

"So why did you sneak into the bookshop? And where did you get the note from?"

Mathilde chewed on her bottom lip and looked down. "It's complicated."

"Just tell me the truth," Bastien demanded. "Last night at the bookshop, you said you could be a friend or a foe. What did you mean by that?"

"And try to explain it in the most *un*complicated way for us," Alice interrupted.

Mathilde looked back up and sighed; underneath the dirt, Bastien noticed dark rings under her eyes.

"I went to the Palais de Justice on the day that Olivier was released. I wanted to tell him who I was and what he had stolen from me. But it was so busy and I couldn't get close to him. I saw that note fall out of Olivier's pocket and onto the floor. He must have dropped it by

80

accident." Mathilde looked Bastien directly in the eye. "I'm telling you the truth."

"So he didn't ask you to deliver the note to me?" Bastien interrupted. "Or anything else to the orphanage?"

Mathilde shook her head. "I promise. I am not working for him."

"Why do you want to track him down?" Bastien asked.

"He owes me a debt." Mathilde spat out her words like sour milk. "I want justice. Just like you. That's why I wanted to give you the note – to show you he is not done with you. That you need to be prepared to fight him again. We could be stronger together. It's why I asked you here today." She slid forward. "I think we should team up."

Bastien looked at Theo and Alice; the expressions on their faces were just as surprised as he felt. "Team up. Like some sort of gang?"

Mathilde shrugged. "Call it what you want. I know you want the same thing. You almost defeated him once. I read all about the Bad Brothers trial in the newspaper and how your discovery led to their arrest."

"Everyone in the entire country read about the trial," Theo interjected. "It's not exactly secret knowledge that means you can join *our* team."

"I'm not like everyone else. I don't believe that Xavier

Odieux was solely responsible for those crimes." Mathilde sat down on the floor of the grotto and indicated for the others to join her.

"I think we'll stand." Alice crossed her arms.

"Suit yourself." Mathilde's eyes turned hard like a beetle's shell. "Maman always told me that Olivier was a puppet-master. He controls and manipulates everything around him. When I read the newspapers, I knew that Olivier was lying. He let his own brother take the fall for his crimes. Olivier Odieux doesn't deserve to be a free man, but he's fooled everyone."

Bastien thought of how Olivier had ordered Xavier to start the fire at the hotel in Cannes that had killed his parents. He'd also sent Xavier to the orphanage, where Xavier had made all of their lives a misery just so he could steal Bastien's notebook. What was Olivier's plan now – find another loyal minion to obey his every command? Bastien wondered who it might be this time and what Olivier could achieve with their help.

"You're right." All at once, fatigue pulled Bastien onto the floor. His legs folded underneath him and he sat down.

"Bastien!" Theo hissed. "What are you doing? Don't let your guard down."

"If I was planning on hurting you, I would've already done it by now." Mathilde held up her hands. "I promise on Maman's life, I'm not here to trick you. It's just me."

Reluctantly, Theo sat down next to Bastien, but Alice still stood at the edge of the stepping stones, eyeing Mathilde suspiciously.

"You want our help, but I don't know anything about you," Bastien said. "It's pretty clear why I want justice. What about you? You mentioned your mother earlier. Is that why you're going after Olivier? Did he do something to her?"

Bastien saw how Mathilde's face wrestled with different emotions. Whatever she was thinking about had clearly gnawed away at her inside for far too long.

Her eyes met his and she took a big breath, as though making space in her throat for the words she was about to say. "I will tell you the truth. I've just never said it out loud before."

"What?" Bastien leaned forwards. "What is it?"

"Olivier Odieux is my father."

8

DAUGHTER OF THE ENEMY

The words rang in Bastien's ears like an alarm. He couldn't fit "Olivier" and "father" together. The words repelled each other, making as much sense as one of Theo's scribbled blackboard calculations.

"He's your father?" Bastien stared at Mathilde, unable to trace any of Olivier's features onto the girl's face. "If you are his family, how can I trust you? Olivier has destroyed so much in my life."

"He doesn't know me," Mathilde replied. "We've never met."

"Never?" Alice's face made it clear she still didn't believe Mathilde.

"Let me explain." Mathilde tapped her feet against

the rock floor nervously. It struck Bastien that the girl was uncomfortable sitting still with such emotions.

"Maman was a brilliant dancer. She was born with twitching toes and could never stay still. At one point, she was the best ballerina in the whole of France, earning more money than she had ever imagined.

"Her life changed the night she met Olivier Odieux. He promised her a happy life and Maman fell under his spell. She agreed to share her money with him as Olivier promised that he would double the amount and they would buy a chateau in Normandy together. All Maman wanted was a family and a home near the sea.

"Obviously, that didn't happen. Olivier made bad investments and his cruelty made Maman weak and sick. When she told him that they were to have a baby, he left and never came back."

Bastien thought of his parents and the fierce love that they'd had in their hearts. He didn't know if he could trust Mathilde yet, but he couldn't deny the sympathy he felt for her.

"Yemma always said there are two different types of love," Theo said. "The kind that fills you up and outpours goodness. The other kind makes you a shell of yourself."

Mathilde sniffed. "Maman did her best to look after us, but it was difficult. Her mind was unwell and she stopped dancing altogether, so I had to find a way to keep us afloat."

"That's a lot of responsibility." Alice's voice softened.

"Six months ago, a police officer caught me stealing food. They took me back to our attic flat. When they discovered how poorly Maman was, they sent her to Sainte-Anne hospital." Mathilde's voice faltered. "I had to go to a correction school on the city outskirts, but I escaped last month. That's why I cut the lights at the bookshop last night. I can't be seen. People from the school are looking for me. They will drag me back the minute they find me. I can't get caught. Not now."

Mathilde pushed her hair from her face. Gone were the tears; only determination glittered in her eyes. "I want to take back what Olivier stole from Maman and make a better life for us. I felt hope when I read about how you saved the writers in the catacombs, hope that there are still people who can see through Olivier's web of lies. Maybe together, we can make him pay for everything he's done."

They sat in silence, which stretched into every crevice and crack of the grotto. Bastien replayed

Mathilde's words in his head. If it was the truth, he could understand Mathilde's motives. She was doing everything for her mother, for love. It struck him that they were more alike than he first imagined.

"I understand your anger," Bastien said finally. "I can never understand your pain, because it is yours alone, but I know just how powerful it can be. It can make you want to tear the whole world in two."

"Does that mean you'll help me get Maman's money back?"

Bastien had always thought he was quite good at reading people. The flare of a nostril, the sharp rise of an eyebrow; all of these things could reveal a person's true nature. Looking at Mathilde, he saw a girl who was lost. Just like him, Theo and the other boys. He saw a girl who fiercely loved her mother and would do anything to right a terrible wrong. But life so far had taught Bastien to protect his heart like a precious jewel. He couldn't risk letting the wrong person in.

"Come to the Orphanage for Gentils Garçons in two days' time," he said. "Six o'clock. You'll have your answer then."

"I understand." Mathilde smiled; it was the type that looked like it had taken great effort. She got to her feet and rubbed a scuff from her ballet slippers. "I promise you can trust me. It is time to stop letting people like Olivier get away with evil. If we don't do something, he will carry on hurting people. Just like he did to us."

The three friends stood.

"*À bientôt*." Bastien turned back towards the waterfall, eager to leave the grotto behind. They needed to get back to the others before the twenty minutes were up.

Then there was a loud *crack* behind them.

"Where did she go?" Theo looked over his shoulder.

Bastien spun on his heels. He spotted a crevice in the rock wall, just wide enough for someone to fit through. Was that where Mathilde had disappeared into? If her mother was living in a hospital, did that mean she had no home to call her own?

Alice tugged on his arm. "We need to hurry back!"

They made their way along the stepping stones and out into the park. While Theo and Alice chatted, Bastien retreated into his thoughts. Who was this girl who had just rocketed into his life like a firework?

Was Mathilde who she said she was?

And, most importantly, could he trust her?

9

FLAMES ALONG THE SEINE

The late afternoon sun had simmered away by the time Madame Gentille led the boys and Alice out of the park and back across the river. Even with a hundred questions swimming around in his head, Bastien took a moment to stop on the Pont Saint-Michel and look out at the violet-coloured sky. He never took a day in his city for granted, even more so after living under Xavier Odieux's rule. Paris was a part of him and this bridge afforded one of the best views in the city.

But moments of peace never lasted long.

"What happened between you and the girl then?" Pascal appeared next to him. "Who is she? Is she working for Olivier? You haven't said a peep since we left the park."

"Her name is Mathilde. She said she wants to stop Olivier too and that we should work together."

Clément appeared on Bastien's other side. "Why should we help her?"

"Bastien will tell you everything later." Alice whisked him away, leaving Clément and Pascal pouting. "We need to talk before I head back to the bookshop." She leaned into Bastien. "What are you thinking?"

"I want to believe Mathilde. I really do."

"But you want proof?" Alice continued his train of thought. "Proof that she is who she says she is?"

Bastien nodded and reached into his memory, trying to remember what his parents had told him about how to separate fact from fiction. But a more recent memory overtook: on New Year's Eve, LeGrand had told him all about the biggest archive in the city. Hundreds of thousands of documents and facts existed at the Mazarin Library archives, the oldest library in the country.

"I have an idea! Remember when LeGrand told me about the archivist who works at the Mazarin Library – Pauline Savoir. What if she can find something that might help us?"

"She comes into the bookshop on Sundays." A wide

grin pulled at Alice's lips. "Always buys a copy of *The World's Hardest Crosswords* and a bag of lemon madeleines."

"If Mathilde's mother was a famous ballet dancer, then there's bound to be a record of her performances in the archives." Bastien pictured rows of dusty filing cabinets full of answers. "And we can find information on the Odieux family history too! If his family past is an important part of Olivier's new plan, then there's no better place to look than the archives. Let's go tomorrow!"

Alice nodded. "I'm helping Papa out in the bookshop tomorrow afternoon, so we can go in the morning."

As they continued walking, a plume of smoke in the distance caught Bastien's eye. It wasn't like a billowing chimney; this smoke was much thicker and darker.

"Do you see that?" Theo cut in between them, pointing to red flickers spilling across the sky like ink blobs across a page. "Over there, a bit further down the Left Bank."

"Maybe it's part of a show?" Alice walked quicker. "They're already rehearsing for the Exposition Universelle. Maman said there's going to be a light spectacle this year."

Bastien thought of the neon-lit signs of the bars and brasseries that often dazzled the city and shook his head. "*Non*. The air feels thicker the further we walk. Don't you sense it?"

"Stay close together." Madame Gentille's voice was taut like a finely-tuned violin string.

"What is that awful smell?" Alice covered her mouth as they turned off the bridge and crossed to the other side of the road.

Bastien looked up at the red flickers and now saw them for what they actually were: rising flames spreading across the sky. He ran to Madame Gentille at the front of the group and followed her horrified gaze. His stomach dropped – and it wasn't the good kind of stomach-drop that you got on a fairground rollercoaster. This was fear, eating Bastien from the inside out.

"Paris is burning."

All along the river Seine, the stalls of the *bouquinistes* were up in flames. Piles of books and paintings were on fire. People rushed back and forth from the river with water in buckets, bottles and wine glasses – anything they could find at nearby restaurants and cafés – but the flames only climbed higher into the sky, reaching the leafy tips of the horse chestnut trees that lined the riverbank.

More flames appeared across the Left Bank and Bastien watched as enormous tendrils of fire swallowed buildings in large gulps. Wisps of black smoke corkscrewed up into the air.

"We have to help!" Bastien looked over at a bookseller, an old woman with her head in her hands, and his heart broke. The *bouquinistes* were special to him. This was where his mother had first met his father. Hugo Bonlivre had sold Margot Auclair a book, and when their hands touched as he handed her the well-worn paperback, their hearts had surged.

Now another part of his parents' story was disappearing right before his eyes.

"There's nothing we can do to help." Madame Gentille herded them away. "It's far too dangerous. We need to get back home."

"But we must do something!" Theo protested.

"We can help getting water from the river!" Timothée suggested and the boys roared in approval.

Madame Gentille raised her voice an octave higher. "You are in my care and I will not let you put yourselves at risk."

But Bastien wasn't paying attention to the director or the argument going on around him. He watched a ball of flames erupt over the Place Saint-Michel. The square was just around the corner from Le Chat Curieux.

"Over there!" he cried. "Another fire!"

"Maman and Papa! Babette!" Alice jerked into action and sprinted into the chaos.

Instinctively, Bastien and Theo ran after her.

"*Arrêtez!*" Even if Madame Gentille had screamed herself hoarse, they would not have listened. Bastien only thought of Jules, Charlotte, their cat Babette and the bookshop where he had spent so many days with his parents.

His heart pounded in time with his heavy footsteps as they twisted further through the streets. The heat of the fires prickled his skin and Bastien looked on with horror at rows of buildings, all engulfed in flames. He tried not to picture Le Chat Curieux meeting the same fate. The bookshop had to be okay! It was more than just a shop made from bricks and mortar – it was a haven for his mind and heart and another piece of his own family history.

Skidding around the corner, he spotted Alice at the fountain in the middle of the square. Jules struggled with a wooden bucket full of water, his daughter's arms

94

wrapped around him like a rope. Dozens of people ran past, plunging bowls and cups into the fountain and an old man desperately swatted the flames away from the florist's with a splintered wooden broom.

Bastien and Theo weaved through the crowd and their cries pierced Bastien's heart. People were losing their homes and their livelihoods. It was all so unfair.

"Is the bookshop okay? Where is Charlotte?" Bastien's breath came in pants once they arrived at the fountain; the smoky flames had seeped through to his lungs.

"And Babette," Theo said. "Is she safe?"

Jules attempted a smile. "Le Chat Curieux is fine – a fire did break out at the front of the building, but we managed to put it out before it could take hold. Charlotte and Babette are safe too." He ruffled Alice's hair with his free hand. "Luckily, Maman was out shopping when the fire started."

Relief rushed through Bastien as he picked up a bucket. "How did this happen?"

"I have no idea." Jules led them through the throng of people and around the corner. A small breath slipped from Bastien's lips as he admired Le Chat Curieux standing defiant. Only black ash stained the pavement in front of the bookshop window. Further down the street, individual fires continued to burn.

"All of these fires remind me of the Great War," Jules added. "I saw Abdou's printing shop on fire from our bedroom window and then more started to appear a few streets over."

"I counted at least five others down by the river and across the Left Bank." Theo coughed.

Fire-engine sirens screeched loudly in the air and the sound cut right through Bastien. A moment later, members of the Paris Fire Brigade sprinted past them carrying ladders and unravelling their water hoses.

"I have to help Abdou." Jules took the buckets from Bastien and Theo, holding all three in his large hands. "You two need to get back to Madame Gentille now."

"Papa's right," Alice said, covering her mouth with her arm as the smoke grew thicker. "She'll be worried sick."

"What about tomorrow?" Despite the panic all around them, Bastien was still thinking about their plan. He hoped that the Mazarin Library would survive the fires. "Will you still come with us?"

Alice nodded. "If it's safe, I'll meet you at the library. Tomorrow morning. Ten o'clock."

"Come on," Theo urged. "Let's go!"

As Bastien turned to leave, he noticed Georges in the bookshop window through a gap in the smoke. The new bookseller stared out at the blazing street, his face expressionless as he watched a firefighter climb down the ladder with a baby in their arms.

How could a frown not tug at Georges's face? And why was he not outside helping Jules and everyone else to work together against the flames? He looked completely different from the person Bastien had met on the night of his book party. Georges didn't look friendly or helpful; he just seemed empty.

As though he'd sensed eyes on him, Georges turned his head towards Bastien. Their eyes locked, and the bookseller's face softened. He waved to Bastien, his face a portrait of kindness. Hesitantly, Bastien waved back.

Then a pile of ash blew across his face and by the time he had rubbed his eyes, the bookseller had disappeared.

Despite the delicious meal that Camille had prepared for dinner, appetites were low. After a quick walk home, with Madame Gentille ushering the boys through the streets while doing her best to reply to hundreds of anxious questions, everyone now sat in silence. There were no answers about what had started the fires across the Left Bank and why they had appeared one by one. Not yet, anyway.

"Anyone for dessert?" Camille asked, her apron splattered with cream and splodges of strawberry.

As much as Bastien wanted a bite, his stomach churned thinking of the fires and the destruction they had caused. He couldn't wrap his head around how they'd spread so quickly.

"I think an early night is needed for our boys," Madame Gentille said. "We can have the *fraisier* for breakfast tomorrow. How does that sound?"

The boys murmured in approval and rose from the table, making their way to the dormitory. Madame Gentille cradled Robin in her arms and placed him on his bed.

"I never want to limit your freedom, but I think it would be prudent if none of you went anywhere by yourself for the next few days," the director said as the boys climbed into bed. "Until we know what or who caused the fires, I want you all to stay in our neighbourhood unless you're with me. If you are to go out after lessons then you must tell me where, when and what time you will be home."

Every head poking out from the duvets nodded in agreement. Madame Gentille smiled and wiped her forehead with the back of her hand. Bastien noticed the deeper lines on her face, as though the fires had aged her by years in one day.

"*Bonne nuit.*" She blew them a kiss and closed the doors.

Bastien squirmed in bed, his restless legs kicking

against the duvet. His pillow was scratchy and rough against his face. Everything felt off.

What had happened today? Had the fires been an unfortunate accident? Or was there something more sinister behind it all? Madame Gentille had said "*who*" – did she think that someone had started the fires on purpose? Or even a group of people? However it had happened, the fires had destroyed buildings, businesses and homes. The lives of so many people had been ruined in a matter of minutes; Bastien could understand how that felt.

He closed his eyes, hoping sleep would come, but instead he saw flames as high as church steeples, thick smoke and Olivier with a twisted look on his face. Bastien scrunched his eyes tighter, but now saw his parents reaching out from the smoke. Beside them, Olivier grew as large as the towering inferno.

Bastien's eyes flicked back open and he rubbed them hard, desperate to erase his nightmare. He didn't want to think about what had happened to his parents; he refused to remember them like that.

Something poked him in the side and he jumped, looking down to find Theo kneeling on the floor. "What on earth are you doing down there?"

Theo grinned sheepishly. "*Désolé*. I've come here to ask you a question from all of us."

"All of us?" Bastien sat up to find the rest of the boys sitting at the foot of his bed.

"We hoped that you might tell us a story." Theo sat down next to Pascal. "We're all having trouble getting to sleep after today."

"Are you saying my stories help you doze off?" Bastien raised his eyebrow.

"Never!" Timothée interrupted, clasping his hands together. "They are the greatest comfort of all."

"Apart from these new quilts Madame Gentille bought for us." Fred pulled the soft fabric around his and his twin's shoulders.

Bastien smiled at the familiar scene in front of him. When Xavier Odieux had overseen the orphanage, storytelling was strictly forbidden, and so Bastien had whispered stories to the boys late at night. The storytelling evenings had kept each of them going during Xavier's reign; that, and their ability to make each other snort with laughter for hours.

Bastien no longer had to tell stories in secret, but there was still something magical about gathering after lights out. He scanned their faces, his eyes settling on

Timothée, and a story started to form. He grinned at his waiting audience. Tonight, he needed this story just as much as they all did.

"Let's begin," he said.

"*Timothée Charrault always remembered the most important advice his mother had given him about acting: 'You must nurture your talent just like I nurtured you as a baby. You must help your talent breathe and feed it. Watch films and plays until your eyes are sore. It is by doing this that you will learn to perform to the best of your ability.'*

"*His mother, Christine Charrault, had been one of the finest actors in the whole of Europe. Like a jester, she had made people laugh and smile, but she had also made her audience feel emotions that they had once squeezed down inside them until they were as flat as a crêpe.*

"*It was no surprise that her son had inherited her artistic ability. Although his mother was now gone, her wise words set Timothée on the path to stardom.*

"*If the Salle Richelieu theatre at the Comédie-Française was the sun, Timothée was the earth, orbiting it daily. With no fixed address, he had made a deal with the kind theatre manager. Timothée would teach the manager's daughter how to act as long as he could spend his nights in the theatre. Satisfied, the manager looked the other way as*

Timothée climbed to the top balcony each evening and slept on the plush velvet seats.

"He watched every single performance, day and night, studying everything – from the way the actors pronounced their lines, to how make-up artists and dressmakers transformed faces and bodies in a matter of minutes. Timothée helped ushers guide the audience to their seats and sat backstage, painting props and fetching candied almonds for the demanding actors.

"No job was ever too small or too big for Timothée, but his biggest dream was to become an actor like his mother. He wanted to make people feel through the power of performance. To do that, he needed to practise.

"And so he performed wherever he could, from alleyways on busy market days to packed Métro platforms, and even the escalator in the Eiffel Tower – which, frankly, did not have the best acoustics. He performed in small theatres from Dunkerque to Dijon and finally, one night, he took to the stage at the Comédie-Française, standing in the exact place where his mother had received hundreds of standing ovations. Now, it was his turn to be admired by the audience.

"As it turned out, someone special had been watching. On his tenth birthday, Timothée received the most special of gifts: a lead role in a René Gide film. The internationally famous director had created a film just for Timothée, all about a Parisian boy who became the greatest actor in France.

"And as much as Timothée loved playing other people, transforming into long-lost kings and savvy detectives, to sold-out theatres and cinema audiences, his favourite role was always the first one he'd ever had: being the son of Christine Charrault, the person who he loved more than anything in this world."

"I told myself I wasn't going to cry. I promised I wouldn't." Timothée flung himself at Bastien. "You made me sound like a star. No less than what my mother would've expected, of course."

Bastien smiled. "That's because you are one already. And every time you perform, she is right there with you."

Timothée smiled. "Sometimes, I think I'm losing her. Her face blurs and the memory of her voice feels like a stranger. But thanks to you, I feel her with me right now."

While the other boys slept soundly in their beds after the story, Bastien still tossed and turned. His mind came alive in the night, as though he needed the dark to see things more clearly.

He pictured how the Mazarin Library archives might look, a dark and dusty labyrinth of filing cabinets that he hoped would hold answers – not just about Mathilde, but Olivier and his family history. If Mathilde was his daughter, determined to take back the money he owed her mother and stop him for good, Bastien would help her just like his friends had helped him against Olivier. He made this promise as sleep pulled its blanket over him.

As his troubled thoughts dissolved, Bastien dared to dream of a hopeful new day.

11
PRINTED LIES AND ARCHIVE SPIES

Concentrating had been an impossible task the following morning, especially when Monday was a day full of mathematics. Numbers didn't add up for Bastien even when he paid attention. Right now, as he stared down at the last worksheet, he could only think of the archive at the Mazarin Library and the answers it might hold.

"You can do this one." Theo's worksheet was long completed, but he sat next to Bastien at the table in the dining hall, which doubled up as a makeshift classroom. Early morning lessons had already finished, and the other boys were enjoying their free time in the Luxembourg Gardens with Madame Gentille. Bastien and Theo were expected to join them in a couple of hours.

"Whenever I think I've got it, the numbers just don't make sense." Bastien punctured his worksheet with his pencil tip.

"You just need patience." Theo took the pencil from his grip and scribbled the calculation. "The numbers are a language. You just need to learn how to speak it."

Bastien sighed. "Words are the only language I understand." He got to his feet. "Shall I go and grab a *goûter* from the kitchen before we head to the archives? If we stay here any longer we'll run out of time to explore them."

Theo's eyes lit up. "I think Camille was making *pain perdu* earlier. Can you grab some?"

"I'll see what I can find and meet you in the courtyard."

Theo waved the unfinished worksheet in the air. "But we *will* do this later."

Bastien rolled his eyes and jogged across the hallway to the kitchen. He cupped his ear to the door. No clanging pans or shouts. Camille's cooking rants normally displayed an impressive vocabulary of rude words.

Certain it was safe to raid the cupboards, Bastien slipped into the kitchen. He followed the sweet smell of sugary, fried bread to the stove oven, where the *pain perdu* sat in a pan. Bastien opened the cutlery drawer and grabbed a knife; hopefully, Camille wouldn't notice two slices missing.

It took a lot to distract him from sweet treats, but an open newspaper on the kitchen countertop succeeded. *La Seule Voix* was a newspaper he hadn't heard of before. Madame Gentille always said that *Le Parisien Quotidien* was the only newspaper in the city that could be trusted.

On the front page was a name that ruined Bastien's appetite.

The knife clattered to the floor as he grabbed the newspaper. Noise from the hallway forced Bastien into the pantry, but even the smell of mouldy courgettes and dried anchovies didn't register. He crouched down between crates of potatoes and read the article as quickly as he could.

LA SEULE VOIX

LUNDI, 9 AVRIL 1923

A NIGHT OF FLAMES SPARKS FEAR
ACROSS PARIS

By Olivier Odieux

ASHES COVER THE COBBLESTONED STREETS THIS morning after our City of Lights turned into the City of Flames. An atrocious spate of fires spread across the Left Bank yesterday evening. The bouquiniste stalls, which have lined the Seine for years, perished, as well as dozens of other buildings and homes.

This morning, the government confirmed that the fires were an act of arson. An investigation is pending. Speaking from the Palais de l'Élysée, President Millefois asked the city for patience and calm.

"I address not only the inhabitants of Paris, but the entire nation. Rest assured that we will bring the perpetrators to justice. Let us not seek to divide, but to unify. Ahead of the Exposition Universelle, when the eyes of the world will be on us, let us show our good grace, compassion and determination for justice."

Dear citizens, how many of you think that the President's words are not good enough? Good grace and compassion mean nothing. Action is everything. Our cowardly President and his government sit safe and secure inside their palace. YOU are at risk while they twiddle their thumbs and decide when their investigation shall begin.

Here at *La Seule Voix*, we are taking action. Charles Fitzmagnat – owner of this trailblazing newspaper – and I will be holding a protest this Monday afternoon. If you, brave-hearted citizens, are as concerned about the fires as us, please join us at the Place de la République at midday.

Come and stand with us. And, most importantly, come and make your voice heard.

Your President might not want to listen.

But we do.

———————————

Bastien gripped the newspaper so hard that the veins in his hands rose to the surface. How was Olivier already writing for a newspaper? It had only been a month since his release. Whatever *La Seule Voix* was, it was clearly a paper that thrived on lies.

Was this what Olivier meant in the note when he said he would do things *the proper way*? Was writing for a newspaper another part of his grand plan that Bastien had even less time to figure out?

The pantry door swung open to reveal a confused-looking Theo. "I thought you were looking for snacks, not becoming one?"

Bastien pulled himself up with the help of a nearby shelf and handed over the newspaper. "Read this."

Theo's eyes darted up and down the page, his thick curls dangling in his face.

Then, he tossed the newspaper on the floor and stamped it under his boot. "What a load of rubbish. Truly."

"Remember what Olivier said in the note? He's no longer satisfied with stories."

"But this is still all a lie. About President Millefois not caring." Theo folded his arms. "That's just not true."

"It's fiction disguised as fact," Bastien explained. "If Olivier's words are in a newspaper, then people might believe what he says. The more people who read and believe this, the more powerful he will become. 'He who controls the words controls the world.' That's what he told me."

"I know that look." Theo nudged his shoulder; Bastien hadn't realized his gaze had turned vacant. "What is it?"

"I think we should go to the protest this afternoon

and see what he has to say." Even imagining seeing Olivier in person was enough to unsettle Bastien's stomach. But he had no choice; he had to protect himself, his friends, and now, it seemed, everyone else. "I thought we had longer to figure everything out, but he's already stirring up more trouble. Mathilde isn't coming here until tomorrow. We might find out where he's getting his money from now. That could help her."

Theo grabbed an apple from the pantry. "Do we have time to do both?"

Bastien shrugged. "We'll have to make time. Madame Gentille doesn't want us going out on our own, but if we're quick then she won't ever find out."

"*D'accord.*" Theo nodded. "Library first, then the protest."

On the way out of the kitchen, Bastien wrapped two pieces of *pain perdu* in cloth and slipped them into his satchel.

"I'll race you there." Theo eyed up the sweet treat. "The winner gets the bigger slice."

Before Bastien could protest, Theo was already gone from the kitchen.

The Mazarin Library sat on the river's edge, mirroring the Louvre on the other side of the water. The dome of the Institut de France appeared, the building that housed the library and archives, but Bastien didn't dare slow down. Theo was right behind him and nipping at his heels. The route to the library hadn't been straightforward, with many of the streets on the Left Bank closed because of the fires. There was still debris to clear before rebuilding could take place. Bastien hated seeing his city like this, half-defeated and in despair.

The yellow stone pillars that stood either side of the black wooden door came into view and Bastien sprinted up the stairs to the library entrance, collapsing in front of a girl's feet. Luckily, it was Alice.

"What are you two doing?"

Words were a stretch too far for Bastien – panting was all he could manage. He pulled himself up from the floor and smiled.

"Not fair." Theo arrived, tiny beads of sweat dripping down his face and shirt.

Alice chuckled. "Racing for dessert again, were you? You two ran all the way here and you're still late! I've been waiting fifteen minutes."

Bastien looked up at the golden clock embedded

above the entrance. They only had one hour before the archive closed at eleven o'clock. It seemed that Pauline Savoir, Head Archivist, didn't like to work long days.

"We got distracted by that newspaper, *La Seule Voix*," Theo said.

"The protest." Alice grimaced. "A customer left a copy in the bookshop. I can't believe they've let Olivier write for them. I *can* believe he's filled their pages with lies, though."

Bastien held the door open and ushered them through.

The Mazarin Library was just as glorious on the inside as it was on the outside and as delicious as a duck's egg. Maybe it was strange to consider a building delicious, but looking at the richly painted ceilings and gilded walls, Bastien was certain that if he took a bite, it would not disappoint.

"Do you know where the archives are?" Alice asked.

The various corridors and staircases all snaked off in different directions, busy with people. Stone columns and marble statues of Greek gods and goddesses lined the different paths from the lobby.

Bastien hesitated. The only time he had visited the library had been almost three summers ago with his parents. He scratched his head as though it would bring forth the memories he needed to navigate these corridors, but he could only picture his father being told off by the librarian and his mother building a book fort in the research room.

"What about him? He looks like he works here."

Bastien followed Theo's gaze to a man in a blue jacket with a face so stern he looked like one of the stone statues.

They hurried over.

"Sorry to disturb," Bastien said, politely. "Could you tell us where the archives are?"

"Top floor," the man replied, without bothering to look at them. "Take the west staircase. *No* running."

"We weren't planning to," Alice sniffed.

The corridor to the west staircase took them past rows of antique books housed in glass cases. After a sharp left turn, the corridor ended at the bottom of a grand stone staircase. Alice jumped up three steps at a time. "Let's see if you can keep up with me this time."

By the fourth floor, Bastien's lungs burned like a candle at the end of its wick, and the three friends agreed to slow to a walk.

On the sixth floor, the staircase changed from stone

steps to wooden slats. The air turned thick and heavy with dust. Theo eyed the wooden stairs, suspicious about their sturdiness.

"I think this will hold." He slowly stepped onto the first slat. "Move carefully."

After twenty treacherous slats, the staircase opened onto a narrow corridor sheltered by a slanted roof. A row of cracked stained-glass windows let through just enough light for Bastien to spot the yellow oak door at the end of the corridor. Such a polished, well-kept entrance looked entirely out of place in the forgotten attic. Black metal lettering above the door read: *By Appointment Only.*

Bastien frowned. "We're not leaving empty-handed." He knocked on the door. The following five seconds felt like an eternity until the door creaked inward.

"*Entrez.*" A stern voice beckoned them in. "Do take a seat and I'll be with you shortly."

12
THE HEAD ARCHIVIST

The walls inside the archive looked like they were made entirely of paper and could collapse with one great breath. Blueprints and long pieces of parchment with scribbles covered the walls and the floors. Bastien spied maps of Paris and cities beyond – Lille in the north and Marseille in the south – plastered across the ceiling. Rows of bookshelves stretched in every direction and filing cabinets, overflowing with documents, looked fit to burst.

The main source of light was a small copper lamp placed on top of a wooden bureau, casting a dingy glow across the room. Alice picked up a yellow parchment page from the desk. "What a strange place."

"Where did that voice come from?" Bastien craned his neck. "I can't see anyone."

And then a woman sprang up from a mountain of paper. "I am Pauline Savoir, Head Archivist, and you would do well not to touch anything without my permission." She plucked the parchment from Alice. "I wasn't expecting children today."

The three friends startled at her sudden appearance. Pauline wore a buttoned white shirt and a jade green skirt with pockets running down each side. Her black bobbed hair was tucked behind her ears, as were a few pens and pencils.

"Have you been sent by *Le Parisien Quotidien*?" she asked. "They were meant to bring their old newspapers here for safekeeping after the fires."

"Not exactly." Bastien stepped forward. "But we're looking for information and we were told that you're the best archivist in the city."

"The entire country," added Theo.

"We need the sort of impossible information that only an incredible archivist could find." Alice smiled.

Pauline took off her glasses and rubbed her eyes. "No appointment, no archive access." She fixed her glasses back on her nose. "No matter how much you try to compliment me, I can't help. Although, I am flattered. You may continue."

Bastien stepped forward. "This information is urgent. Please, won't you help us?"

"Everyone who comes to my archives claims that what they need is urgent." Pauline turned back to her filing.

Bastien shrugged off this rejection. Pauline Savoir was going to help him. He just had to make her listen. "A friend of mine, Gaston LeGrand, told me that you might be able to help. My name is Bastien Bonlivre."

Pauline slammed the cabinet shut and looked back. "Bonlivre." She rolled the name over her tongue, searching for its familiarity. "You're Margot's son? She used to visit whenever she was working on a new story. I quite miss hearing her wicked laugh. It could cut through glass."

Bastien smiled. It was easy to imagine his mother spending hours poring over old documents. Researching a book idea had been her favourite part of the writing process. He liked learning about his parents from other people; each memory was a new way of looking at them and the type of people they had been.

"I read about what happened to your parents, in the

reports of the Bad Brothers trial." Pauline's face softened. "I'm pleased justice prevailed. You and your friends were so courageous."

Bastien bit his tongue. Justice most certainly had not prevailed, not in a world where Olivier Odieux walked free and continued to write dangerous words.

"What are you looking for?" Pauline retrieved a pencil from behind her ear. "I suppose I can make an exception. Just this once."

"We're trying to find out more about a famous ballerina. Her name is Lucienne Méchante. Might you have any records on her?"

Pauline's brow furrowed. "Dancing isn't my speciality. Let me go and look. I'll be back in a moment." She turned to Alice, a wicked glint behind her glasses. "And don't touch *anything*. History is irreplaceable, unlike children."

Bastien and Theo held in their laughs until Pauline had disappeared down a dimly-lit corridor.

Alice shot them a look that could have sliced the toughest steak in two. "Remind me to throw you both into the river on the walk home."

A minute later, Pauline emerged from the corridor with wild hair and glasses smudged with ink. "As it turns out, we have quite a few documents about ballerinas.

Who knew?" She held up a thick folder and dropped it onto the desk.

Theo whistled. "That looks like it could do serious damage."

"No one is better armed than an archivist. I have books and document stacks more damaging than any weapon." She cracked her knuckles and opened the folder, flicking through each page with incredible speed. Bastien wondered how many books he could read if his eyes moved that quickly.

"Here we go!" Pauline smacked her hands on the table. "Lucienne Méchante was Prima Ballerina at the Opéra National for ten years. There are pictures and articles in here."

The archivist held up the first photograph and Bastien knew that Mathilde was telling the truth. The photograph of Lucienne Méchante was like staring into Mathilde's future. They both had the same fierce, hungry look in their eyes.

Pauline removed a small magnifying glass from her desk drawer. "The print in this article is so small. Like it was made for only ants to read. Ah, it says Lucienne retired from dancing when she was expecting her first child."

"Does it say who the father is?" Alice asked.

"It doesn't say anything other than a 'French nobleman'." Pauline harrumphed and stuffed the article back into the folder. "Is there anything else I can help you with?"

"There was one more thing," Bastien said. "The Odieuxs."

Pauline flinched as though a gob of spit had just hit her. "Why do you want to look into the Odieuxs? I—"

"Pauline!" The archive door flew open with a loud bang, revealing a short, stocky man dressed in a dark grey herringbone suit. A black bowler hat covered his head, and his hands were fixed on his hips. He had, what Bastien's mother would've called, a face that refused the word no.

"Monsieur Trapu." Pauline curtsied. "I wasn't expecting you until eleven o'clock."

The stocky man slumped in a chair across from Pauline's desk and took a handkerchief from his suit pocket to dab his brow. "I must go to the Élysée Palace earlier than scheduled. President Millefois needs urgent assistance. Come and help me." He paused and sneered. "I didn't realize children were allowed in here."

"Do you mind if we have a look ourselves?" Bastien ignored the man.

Pauline wiped her glasses on her shirt. "I don't normally allow it."

"I'm waiting," Monsieur Trapu called.

"We'll put everything back in its correct place." Bastien looked down the archive corridors. He couldn't actually see where they ended. Any time searching through them wouldn't feel long enough.

Pauline's head swivelled like an owl's between Bastien and Monsieur Trapu. "You have twenty minutes," she decided. "Put everything back in its correct place. I will know if you don't."

"*Comment?*" Alice couldn't help herself.

Pauline smiled. "Just call it a sixth sense of mine. I have worked here for twenty years. Nothing goes unnoticed." And with that she sat back down behind her desk and attended to the impatient man.

"That's us warned." Bastien eyed up the maze of never-ending corridors in front of him. Now that they knew Mathilde was telling the truth, they could focus solely on figuring out what Olivier was up to.

The words in his note repeated in Bastien's mind. If the Odieux family history was the key to Olivier's next plan, then the archive was their best bet. Could Bastien find what they needed to stop Olivier spreading his lies in the newspaper and beyond?

"Come on." Bastien slipped through the narrow entrance between two crooked cabinets. "Let's go and dig up the past."

The archive corridors were no place for claustrophobic people. The metal filing cabinets towered all the way to the ceiling and formed an arch above their heads. Bastien felt underprepared. He also really wished that he was wearing a helmet.

He led Theo and Alice past a structurally unsound newspaper tower, his eyes darting all over. "I'm starting to think that twenty minutes is nowhere near enough time." Bastien peered at the filing-cabinet labels. *Paris Theatres & Cinemas* next to a cabinet called *First World War Cavalry Regiments*.

Theo blew a layer of dust from another label. "This one is a file on every single left-handed person in Paris!

125

They're not in any sort of order."

Bastien scrunched his nose. They only had twenty minutes to search and then they'd have to sprint to the protest if they were going to meet Madame Gentille and the others in the park. He didn't want to make the director suspicious, and time was *not* on his side. "We need to move quicker!"

They hurried to the end of the narrow corridor. It opened up into a circular space with two separate corridors trailing off it. In the middle of the black and white chequered tile floor, a blackboard sign stood on top of a large oak table.

"Finally!" Bastien looked at the chalk scribblings on the blackboard. "This is the directory. The cabinets from here are alphabetically ordered. A-M is on the left, N-Z on the right."

Alice tucked her hair behind her ears. "Right it is."

Bastien startled at the sound of Pauline Savoir's commanding voice. He didn't want to get on the wrong side of her and he had a feeling that this would be their only chance to explore unsupervised.

They started down the right-hand corridor. Most of the filing cabinets this far back had turned different shades of rust, a mixture of dark orange and pale green.

Bastien covered his mouth with his sleeve and slipped underneath a black metal ladder that was bolted to the wooden shelves. "O shouldn't be too far."

Alice narrowly dodged a stack of thick newspapers that toppled from a pile and landed with a thump.

"*Oups,*" she said, quickly scooping them back up.

"Found it!" Bastien spun towards Theo, who was pointing upwards. "Documents beginning with O!"

The tall metal cabinet stretched high, its handle out of reach.

"I knew I should've brought my extendable arm with me," Theo muttered. "Can either of you reach? I'm counting myself out for, you know, obvious reasons."

"Not by myself." Bastien looked over at Alice. "I can reach if I climb on your shoulders?"

Obligingly, Alice crouched down and positioned herself in front of the cabinet. "If you pull my hair, I'm dropping you."

"Noted." With a hand from Theo, Bastien carefully climbed up Alice's back and onto her shoulders. Standing at full height, he rose onto his tiptoes, his fingers spread wide in anticipation as he reached for the cabinet drawer. The handle squeaked, but refused to move. He tried again but it was no use.

"It's stuck with rust!"

"An inventor is always prepared." Theo patted down his shorts pocket and produced a small vial of oil. "*Voici*, this should do the trick. Catch!"

The glass vial flew up into the air and Alice shuffled to the left, allowing Bastien to catch it.

"Do I want to know why you always carry oil with you?" Alice asked.

Theo grinned. "I told you. It pays to be prepared."

Bastien rubbed a couple of oil drops around the rusted edges of the drawer. After waiting a minute, he tugged on the handle and it flew open to reveal rows of folders.

"We're in!" Bastien flicked through each folder as quickly as he could, searching for a name that had unfortunately become all too familiar to him.

"I've got something!" His eyes landed on a thick folder, bursting with papers. *ODIEUX* was printed in dark red letters. He grabbed the folder and clutched it to his chest as Alice slowly lowered him back down.

The folder spilled open as the three friends dropped to their knees in the archive corridor. The floor was cold, but none of them noticed.

Bastien scoured through newspaper clippings, papers and documents, willing his eyes and mind to focus. What had Olivier meant in his note when he'd said he would use his family's past to help his future? There had to be something in here that would help them understand. Bastien had to figure out *what* Olivier was planning and *how* to stop him as quickly as he could.

Alice slapped her hand down. "Go back to the page before."

It was an old newspaper clipping, the paper as brown as mud, and Bastien flattened its creased edges.

"What is it?" Theo asked.

"It's an obituary. For a man called Victor Odieux." Bastien held the clipping up to the light to read.

Le Parisien Quotidien

VENDREDI, OCTOBRE 10 1890

OBITUARY

VICTOR ODIEUX died last night, aged seventy. He passed peacefully at his home in Boulogne-Billancourt, surrounded by his family, after suffering from a short illness.

Victor Odieux was a renowned political advisor, helping the all-powerful Emperor Napoléon III to make important decisions, pass new laws and strengthen France's military power.

However, with the news of Odieux's death reaching many today, it is expected that his career will not be what he is best remembered for, but instead, the double life that Victor created for himself.

It is believed that Odieux was a co-founder of the Red Ink Society, an underground political group who sought to restore a ruling king to the country and to maintain the privileges of the French elite.

What will become of the Society following the death of one of its founding fathers? Will a new leader emerge, ready to challenge the government, or will the Red Ink Society retreat into the shadows? Only time will tell.

Victor leaves a wife and three sons.

———————————————————

"The Red Ink Society." Bastien rolled the name around on his tongue. It felt familiar. But why? He broke down the name in his mind. Red ink. To write with. A pen. Where there was a pen there was always an inkpot. And then it all clicked into place.

"Remember there was a symbol on that note from Olivier? Of a red inkpot and pen?"

Theo nodded. "And the fountain at Olivier's old house. That was shaped like an inkpot and pen too, wasn't it?"

"And the same symbol was inside Olivier's book that arrived at the orphanage yesterday morning." Bastien followed his trail of thought. "It has to be a symbol for the society. What if that is what Olivier is trying to do? To revive the Red Ink Society and bring back a king! He said in the note that he didn't want to write about kings any longer. He wants to *be* one."

The three friends stared at each other and Bastien's thoughts sped up, as though his own mind was too afraid to linger on them for longer than necessary.

The Red Ink Society believed only a ruling king could control France and Olivier wanted to become the most powerful man in the country. He had made that much clear the night that Bastien had escaped from his house in Montmartre. And in the little time that he had been a free man, Olivier had somehow managed to convince a newspaper to support him.

If he could bring back the Red Ink Society, gain support from other members and grow his power, then Olivier Odieux could dust off the golden throne and place the jewel-encrusted crown where he felt it belonged: on top of his head.

Despite the warm and stuffy atmosphere of the archives, Bastien shivered.

"It doesn't surprise me that every generation of Odieuxs was just as awful as the next," Theo finally said.

Alice nodded. "I'd laugh if that wasn't depressingly true."

Bastien placed the newspaper clipping to one side and took the remaining documents from the folder. "We don't have much time left. Prioritize looking for anything that mentions the Red Ink Society."

The three friends got to work. As Bastien trawled through censuses and book reviews, it dawned on him that Olivier's plan was much bigger than just the cruel, calculated moves of one man. He was trying to re-establish a whole organization that shared his poisonous beliefs and would help him take power.

"I've got something." Theo passed a small red booklet

to Bastien. "See that?" The young inventor pointed to a small stamp at the bottom of the cover. "It's the Society symbol."

Bastien opened the booklet and his heart felt as heavy as iron when he realized what it was. "This is a manifesto."

Theo's mouth formed a perfect circle. "A what?"

"A manifesto is a published piece of writing by a political group or individual," Alice explained.

"It's their way of explaining what they believe in and what they want to accomplish," Bastien continued. "Look at this first sentence. *We seek to re-establish one ruling figure to lead our great country of France. Only a king can keep total control.*"

"And the one beneath it!" Theo growled. "*The Society believes in the superiority of the noble French class. We believe that noblemen should possess all rights and that any lesser citizens should have restricted rights as dictated by us noblemen.*"

Sickness curled in Bastien's stomach. "This is as disgusting as it is dangerous." He turned to the last page, where a list of names and signatures filled the space.

Beside him, Theo traced his finger down the names. "The Odieuxs, the Fitzmagnats and the—"

In the distance, a door slammed. Bastien jumped to his feet, the booklet in his hands.

"That silly man must've gone." Alice stood up and brushed the dust from her palms. "Pauline will come looking for us soon. Our time's almost up."

"What was the last name?" Bastien asked. "Of the founding families?"

"The Nineys," said Theo.

Bastien didn't feel the sturdiness from his legs disappear, but suddenly he stumbled back into a cabinet. The metallic thud echoed through the room. "Niney is the surname of the replacement judge in the Bad Brothers trial. Pierre Niney! The one who let Olivier go!"

"It was corrupt. The whole trial." Alice paced, her footsteps now stomps. "The judge is a member of the Red Ink Society."

"But why did he find Xavier guilty if he let Olivier go?" Theo asked. "It doesn't make sense."

"That's what we need to figure out." Bastien picked up the manifesto and realized he didn't want to let it go. It was wrong to take anything from Pauline's archive, but this was important proof that might help him figure out how to stop Olivier.

With a sleight of hand to rival the magicians at the Cirque d'Hiver, Bastien slipped the manifesto into his satchel. Theo and Alice stared at him, the worry on their faces now replaced with delighted grins.

"Bastien Bonlivre, library and archive rule-breaker." Theo chuckled. "I never thought I'd see the day."

"I hope you've never stolen a book from Le Chat Curieux!" Alice winked.

Heat flooded Bastien's face. "Of course not! But we need this manifesto. It could be the key to stopping Olivier." He stuffed the rest of the documents back into the folder. "I'll bring it back once this is all over. Let's go before we get caught."

"We?" Alice raised her eyebrow.

"Don't drag us into your criminal activity," Theo sniggered. "We've already got one villain to stop."

Once they'd stopped their teasing, Alice and Theo helped him put the folder back into the cabinet. As Bastien followed them back through the archive corridors, a new purpose rose in him. He didn't just want to stop Olivier, but he had to halt the sickness of the Red Ink Society from spreading through the country too.

People believing the lies Olivier wrote in *La Seule Voix* newspaper would only be the beginning of something far more dangerous. The type of king that Olivier wanted to be – a selfish leader who ruled with unlimited power – only belonged in history books.

Soon enough, Bastien hoped, Olivier Odieux would become history too.

THE RETURN OF OLIVIER ODIEUX

LA SEULE VOIX

Not far from the Mazarin Library, the Place de la République was abuzz with anger. Olivier peered out of the window as his taxi slowed to a stop on Boulevard Voltaire. It had just turned midday and he couldn't see a free square of the street.

Olivier felt a swell of triumph rise in him. Hundreds of angry citizens had read his article and turned up to the protest. It was heartening to think that so many people agreed with him. Plus, he liked anger. He knew what to do with it; how to bend and shape it into something that he could use to his advantage.

"I can't go any further, Monsieur Odieux," the driver said. "There are too many people."

Olivier met the driver's gaze in the mirror. "But I paid you to take me all the way. Do you not value your job? Or your life, for that matter?"

From the backseat, Olivier watched the driver's neck hairs stand on end.

He smiled, enjoying the man's discomfort. "It was a joke. I will walk." Olivier climbed out of the car and threw a handful of coins through the window. Turning towards the noise, he took a deep breath, pulled up the hood of his coat and slipped into the crowd.

Everyone was here because of him. Olivier had promised Charles Fitzmagnat exciting news stories, and mysterious fires spreading across Paris certainly counted as exciting.

Olivier swerved to avoid a woman waving a placard that read: *WE DEMAND ANSWERS*.

"Protect our city!" a young man chanted, his friends clapping their hands and stamping their feet in unison.

Olivier smirked; the level of anger in Paris was far higher than he could have imagined. And in all honesty, did they even know what they were truly angry about? People were so easily manipulated.

Organizing the protest quickly had been a stroke of genius on Charles's part. That much Olivier had to admit. Cunning admired cunning. And now, looking around at the number of people – the old and the young – Olivier felt a surge of power flow through his veins. His plan was working.

He reached the middle of the square, where a small makeshift stage stood in front of the Marianne monument, the bronze Goddess of Liberty surveying everything below her firm feet. Through the glow of the sunshine, he spotted Charles Fitzmagnat standing next to his colleagues. Olivier walked towards the red tape that encircled the stage, lowered his hood and checked his hair. Appearance was everything.

"Charles!"

The newspaper tycoon turned around. His eyes shone like polished coins. "Not a bad turnout with only a morning's notice!" Charles lifted the red tape to usher Olivier through. "You have quite the audience for your return to the public eye."

"Indeed." Olivier sniffed the potential in the air. Soon, every single person in the square would hear his speech. They would no longer think of him as the disgraced author who had been roped into his brother's kidnappings and other dastardly crimes. Once they heard from him, his past would disappear as quickly as a vanishing act.

And then he could rebuild and conquer.

"We've been reprinting all morning," Charles said, his voice thick with smugness. "We were the quickest newspaper to report on the fires. And one of the few news buildings to remain undamaged."

Olivier cracked his knuckles and grinned. "How fortunate."

"Come and meet the newspaper's board." Olivier followed Charles and shook the hands of wrinkled old men, whose hair and conversation skills were as grey as newspaper print. Once they'd left, Olivier pulled Charles to the side of the stage.

"You remember the other thing we discussed at dinner?" Olivier could smell the garlic *escargots* that Charles had eaten for lunch. "About your son."

"As promised, he has made contact with the boy and his friends."

"But just how capable is he?"

"My son is a Fitzmagnat," Charles hissed.

"I don't doubt your son's heritage." Olivier spoke calmly; he couldn't afford to anger Charles. "But the Bonlivre boy is craftier than he appears. He escaped from my clutches once, along with his notebook. Hugo and Margot knew—"

"You've made clear what is at stake for you," Charles interrupted, "but I would rather disown my son than let him disappoint me. It is being handled, so please, no more direct threats to the boy that could be traced back to you. A move will be made when the time is right." The newspaper owner checked the time on his diamond-encrusted watches. "Anyway, it's almost time to begin. Are you ready?"

Olivier removed his coat to reveal a sharp black suit. Pinned on his lapel was a small emblem: a red inkpot and pen.

"Why, yes." Olivier waved away Charles's offering of a megaphone; he didn't need any help in making his voice heard. "I don't think I've ever been more ready for anything in my life."

15

PARIS IN PROTEST

Emerging from the Mazarin Library, Bastien felt like he was underwater. His feelings swam up and down and his thoughts were bubbles, scattered and unsolid.

The fear of Olivier had never really left Bastien, but to know that Olivier had corrupt judges on his side and that they were all part of some sinister society working together to bring back a king to France – it was too much to even imagine. Overcome, Bastien leaned against the library's stone wall to catch his breath.

History was something that Hugo Bonlivre had been able to talk about for hours; whether anyone was paying attention was another matter. Still, some evenings Bastien would listen as his father explained how many years ago, people had grown fed up of being ruled by a royal family and brought it all to an end. Some of it had been too difficult for him to understand, but Bastien remembered how his father had told him that one person should never have absolute power. And definitely not a whole family. It was why the country now had a president who made decisions with the help of other people in the government.

But how could Bastien fight against all of this if his parents had failed? They had both possessed more courage and intelligence than he could ever hope to have and Olivier had still somehow got the better of them.

Alice placed her hand against Bastien's forehead. "You don't look too good."

"I'm just afraid of what happens next. Olivier might have a grander plan, but he's still going to come for me. And the notebook."

"He might not," Alice said quietly.

"You know he will. He's threatened me twice already!" More questions flitted around in Bastien's mind like flies. "And his plan is already in motion. Olivier said what my parents knew could ruin everything. He must've been talking about the Red Ink Society and how it will help him take power. The secret in the notebook has to be linked to all this. And I still don't even know what it is!"

The friends looked at each other blankly, desperately trying to figure out what to say.

"Just a thought," Theo said, "but maybe we don't need the help of a hidden secret. Maybe we can figure this all out for ourselves. We've come this far without the notebook clue, right?"

"Protest at the Place de la République! *La Seule Voix* and friends challenge the government!" a boy wearing a grey flat cap interrupted, shouting out the day's news in his foghorn voice.

Olivier's newspaper article came hurtling back to Bastien, one word at a time. He closed his eyes and pictured a name in block print, one that Olivier had mentioned.

Charles Fitzmagnat.

"I forgot about the protest – we need to go to it!" A new wave of energy rushed through Bastien. He had allowed doubt to drag him down, but Alice was right. Even without his parents' help, they could stop Olivier's dangerous and twisted dream from coming true.

"Now?" Alice asked, surprised. "I don't have long until I need to get back to the bookshop."

"If we hurry, we can get to the Place de la République in time." Bastien broke into a jog as the bridge came into view. "The founder of *La Seule Voix* is called Charles Fitzmagnat. He's the one who organized this protest and invited Olivier to speak. Fitzmagnat was the other name in the manifesto. They are the last founding family. They must all be working together again!"

The journey to the Place de la République took twice as long as usual. People spilled from the pavement and onto the streets like knocked-over inkpots. The atmosphere of the crowd thickened as they turned off Rue du Temple and crossed over to the square.

"I didn't think there'd be this many people." Bastien stood on his tiptoes to look through the crowd. There was a wooden stage in the middle of the square, but the figures standing on it looked as small as ants.

Theo jumped. "Can you see him?"

"Not yet." Bastien squinted. "Let's get closer. We don't have long before Madame Gentille suspects we're somewhere we shouldn't be. We're supposed to meet them in the Luxembourg Gardens right about now."

"Better make it count then," Theo said.

As they weaved in and out of groups, Bastien noticed old men with greying beards, young children wrapped around their parents' legs and babies swaddled across their mothers' chests. A group of teenagers spat in the air as they chanted furiously. Did all of these people really want to hear what Olivier had to say? Did they truly believe that he had nothing to do with the crimes that Xavier had taken the fall for? Bastien knew how fear could twist people's minds into believing the wrong things, but he still despaired to see such support.

"Over there!" Alice pointed to the honey-locust trees that lined the right-hand side of the square. "We'll be able to see the stage better."

The gap between the trees did give a clearer view of the stage and Bastien spotted a familiar stocky figure standing with their arms stretched out wide. Although the figure's back was turned, Bastien could never mistake Olivier Odieux.

Theo hopped. "I can still only see the bottom half of the stage."

Alice pulled him back by the collar of his shirt. "Here, sit on my shoulders."

"And you won't drop me?"

"Not on purpose." Alice squatted and tucked her hair behind her ears.

Theo jumped onto Alice's back, his dirty boots grazing the sides of her canary-yellow dress.

"Keep those off my new *robe*!"

Bastien silenced his squabbling friends with a flap of his arm as Olivier walked to the front of the stage. "He's about to speak."

Like a conductor leading an orchestra, Olivier dropped his arms. Silence fell across the crowd.

"Dear citizens," Olivier's voice boomed. "*Merci* for joining us today. Some of you will know who I am, for all the wrong reasons. I hope you will listen to what I have to say and judge me as the man standing in front of you, not for the crimes I was wrongly accused of."

Bastien bit his tongue. How could Olivier stand up there in front of hundreds, possibly thousands, of people and spew such lies?

"We all share something," Olivier continued, "and that is anger. Anger at President Millefois and his government for letting our city burn. The fires were clearly an attack against Paris, perhaps a warning for what is to come for the rest of the country. Whoever is responsible for these fires must be stopped."

Was it Bastien's imagination or did a smirk just flash across Olivier's face? He rubbed his eyes, but it was still there.

"But the President has done nothing!" Olivier shouted. "His staff make every decision for him. He is spineless and certainly not fit to lead us through such an emergency."

Bastien looked around nervously at the faces in the crowd. Some nodded their heads, their mouths moving and chewing on the words that Olivier fed them. Others roared, shouting *with* him and believing every hateful word he said.

While a storm raged inside Bastien, he still noticed that something was off about the way Olivier spoke of the fires – he felt it from the tips of his toes to the fair hairs on his head... And why had he smirked when talking about them too?

"My grandfather Victor Odieux was an influential government figure and a man of great nobility. Remember, we Odieuxs are royal descendants, after all." Olivier's words hung in the air for a few seconds. "He taught me about our society and how it operates. If there is one thing I learned from him it is this: the people hold the power."

The crowd roared again.

"*La Seule Voix* is the only paper concerned with delivering the news you deserve." Olivier stood even taller. "Our people need a strong hand. Will there be more fires? Will we feel truly safe again? The Exposition Universelle is less than a week away now and we need someone to protect our citizens and guests from all around the world! I hope you might consider me as the man qualified for this important job."

Uneasiness crept further up Bastien's body. Everything felt off-kilter, from Olivier's speech to the look on his face. He'd talked about the fires almost as though he was proud of them, trying to hide a constant smirk. Bastien knew a thing or two about how to read people; how you could open them up like a book and delve into the parts of themselves that they tried to hide.

He also knew Olivier Odieux, and the thoughts that had been swimming around the dark pond in Bastien's mind became clearer until they finally sparkled like crystal-clear water.

He turned to Theo and Alice. "I think Olivier is responsible for the fires."

"*Quoi?*" Theo twisted too quickly and fell from Alice's shoulders. People nearby turned and tutted.

"Come on," Bastien said. "Let's get out of here before we draw any more attention to ourselves." He hurried through the trees and waited for Theo and Alice on the other side of the street, across from the square.

"Repeat what you said," Alice instructed.

"Olivier spoke about the fires as though he was proud of them," Bastien said. "Like he was boasting and it made me think: what if he started the fires on purpose?"

Alice frowned.

"I've come face to face with Olivier before and I can read him," Bastien continued. His best friends had to trust his instinct. "I can see through his lies. He's pretending to be reasonable, but he'll do anything to get what he wants."

"Even burning down half of Paris?" she asked.

Bastien nodded. "Even that."

Theo's nostrils flared; the look on his face reminded Bastien of the moment just before he fixed a problem.

"Olivier wants to get rid of President Millefois and turn the people against him," Theo said.

"Exactly!" Bastien replied. "We know his ultimate goal is to become king. A good way to turn everyone against the President is to create chaos. Once Olivier has Paris on his side, he will spread his lies to the rest of the country and the influence of the Red Ink Society will help him do just that."

The three friends crossed the river and returned to their side of the city. Even though they'd put some distance between them and the protest, Bastien still heard cheers of support.

"If we're going to expose Olivier, we'll need proof that he started the fires. He must've had help too from his society friends." Alice kicked a cobblestone in frustration. "But Pierre Niney is still the Head Judge at the Palais de Justice. Even if we can get Olivier arrested again, he will walk free."

Bastien knew that his suspicion was nothing without solid proof and, even then, they would have to battle against ancient societies and corruption. Olivier had already caused so much destruction. What would he be capable of with thousands of people behind him?

The idea terrified Bastien into action.

"Mathilde was right," he said. "We need to work together if we're going to take Olivier and the Red Ink Society down. If they're not playing by the rules then neither should we. But we have to be careful; this is bigger than anything we've gone up against before."

What Bastien didn't say aloud was another thought

that flashed like neon in his brain. Olivier had his grand plan to carry out, but he was still not finished with him. Bastien knew that the threats would soon turn into real danger; that Olivier would find a way to get to him and his notebook just like he'd always said.

Alice clapped her hands together. "What comes next then?"

A rumble escaped from Theo's stomach. "Food, preferably. We've probably missed Madame Gentille's picnic!"

"First we eat," Bastien said, swallowing down his fear. "Then we assemble our team."

The rest of Monday had unfortunately afforded Bastien and Theo little time to plan how to prove Olivier was behind the fires. Alice had rushed off to get back to the bookshop and they had quick-footed it to the Luxembourg Gardens, where Madame Gentille and the rest of the boys were picnicking. Thankfully, there had still been two caramel éclairs left and they had quickly shoved them into their mouths, making it impossible to answer the director's questions about why they were so late.

Once they had arrived home, Bastien had surprisingly fallen into a heavy sleep. The human body had a remarkable gift for knowing when it was time to reset.

And Bastien had so desperately needed to let the weight of everything float away into the sky, if only for one night.

During Tuesday's lessons, his mind trailed back to his parents. He wondered if they would be proud of everything he had uncovered so far, even if he still hadn't cracked their notebook secret. Now Bastien knew about the Red Ink Society and the names of the other founding families. Judge Pierre Niney would never find Olivier guilty of any crimes and Charles Fitzmagnat was giving him the platform to spread his lies about the fire and the President. But what could Bastien and his friends do about it?

By dinner, Bastien was still chewing on his thoughts like the last of the green beans that currently sat on his plate. Mathilde would arrive at the orphanage soon. Although he knew that working together was the best option, he still had to come up with a plan. Maybe she would have an idea? That was the advantage of working in a team, after all.

Going up against the two evil Odieux brothers had been challenging enough, but to stop Olivier and the Red Ink Society from overthrowing the government... well, it felt hopeless. Especially with Bastien's looming fear that Olivier would come for him again when he'd least expect it.

Still, Bastien knew that hope was not a solid thing but ever changing. It could be stretched and squished to fit into the smallest of situations and, as long as he held onto that little bit of hope, he knew it could grow. Right now, his hope came in the form of him and his friends, old and new, banding together to stop evil from spreading in their city.

"Earth to Bastien!" A hand in front of his face jolted him from his thoughts. Theo stood on the other side of the dining table.

"*Désolé*. I was in my head."

"Your favourite place to be." Theo grabbed a green bean from Bastien's plate and popped it in his mouth. "Mathilde should be here soon. Shall we go and wait for her in the courtyard? Madame Gentille and the others are listening to Felix in the music room."

Bastien dropped his plate off in the kitchen before he and Theo headed towards the entrance.

The courtyard had always been one of Bastien and Theo's favourite places to sit and chat. When the first signs of spring had bloomed, Madame Gentille had enlisted the help of all the boys to plant flowers, of every kind, and now the courtyard was their very own Eden in the heart of the fourteenth arrondissement. They took it in turns each week to water the lilies and roses, although Clément was banned from using the pruning shears after almost cutting off the ear of a passer-by while attempting to cut the hedge.

"Do you think she'll come?" Theo plucked a nearby daisy and twisted it into a loop.

"*Qui*? Mathilde? Why wouldn't she?"

Theo shrugged. "We weren't exactly welcoming to her."

Bastien thought back to the grotto, where their worlds had collided with the mysterious girl. "Trust doesn't come at the click of a finger. Also, were you really expecting to meet Olivier's secret daughter that day?"

"Even I didn't see that one coming." Theo grimaced. "Poor girl. Imagine having Olivier as your father."

A crash, from the other side of the courtyard, forced the boys to their feet.

"Mathilde," Bastien called. "Is that you?"

A dirty ballet slipper appeared from behind the angel statue in the middle of the courtyard. Mathilde's hair was tied in a scruffy ponytail and she looked awfully sheepish.

"Why were you hiding from us?" Bastien pretended not to notice the smashed flowerpots that she'd knocked over. "We invited you here!"

"I wasn't hiding." Mathilde shrugged. "I just wasn't sure if you'd be pleased to see me or not."

"We believe what you said about Olivier destroying your mother's life," Bastien said. "We will work as a team and help each other. Olivier's plans are even bigger than we thought."

A crooked half-smile broke across Mathilde's face. "*Merci*. I promise you can trust me." Then her expression darkened. "What have you learned?"

A loud rumble that sounded like a tired engine escaped from Mathilde's stomach. She wrapped her arms around her waist.

"There are some leftovers in the kitchen," Theo said. "I'll go get them. You don't want to hear this story on an empty stomach."

While Mathilde savoured every bite of her *poulet roti*, Bastien and Theo sat beside her on the steps and recounted everything they had learned at the archives. Bastien spoke quickly, not wanting to dwell on the details – it would only make him worry. Right now, he needed to focus on what he could control.

Mathilde paused mid-bite, a forkful of roasted chicken lingering in the air. "So you want to find evidence that Olivier started the fires and that it's all part of a larger plan to make him king. I want to help you do that, obviously, but I want to get Maman's money back too."

"Simple." Theo smiled.

"Good thing we're a team then." Mathilde wiped her mouth. "How are we going to do this?"

A seed of an idea had planted itself in Bastien's head. It was a wild idea, but it grew all the same. He thought of Olivier's old house in Montmartre, where richness and secrets had dripped from every wall. That house was now a pile of ash, so where was Olivier staying?

"We need to find out where Olivier is currently living." The three of them huddled closer together as Bastien spoke. "If we can find where that is, then I'm certain there'll be proof inside. The note you found, Mathilde, made me realize that Olivier will never stop. He sent me another threat directly to the orphanage, saying not to get in his way. I'm scared, but I've been scared ever since I first met him. But being afraid isn't a bad thing. It means we will be smarter about sneaking right under his nose."

"Another break-in?" Theo's eyes began to dance. "We'll need upgraded tools to help us."

But Mathilde only looked partially convinced. "And you're certain about this?"

Bastien nodded. "I don't think Olivier truly trusts anyone other than himself. He might have the help of the Society this time to get what he wants, but we have something even more powerful. We have each other."

Mathilde laughed. "That's a bit…sentimental."

"We all want the same thing." Bastien ignored her teasing. "We're not competing against each other. None of us wants to be the most powerful person in this country. We just want to do what is right. For our loved ones and ourselves. And that is what is going to give us an advantage."

The last of the evening sun had almost disappeared behind a large cloud in the sky. Another day was ending, but something was starting inside Bastien. He felt more than just hope. He had belief.

"If we're going to break in, we will need disguises." Mathilde looked down at her shirt, the colour of dried manure. "I don't exactly have anything else to wear."

Theo waved her worry away. "Leave the disguises

159

to me. I like a challenge. After all, Yemma always said that the best coral lives in dirty water."

Mathilde frowned. "You should really work on your compliments."

The door to the orphanage creaked open. Bastien turned to find Madame Gentille standing in her dressing gown, its lilac fabric a stark contrast to the dark and stormy look on her face.

"What's going on? I realized you two were missing from Felix's concert and came to collect you, but I see you're out here gossiping like two grandmothers with…" The director raised her eyebrows in Mathilde's direction, taking in the dirt and scratches on her face.

Mathilde jumped up and the dinner plate fell from her lap. It smashed into pieces on the concrete. "I'm no one. I should be going."

"You're safe here." Bastien reached out to her. "You don't need to leave."

But she shook her head and pulled away. "I can't be anywhere for too long. They might find me."

"Are you in trouble?" Bastien didn't detect anger in Madame Gentille's voice, only compassion.

Bastien wouldn't have taken Mathilde for a girl who'd be afraid of someone in fluffy slippers, but from the way she stood, ready to run and her shoulders hunched defensively, she looked positively terrified of Madame Gentille.

He turned to the director. "Mathilde is a friend, and she needs our help. She was sent to a correction school, but she doesn't belong there. Can she stay with us for a while?"

Madame Gentille looked back and forth. There was doubt in her face, but also sympathy and curiosity.

"In this house, we never refuse a friend. Do come in, *ma poulette*." She held the door open and Mathilde hesitantly tiptoed into the hallway.

Once she was out of earshot, Madame Gentille turned to Bastien and Theo. "And I think it's about time us three had a chat, don't you?"

17
THE OTHER SIDE OF MADAME GENTILLE

"I'll be fine, honestly."

Robin and Fred lingered in the entrance hall, staring curiously at Mathilde.

Bastien frowned. "You're sure?"

Mathilde picked up a pile of folded blankets that Madame Gentille had retrieved from her office. "Fred is going to introduce me to the other boys. And Robin said he'd show me to my room after. My *own* room."

"It's one of the few places where you can't actually hear Fred's snoring," Robin giggled.

"Better she hears my snoring than your babbling," Fred muttered.

Madame Gentille poked her head out of the office door. "Bastien, Theo. Shall we?"

"See you soon," Bastien said. "Hopefully."

Mathilde nodded and skipped upstairs, Robin and Fred running to keep up with her.

Turning towards the office door, Bastien's steps were heavy with indecision.

"How much do we tell her?" Theo said.

"I don't know. Will we ever live a peaceful life if we tell her the whole truth?" Bastien whispered. But not quietly enough.

"I'll be the judge of that." Madame Gentille ushered the boys inside.

Her office was the old cloakroom and just about fitted a small desk, a few chairs and enough wall space to display an impressive amount of swimming medals and awards. Bastien glanced at a silver trophy perched on the desk. *Gabrielle Gentille*. Was that Madame Gentille's actual name? He didn't know much about the director's life before she took over the orphanage.

"Tell me everything about how you met this new friend of yours." The director sat back in her chair and kicked off her fluffy slippers, her green-painted toenails resting on the tabletop. "And don't leave a single detail out. You've both been acting strangely since Bastien's book party. I haven't wanted to push you – I'd hoped you would come to me in your own time. But the world around us is growing more dangerous and it is my job to protect you."

An agreement passed between Bastien and Theo with a single look. They wanted to trust Madame Gentille and so they would tell her the truth. Most of it.

"I don't even know where to begin," Bastien said.

"As a storyteller," Madame Gentille said, "you should know that the start is usually a good place."

By the time Bastien and Theo had paused for breath, the clock behind the director's desk had just struck half past seven.

"I know the fires have frightened everyone, but you can't ask us to just stay inside and do nothing," Bastien said. He hoped Madame Gentille would hear his final plea. "We have to stop Olivier from turning the city against President Millefois. We have to stop him before he hurts other people, just like he did to me and might do again."

Madame Gentille looked as though she had received

a year's worth of bad news in a single second. "Why didn't you tell me about the note that Mathilde found? Or the threat that Olivier sent directly here! This is your home – somewhere you should feel safe."

"Because it wouldn't change anything!" Bastien bit back his frustration. "The rules don't apply to Olivier. The police couldn't help us before and they won't now, with a corrupt judge. We're on our own."

"I understand how much you boys have faced," Madame Gentille said softly. "I know how the hurt you've been through has built a cage around your hearts. But just like you have let Mathilde in, there is strength in numbers. And this isn't something you should deal with alone. Promise me you won't."

When Xavier Odieux had run the orphanage, Bastien and the others had grown used to the deviousness of adults. Apart from Alice's parents, Charlotte and Jules, Bastien hadn't been able to trust any grown-ups. Adults had more than one face and they swapped their kindness for selfishness as often as market sellers trading goods.

Yet Madame Gentille had helped Sami get home to Morocco last year; she had listened to him when so many others had not. That was worth something, but was it worth all of Bastien's trust?

"I know," Bastien said. "We do need your help." Still, he crossed his fingers behind his back, because he couldn't make the promise she asked for. Life had taught him that the unexpected was normally just over his shoulder, waiting for its moment.

"There are many of us who don't agree with Olivier's article in *La Seule Voix*," Madame Gentille said. "What you found out about Olivier and Charles Fitzmagnat and this Red Ink Society doesn't surprise me. Some people don't want our world to change. They want to stay firmly rooted in the past, because it suits them better."

The director stood and opened a small wooden cabinet under the window. From inside, she produced a stack of newspapers in different languages. Bastien recognized words in Flemish, Italian and German.

"Before he returned to France, Charles Fitzmagnat travelled around Europe. My friends in different countries sent me these newspapers." Madame Gentille dropped the stack on the desk and Bastien and Theo flicked through them. "Fitzmagnat believes dangerous things just like Olivier." The office was warm, but the director shivered. "Together, they are an alarming duo. I'd hoped that Olivier would disappear, but it seems as though he is making himself impossible to ignore."

"I don't want to ignore him," Bastien said. "I want to stop him."

"And we will," Madame Gentille replied. "We will get justice for your parents, Bastien, and every other person whom Olivier has wronged, but we will do it the proper way."

"Proper?" Bastien faltered. "What do you mean by that?"

The director took a small address book from her drawer and rifled through the pages. "I'll make a few calls. I have friends from my old job who know how to handle such delicate situations. They will want to help fight against this corruption."

"What was your old job?" Theo asked.

Madame Gentille brushed off the question. "That's not important. What is important is that you don't do anything *else* foolish. Mathilde can stay until she is reunited with her maman. I don't believe in reformatory schools. I would never wish to change a child. Help them find their own path in life? Yes, of course. But to change…" She grimaced. "*Non*, each of you are moulded in your own way. Mathilde is no different."

The clock struck quarter to and a small wooden bird popped out.

"Anyway, I'm sure Mathilde needs saving from the others – why don't you go and make sure she's okay?" She rose to her feet and kissed the boys goodnight. "I promise you are not alone. I am here to help."

Bastien slipped out of the office with Theo close behind him. He felt a mixture of emotions. Guilt for not telling Madame Gentille the whole truth about their plan to find Olivier's new house and break inside. Happiness that she wanted to help them stop him. Frustration that she didn't understand the level of urgency needed to stop Olivier.

"We can't just wait for Madame Gentille to make phone calls," Theo said, halfway up the stairs. "We're going through with our plan still, aren't we?"

Bastien nodded. "There's no 'proper' way of doing things when it comes to Olivier. He's already growing his power and popularity. We have to do something now."

They crossed the hallway and opened the dormitory doors to an unexpected scene. The beds had been pushed to the edges of the room to create a dancefloor. Everyone watched Mathilde as she danced across the room, twirling through the air just like a spider unravelling from a silky web. She landed on her tiptoes and spun like the carousel in the Tuileries Garden.

Finishing with a perfect plié, Mathilde curtsied, and the boys broke out into raucous applause.

"*Incroyable!*" Timothée swooned. "You must perform at the Exposition Universelle. It's only five days away now."

Mathilde shook her hair forward. "I'm not as confident as Maman. I couldn't perform onstage."

"Will you teach me?" Robin asked. "To do one of those jumpy things?"

Mathilde smiled. "Of course, little one. Now, I just need to speak to Bastien before you show me to my room, *d'accord?*"

Mathilde already seemed different from the first time they had met. She had been so withdrawn and angry at the world then, but now she was as light as her ballet slippers. Bastien was glad that she was in his life, even though her arrival had been sudden and scary.

"I can never thank you enough, Bastien." Mathilde carefully undid her slippers and tucked them under her arm. "You trusted me when every bone in your body was probably telling you not to."

He perched on the edge of his bed. "Everyone has their own story and reasons for the things they do. But you've shown me that the unexpected doesn't always have to be bad. I'm glad you're here. Together, we will make things right."

Mathilde smiled in return. "You've already helped me more than you know. I mean, I'm going to have my own bed for the first time in months!"

A loud shout interrupted their conversation. Theo was standing on top of the unlit furnace, which hadn't been used since January.

"In honour of our new friend, shall we celebrate with a story?"

The boys cheered and whistled in agreement.

"What's going on?" Mathilde asked.

"Storytelling evenings are a tradition around here," Bastien replied.

"It used to help us forget about Monsieur Xavier and his wicked ways," Robin whispered.

"Stop calling him Monsieur." Pascal tutted.

The mention of the former director reminded Bastien that Xavier was Mathilde's uncle. He wondered if she knew much about him and decided now wasn't the time to ask. He was glad that Mathilde was more like Louis than the other, bad Odieux brothers.

"Sounds good." Mathilde grabbed a pillow from the bed and sat between Theo and Felix on the floor.

"What's the tale for tonight then?"

Bastien didn't need to pull an idea from the back of his imagination. He looked at Mathilde and the words magically fell into place. "It's all about you."

"Mathilde Méchante was not your average fourteen-year-old girl, so perhaps it was no surprise that one day she received a most unusual letter in the most mysterious fashion. She was climbing the staircase of the Paris Opera Ballet School to head to her lodgings on the top floor, when an envelope seemingly fell from above and hit her in the face.

"Mathilde looked around, wondering if someone was playing a trick on her. The other kids at the school were snobbish about her second-hand ballet slippers and mean when she was only ever kind in return. So who had written her name on this envelope? Too intrigued to wait, she tore into the letter.

"Mathilde,
You and your talented feet have what it takes to do good in this city. Come to Saint-Ouen flea market tomorrow at 10 a.m. Stall 313. Present this letter. We will explain the rest.
BDB

"For the rest of the day, the letter plagued Mathilde's every thought. What did it mean? And who was BDB? She tried to

make sense of it as she stirred her soup on the stove in her small attic apartment. By bedtime her whirring brain had worn her out more than any dance rehearsal ever had. As she tucked her blanket around her shoulders, she knew then that curiosity would win out.

"The next morning, Mathilde rose early and snuck away from school. She was the best dancer; missing one rehearsal wouldn't hurt. She took the Métro north to the flea market in Saint-Ouen and navigated her way through a maze of antique dealers and art merchants until she arrived at the address. Nestled between a Tunisian pastry-seller and a book-buyer was Tiphaine, an old woman who specialized in silk and lace fabrics.

"Mathilde checked the letter again. Stall 313. This was definitely the right place. So what exactly was going on?

"'Can I help you?' Tiphaine peered up from the Breton lace in her lap.

"Mathilde showed her the letter. 'I'm here because of this.'

"Tiphaine beckoned for Mathilde to come closer. The old woman's eyes were glassy and not as strong as they had once been. 'Ah yes, please come this way.'

"Mathilde watched as she pulled back a long drape of mulberry silk. Behind the fabric was an open wooden door.

"'You want me to go down there?' Mathilde's heart thumped wildly.

"'You are amongst family here,' Tiphaine urged. 'Do not be afraid.'

"As a ballerina, Mathilde knew how important it was to trust your instinct. It was the difference between a misstep and a serious injury. Looking at the old woman's face, she knew, somehow, that walking through that door was the right thing to do.

"The door led Mathilde down a metal staircase, which opened up into a tunnel. She could hear rushing water nearby and the air smelled damp and musky. Something furry and quick hurried over her ballet slippers. Was she in the sewers?

"'Is anyone here?' Mathilde called.

"A light illuminated the tunnel and Mathilde found six faces smiling back at her. They looked about the same age as her.

"'Who are you all?'

"'We are the Bande des Ballerines!' A tall girl wearing a white satin dress stepped forward. 'And you, Mathilde Méchante, have been invited to join us. We have heard of your nimble feet and good heart.'

"'And those are the only requirements for our gang,' a boy wearing golden slippers added.

"'What does it mean to be a part of your gang?' Although

173

she was confused, Mathilde couldn't deny the thrill that fizzed in her blood.

"'We right the city of all its wrongs.' The tall girl smiled. 'We move through the streets, light on our feet. No one ever detects us, for our skills make us discreet. We stop bad people from taking things that don't belong to them and we help people in need. Will you join us?'

"It didn't take Mathilde long to decide. All her life she had wanted, more than anything, to truly feel part of something. She jumped into the air, pirouetting until her head turned dizzy with excitement.

"'When do we start?'"

Bastien's throat was dry and ticklish. The story had told itself, leading him right through to its end.

"Bravo!" the boys cheered, before slowly making their way to bed.

Mathilde sprang up and knocked the wind from Bastien as she wrapped her arms around him. The light of the moon trickled in through the dormitory window and illuminated the outline of her face. "I will always treasure that story. Thank you for being so kind."

"It's not difficult to be kind."

A yawn escaped from her lips. "You'd be surprised." Mathilde walked over to the door, where Robin stood, waiting to show her to her room.

"*Dors bien*," Bastien called. "Tomorrow is the start of a new beginning."

As it turned out, he was completely wrong.

ESCAPE FROM LA SANTÉ

In the east of Montparnasse, as the dark cloak of midnight wrapped itself across the sky, a prison break was about to take place. Inside La Santé prison, an overgrown fingernail tapped impatiently on a mahogany desk. This prisoner had no reason to be impatient, for he had the finest cell in the whole of France. He passed each day in luxurious solitude: writing letters with the finest inks, going to bed wrapped in a feather-down duvet and waking every morning to a breakfast of fresh fruit, croissants and scalding black coffee.

The prisoner looked up at the clock. The evening was seeping into morning, and he thought about the city outside. Soon, he would breathe in fresh air for the first time since he had been locked away on that cold winter's morning.

Finally, help was on its way.

La Santé prison was a fortress built to confuse those on both sides of its high grey-green walls. Two guards stood watch outside the gates and Olivier noticed how particularly useless they looked. The guards were in deep conversation, perhaps even arguing. If these were the sort of men guarding France's most notorious criminals, then the next part of his plan would be easier than expected.

The cheering of yesterday's crowd still echoed in Olivier's mind as he walked towards the gates. There had been some people who had left the protest, but that hadn't mattered. Most of the crowd had been on his side, nodding like obedient dogs. He afforded himself a chuckle; the city was lapping up his words and turning against President Millefois, just as he had hoped.

The taller guard spotted Olivier approaching and nudged the other guard with the butt of his rifle.

"Who are you?" The smaller guard stepped forward.

Olivier crunched his teeth together. "I'm Olivier Odieux. You haven't heard of me?"

Petit Guard shrugged. "Can't say I have."

"We're dedicated to our jobs," Grand Guard added, saluting. "We only have time to protect the people of Paris."

Olivier tensed every muscle in his face to stay calm. "I'm here to meet Director Grimot, so I reckon you should stop waffling and let me in before he hears how much of my precious time you've wasted."

Grand Guard swallowed and shoved Petit Guard in the back. "You heard Monsieur Odieux. Open the gates."

Olivier followed the two guards through the concrete courtyard and past the small inspection house, where another guard was hunched over a desk, fast asleep.

At the end of the courtyard, Petit Guard opened a rusting door. It led into a long corridor of thirteen cells, where the most dangerous prisoners were housed. The shouts and grunts of inmates echoed loudly, and an unpleasant smell lingered in the air. It reminded Olivier of the blue cheese he had eaten with Charles at Le Malheur last night.

"The water hasn't run clean for the last couple of weeks." Grand Guard shrugged.

The exaggerated sound of someone clearing their throat echoed down the corridor and the guards flinched. They turned on the spot and saluted an old man with grey hair and a salt-and-pepper beard walking towards them.

"Director Grimot," the guards barked. "Monsieur Odieux is here." They bowed and scurried back out into the courtyard.

Olivier held Director Grimot's gaze. The man was broad and tall, but looked as old as the half-timber houses on Rue Volta.

"I presume you're here to see him?" Director Grimot finally spoke.

"*Oui.*"

Director Grimot unclipped a heavy set of keys from his belt. "Very well. Follow me."

Olivier walked down a wooden staircase and into a cleaner-smelling basement, where Director Grimot fiddled with the keys on a chain. Five of them were required to open the VIP cell entrance.

"Only I have the keys to access his cell," Director Grimot explained.

The door clicked and swung open and a musty odour tingled Olivier's nostrils. It smelled of eau de cologne.

"You have ten minutes until I raise the alarm. That should give you enough time to escape unnoticed. Use the basement tunnel if you need to." Director Grimot nodded towards a small cupboard door in a dingy corner. "It leads to the city observatory." He folded his coat collar up to reveal a badge of a red inkpot and pen. "Go well."

He disappeared back up the stairs and Olivier walked into a prison cell that was masquerading as a hotel room.

"*Bonjour, petit frère.*"

Xavier Odieux sat in the middle of a four-poster bed in a silk dressing gown, cutting his fingernails and flicking the clippings onto a plate of half-eaten quiche. He looked up. "What took you so long?"

"It's good to see you too." Olivier smiled and leaned against the cell wall. "Nice haircut, by the way."

Xavier put a hand to his shaven head and muttered under his breath. "They do this to every inmate." He walked over to Olivier and prodded him in the chest. "You didn't answer me. Why have you kept me waiting?"

Olivier suppressed the urge to bounce his brother's head off the wall. "I've been busy. It might've looked slightly obvious if you'd escaped from jail the day after sentencing. Get dressed, will you? We don't have much time."

Xavier pulled the robe tighter across his chest and walked behind a black dressing screen. "I've been bored senseless in here."

Olivier looked around the cell. In one corner was a freestanding bathtub and in the other a pile of books and board games. "The time of boredom will be long gone after tonight. It is time for our second act."

Xavier stuck his head around the dressing screen. "*Second?* Does that mean...the fires? They've already happened?"

Olivier nodded.

"I didn't think you'd start without me." Xavier appeared fully from behind the screen, dressed in his long black cloak, pinstripe black trousers and worn leather boots. "That wasn't part of our plan," he whined. "You said we would bring back the Society together. You promised we would do it *all* together this time. You—"

Just like a thread snagging on a thorn, Olivier's patience tore in half.

"Believing in promises is foolish." He lunged forward, grabbed the china plate from the bed and threw it like a discus across the cell. It narrowly missed Xavier and shattered against the wall. "This was *my* plan, *petit frère*. *My* dream. Every cause needs a leader, a face people will look to for guidance. We all have our parts to play. I needed to distance myself from you to appear legitimate and build back support. Do you understand? I didn't abandon you, despite you already failing me once. Now, do you wish to test my patience again?"

"Very well," Xavier said, through gritted teeth. "Lead the way."

"One more thing." Olivier smoothed the creases of his shirt. "I didn't forget about you. I wanted you to gather your strength for what comes next."

"And what is that?"

Olivier noticed how Xavier's face changed. Where it had been hard as a rock from the moment he'd walked into the cell, now his brother's features softened slightly. "Freeing every inmate in this prison," Olivier replied.

They exited the cell and walked back up the stairs and into the corridor. The noise from the cells was deafening now. From his suit pocket, Olivier removed a heavy key chain. Director Grimot's keys. He handed them over and a smirk of realization appeared on Xavier's face.

"Will you reintroduce the most terrible humans in here to the city?" Olivier cocked his head. "Such an outbreak will only tarnish President Millefois's reputation further. Meet me at our grandfather's house once you are done. We shall celebrate."

With a curt nod, Xavier hurried down the cell corridor, his hands shaking with excitement as he fitted different keys into the various locks.

Olivier reached the end of the street just as the alarm began to blare throughout the prison. He turned back to see inmates spilling out of the gates like ants from a mound, ready to infest the city.

The thrill of it all was almost enough to make him forget about the Bonlivre problem. Almost.

What Hugo Bonlivre had stolen from him, and hidden away with his interfering wife Margot, was Olivier's only weakness. It was the chink in his armour that Olivier worried would reveal itself at any moment. Hidden in their son's notebook was the truth about who the Odieuxs really were. It was more than just reputation; the Odieux family secret was the difference between his dreams of domination coming true and floundering completely.

But Charles had told him not to worry and that his son would take care of it. Olivier had to trust it was all in hand, especially after Charles had instructed him not to send any more threats directly to Bastien. Olivier didn't like being told what to do by other people – especially when he wanted to further terrorize the Bonlivre boy – but he'd bitten his tongue and promised for the sake of his grand plan.

Olivier turned a corner as a gaggle of freshly released prisoners ran past him, kicking the shop shutters and howling into the night. He allowed himself a smile.

That was the thing about chaos. It was a vacuum, sucking in everything in its path. The chaos he had created would protect him until he was, finally, where he needed to be.

On top.

19

PANDEMONIUM IN PARIS

LA SEULE VOIX

Waking up to bad news always made Bastien wish it was possible to live in his dreams instead. The following morning was no different, when he found Theo and Mathilde standing over his bed. The other boys paced up and down the dormitory anxiously, just like the lonely lion at the Jardin des Plantes zoo.

"Monsieur Xavier is coming back!" Robin cried, clutching a ragdoll to his chest. "We're not safe. We have to hide!"

Bastien shot up, rubbing sleep from his eyes. "What's going on?"

Mathilde nudged Theo. "You tell him."

"Xavier has escaped from La Santé."

Flashes of the evil that Xavier had put Bastien through – locking him away in the Isolation Chamber, stealing his notebook and, above all, taunting him with his parents' fate at every moment – all returned and made his brain spin. He rubbed the side of his head, hoping he was still dreaming. "Say that again."

"There was a prison break last night." Theo exhaled. "Xavier Odieux has escaped La Santé, along with a hundred other criminals."

Bastien jumped out of bed and grabbed a shirt from his trunk, pulling it on over his vest. He tried to stay calm as he looked around; Pascal sat sobbing at the foot of his bed and Clément and Timothée rocked Robin back and forth. Fred and Felix stared mindlessly out of the window.

Mathilde thrust the open newspaper she held into Bastien's arms. "I found this in the kitchen bin."

LA SEULE VOIX

MERCREDI, 11 AVRIL 1923

PANDEMONIUM IN PARIS

BY OLIVIER ODIEUX

MORE THAN A HUNDRED PRISONERS ARE ON THE run in Paris after escaping from La Santé prison in the early hours of this morning.

Authorities said a dozen prison guards have been injured following the mass escape, including the director, Gilbert Grimot. The prisoners who fled were housed in XIII wing, infamous for its thirteen cells that hold the most dangerous inmates. One of those who fled was Xavier Odieux, my own brother, recently charged with the kidnapping of multiple authors as well as the deaths of celebrated writers, Margot and Hugo Bonlivre.

Witnesses report hearing screams at half past midnight on Wednesday morning and prisoners were seen running from the prison shortly afterwards. It is still unclear how the prisoners managed to escape. Will President Millefois and the government recapture the criminals? With no further news on their investigation into the fires that recently plagued our city, this paper questions whether the President can look after his entire country.

Once again our beloved city has been dealt a most unfortunate and unexpected hand. I cannot understand how this terrifying event has happened, but I can promise you this: I will do everything within my power to find my brother and put him back where he belongs, alongside every other criminal.

My promises are not fragile like bone china. They are made of titanium. That is more than President Millefois can ever offer.

Sitting in my old family home on the edge of the city, I can only imagine the disappointment our esteemed grandfather would feel towards Xavier. Victor Odieux believed in order and control. Just like me.

Along with the owner of this newspaper, my dear friend Charles Fitzmagnat, I will be holding another protest tomorrow evening, 7 p.m., at the Place de la République. There is safety and strength in numbers. If President Millefois will not protect us, then we shall look after each other.

———————

Bastien looked up to find two suspicious faces staring back at him. "Are you thinking what I'm thinking?"

Theo nodded. "That Olivier is behind the prison break too?"

"Olivier is using the prison break to his advantage," Bastien replied. "He can claim that President Millefois can't keep Paris under control and people will believe him. Just like he did with the fires."

He turned back to the newspaper, pushing away the thoughts of Xavier creeping around the city. There had to be something in Olivier's words that would help them.

At the bottom of the page, a sentence jumped out at him. "See that?" Bastien pointed. "It says Olivier is in his old family home. That must be where he is staying."

Mathilde twirled in delight. "Good spot!"

"But the edge of the city could be in any direction," Theo said. "How do we narrow it down?"

Bastien knew the answer was already somewhere in his head; he just had to coax it out. He thought about what his mother had always told him about the art of writing.

"Writers notice the things that others may miss," she would say. *"We collect details like magpies collect material for their nests."*

What details had Bastien collected over the last few days? He thought about their trip to the archive and the documents in the dusty filing cabinet. He turned back to his trunk and rooted through its contents, an idea forming in his head.

"There might be an address in the Red Ink manifesto." Bastien grabbed the booklet and flicked through its pages, but all it contained was more of the same dangerous ideas.

"Anything?" Theo asked.

Bastien shook his head. He had to concentrate, think harder and deeper about what else he had seen in the archive.

And then it came to him.

"There was something else! The obituary for Olivier's grandfather. It said that Victor Odieux lived in Boulogne-Billancourt."

"That's on the western edge of the city," Theo said. "I used to go to the woodlands there with my parents. That means Olivier is living in his grandfather's old house."

"But that's a big neighbourhood," Mathilde said. "We still need the actual address! How—"

The dormitory doors were flung open. Madame Gentille and Chef Camille hurried inside, both still wearing their pyjamas. The director picked Robin up and planted kisses on his head.

"I see I'm too late to stop the news from reaching you all." Madame Gentille looked over at Bastien's bed where *La Seule Voix* lay open. "Please don't take things from the kitchen bin, especially when the newspaper is actually rubbish."

Mathilde tapped her feet anxiously. "*Désolée*," she whispered.

"Let's go eat some breakfast, shall we?" Camille waved her spatula. "I've made mushroom omelettes!"

Madame Gentille carried Robin and the rest of the boys ran after Camille, but Bastien, Theo and Mathilde still lingered in the dormitory; even the promise of breakfast hadn't distracted them from their thoughts.

Theo pulled a coffee-stained envelope from the hidden lining in his trousers. "Before we do anything else, you might want to read this. It came this morning when you were still asleep. I thought I'd wait until it was just us."

Immediately, Bastien recognized the neat cursive handwriting of Louis Odieux, the oldest of the Odieux brothers. Bastien ripped it open, silently wishing the letter in his hands would hold the answer they needed.

Cher Bastien,

Please forgive me for the lateness of this letter. Philippe and I have not long returned home from our travels and I've only just found your letter. The postman often ends up leaving our post in the foyer as we're on the fifth floor. Philippe insists on being able to live as close to the skies as possible.

I'm afraid the bad news seems to have stacked up in my departure. How can I ever apologize enough to you, Theo and the others for the destruction that my bad brothers have caused? I cannot understand how Olivier is a free man.

I have had letters from other Parisian friends who have told me about La Seule Voix*. I see that Olivier is using his words as a weapon in a manner even more terrifying than before, although I don't recall ever having met Charles Fitzmagnat myself.*

As for what you asked about our family's past, I have spent time rooting through my memories as though they were a dusty attic. I was close with my mother, but the rest of my family were never truly accepting of me, always keeping me at arm's length.

Olivier was extremely close with our grandfather and worshipped him as though he was a god. Our grandfather, Victor Odieux, talked often about his belief that only a king could rule our country. Whenever we stayed with him, he would have large gatherings with friends to discuss his ideas, all of them dressed in red cloaks. They would lock themselves away in the office and talk until the early hours of the morning. Naturally, Olivier, the favourite grandson, was allowed to join them. Xavier desperately wanted to be a part of it all, but Grandfather said he was too young to understand.

I had no interest, other than trying to figure out what my grandfather kept in his office safe.

Olivier must be trying to achieve what my grandfather could not. If he is in Paris, then he will surely be staying at our grandfather's house. The mansion at 7 Rue des Princes has always been in our family. Mother refused to sell it after Grandfather died.

Please don't go there, Bastien. Keep your head down and stay away. Philippe and I are coming back to Paris. By the time you receive this letter, I might already be halfway across the Channel.

I will do what I should've properly done years ago: I will stop my terrible brothers.

You allowed me to escape from my past, and I owe you that much in return.

À bientôt,

Louis

"There's an address!" The heaviness that Bastien had felt only moments ago lifted. "And Louis is coming back." He knew how much courage it had taken the eldest Odieux to walk away from his brothers; to come back required even more of the stuff.

Mathilde's face softened. "Maman mentioned the name Louis before. She said I had an uncle who would be glad to know me." She balled her fists and glided over to the door. "But all I care about right now is getting into that house and taking back what belonged to Maman. So what are we waiting for? We can take the Métro and be in Boulogne-Billancourt by midday."

"We can't just go straight away," Bastien replied.

"Why not?"

"Because we don't have a plan yet," Theo said. "Not a proper one."

"You said you would help me!" Mathilde grabbed a pillow from the nearest bed and threw it in Theo's direction. He ducked just in time. "Getting Maman's money back was *my* plan. I know what I'm doing, so why should I wait for you both? My new life is so close."

"Because of this!" Bastien waved the letter above his head. "The secret gatherings that Victor Odieux used to have – that was the Red Ink Society! Their grandfather's old house was the society headquarters. Maybe it still is. If we go there, it's not just Olivier we have to prepare for, but Xavier and the others."

"I'll destroy them all!" Anger and desperation radiated off Mathilde in huge waves.

"We want the same thing, remember?" Bastien had to make her listen. "Your new life won't happen unless we find evidence linking Olivier to the fires and the prison break. We need to expose his lies and make people listen. Because if we can plant a seed of doubt in the minds of everyone who is supporting him…then we might just stand a chance of taking him down along with Xavier and the rest of that awful society." He paused to catch his breath. "And I can finish what my parents started. But not without your help."

Mathilde wiped her runny nose. Her eyes were still glossy, but the storm behind them had calmed. "Louis mentioned his grandfather had a safe in the office. What if it's still there?"

"*Oui*. If Olivier is hiding anything – proof of his guilt and the money he's made from his articles – it's likely somewhere secure." Bastien turned to Theo. "How good are your safe-cracking skills?"

"Can't say I've ever tried to pick a safe lock, but I'm up for the challenge."

"So what do we need to do?" Mathilde asked.

"As a very wise friend once told me…" Bastien smirked at Theo. "It pays to be prepared."

The rest of Wednesday passed by in a blur of scribbled notes, sweat and grease. After omelettes and fresh milk for breakfast, Madame Gentille declared there would be no lessons that day.

"I'm certain you can all keep yourselves amused for a few hours inside," she said, her eyes lingering on Bastien. "Camille will look after you. I have important neighbourhood business to attend to."

"Don't go outside," Robin squeaked. "It's not safe."

"Don't worry," Madame Gentille said. She shrugged on a light jacket. "I spoke to our closest neighbours this morning and we have decided to create a watch group. The Petit-Montrouge Protection will look after each other and ensure that our neighbourhood is safe while the police track down the remaining prisoners."

With a wave and a kiss, the director headed for the front door, leaving Bastien with an important life lesson:

that bravery took all forms and sometimes it wore a lime-green jacket and an old feather in its hair.

Theo was eager to get inventing, muttering about head torches, climbing gloves that could stick to buildings and silent shoes that would be forgiving on an old house's creaky floorboards.

"Don't overdo it," Bastien said. "We don't need all of that."

But Theo could only nod, one hand scribbling down calculations as he hurried down the cellar stairs to his workshop.

"Better to leave him to it when he's in this mood. His mind is like a steam engine. It's constantly moving until it runs out of fuel." Bastien laughed. "Let's head to the library."

"I sort of know how that feels." Mathilde skipped up the stairs. "But it's more in my feet than my mind."

"Do you still want to be a dancer?" Bastien led them through the door to the east wing. "Last night you said you wouldn't perform on a stage."

Mathilde turned away from him slightly, looking at the portraits lining the corridor. Madame Gentille had paid for a group of artists to paint each boy.

"Growing up, I always wanted to be like Maman."

Mathilde ran her hand along the wall. "She wanted me to go to ballet school, but then Olivier stole from her. I've barely danced since we've been apart; last night was the first time. I just haven't felt safe enough to do it." She paused. "Am I making any sense?"

"Completely." Bastien climbed the small flight of steps to the library door. "Storytelling with my parents was my most favourite thing in the world. I love telling tales to the boys, but that night at the bookshop was different. When I had to read from my own book, I didn't know where to look. There were too many people. Too many strange faces."

Mathilde coughed, a sheepish look on her face. "I don't think I ever apologized for giving you a scare that night. I'm really sorry. I just didn't know who I could trust."

Bastien waved her apology away. "Don't worry. It's all in the past. But let me ask you one thing: did dancing last night make you feel good?"

An outline of a smile formed on Mathilde's face. "It really did."

"Then you should keep on dancing. That's why I tell stories."

"But doesn't it make you miss your parents more?" Mathilde paused at the library door. "You don't have to answer that. Dancing just always makes me want Maman by my side."

A reel of his favourite memories played in Bastien's head – of nestling in between his parents on a Sunday morning and writing together. "It's like you said. I pick up a pen and I can feel them looking over my shoulder. Sometimes it makes me sad, but usually I feel better. Stories are my medicine."

Mathilde nodded.

"Here we are." Bastien opened the door. "The library."

Mathilde's face lit up and she bolted into the room. "*Génial!*" She jumped up onto the wooden ladder attached to the bookcases and pushed herself over to the other side of the room. "There was a library at the correction school, but this one is a hundred times better."

"It's my favourite place." Madame Gentille had entrusted Bastien with decorating and filling the shelves with as many brilliant books as possible. He had made fifty return trips to Le Chat Curieux, enlisting the help of Charlotte, Jules and Alice to help him carry the books.

"I can see why!" Mathilde jumped down and landed in a plush velvet chair. She placed her hands behind her head and sank into the cosy reading spot. "So, what are we here for?"

"We need to look for city maps." Bastien pulled a wooden chest out from under the chair. "Madame Gentille likes to collect maps of Paris from different time periods. The city has changed a lot in the last seventy or so years, but if we can find Rue des Princes on one of these maps, we'll know where to go."

The lid swung open and burped dust into his face. Bastien pinched his nose, scooped out the maps and placed them on the floor. "Let's get searching!"

They pored over each map for some time, their eyes scanning the squiggly lines that ran across the paper. Bastien remembered his father telling him about the architect, Georges-Eugène Haussmann, who had transformed Paris by building great boulevards and parks.

Now Bastien felt fear for what might happen to Paris if Olivier was successful in his bid for absolute power. What else would he destroy because of his need to be number one? Bastien had already lost so much because of it. Olivier and Xavier Odieux had killed his parents because they'd known too much and got in the brothers' way. There were truly no lengths that Olivier wouldn't go to in order to get what he wanted. Bastien feared for every person in his city, and beyond, as to what might happen if Olivier and the Red Ink Society came out on top.

It was a worry that followed Bastien like a shadow, but he knew what he and his friends had to do. They had to fight, just like his parents had done.

"Found it!" Mathilde squealed. "Rue des Princes is right here!" She pointed to a street on the edge of the city centre, not far from the river. "We'll get in and out, no problem. I am a recent escapee of a reformatory school, after all."

Mathilde's confidence gave Bastien his own boost. He had spent so long worrying about whether Xavier and Olivier would come after him again, imagining them waiting in the shadows, when he should've been focusing on taking charge. Like Mathilde, he had a wrong to right; they could change their own future.

The door burst open and in ran Theo. Even wearing his smudged goggles, Bastien saw the frantic flitter in his eyes; his hair clung to his head and various pens and pencils were lodged behind his ears. "I've finished! Come and see what I've made."

"You've got something on your cheek." Mathilde pointed at his face.

Theo dabbed his face with his sleeve. "Grease makes a good moisturizer."

Bastien put the rest of the maps back in the trunk and carefully folded up the one that would lead them to Olivier, slipping it into his pocket. "Let's see what the Talented Theo Larouche has made!"

Bastien followed his friends from the library. Hope and belief gelled together and he found he had a spring in his step. The fear that Bastien felt about breaking into Olivier's house wasn't as strong as the feeling that told him this was the right thing to do. He wouldn't look away from this, no matter how many threats came his way.

Olivier and Xavier Odieux had spent their entire lives spreading fear, but soon enough, they would be the ones who would be truly afraid.

Because Bastien and his friends were going to find what they needed to take the bad brothers down for good.

20
THE MANY INVENTIONS OF THEO LAROUCHE

A loud knock at the front door reverberated around the entire orphanage as Bastien, Theo and Mathilde were halfway to the workshop. All at once, the other boys raced into the hallway, looking for places to hide. From the bottom of the main staircase, Bastien watched Fred and Felix dive into Madame Gentille's office.

"It's Xavier!" Pascal cried from inside the ornate vase that doubled up as an umbrella stand.

"Everyone hide!" Clément stood at the door with his fists up. "I'll hold him off for as long as I can."

"Calm down!" Camille scuttled out of the kitchen, picking a fishbone from her hair. "Criminals aren't going to walk right up to the door."

Pushing Clément aside, she unlocked the front door. Unsurprisingly, it wasn't a criminal, but Alice. She held a cake box in her arms. As Bastien hurried towards her, he noticed Georges, the new bookseller, standing there too.

"Excuse the smell." Camille ushered them in. "I'm working on a new *bouillabaisse* recipe. I hope you can calm these boys, Alice. They're petrified that every criminal in Paris is coming here."

"We're not petrified," Clément replied. "Just cautious. You didn't meet Xavier. He was awful."

"Truly." Timothée stepped out from behind the grandfather clock.

"Better to be safe than sorry," Georges said. "The bookshop has been incredibly busy and her parents couldn't get away, so I offered to walk Alice here."

"I didn't need an escort," Alice muttered.

"How nice of you." Camille turned back to the kitchen. "Now, who wants to come and try my new recipe?" The other boys nodded and traipsed after the chef, leaving the four friends alone with the bookseller.

Georges laughed awkwardly and turned to Bastien. "How is Paris's youngest storyteller? Working on anything new in that notebook of yours?"

Bastien stuttered, caught off guard by the mention of his notebook. "Not really, no. I've been busy."

"Busy doing what?" Georges glanced at Mathilde. "And who is this? I don't believe we met at the bookshop. How do you know each other?"

"*Euh,*" Mathilde started.

"We can't stop to chat," Bastien interrupted. "We're off to Theo's workshop."

Alice waved Georges away. "You can go now."

"Can't I join in with your gang?" He pouted. "Looks like you're all up to something fun!"

Bastien felt uneasy standing in the hallway with Georges. Just like the whiff of Camille's fish soup drifting from the kitchen, something smelled off about Georges too. Why did he ask so many questions, but never answer any about himself? At the bookshop, Georges had changed the subject each time Bastien had asked him a question. And what about the day of the fires? Georges had just stared out at the destruction before him and done nothing to help. What type of person did that?

"Our gang is invitation only," Alice replied, heading towards the cellar stairs.

"Well don't go running around the city," Georges

called. "It's dangerous. Who knows what trouble you kids might find yourselves in. Anyway, *au revoir!*"

But Alice had already disappeared down the stairs with Theo and Mathilde. Feeling awkward, Bastien waved back to Georges and walked after his friends. He didn't want to stay a single second longer alone in Georges's company.

Which was a shame. Because if he had turned around one final time, Bastien would have seen Georges only pretending to leave before he slammed the orphanage door shut.

Bastien liked to think that Theo's workshop looked the same as the inside of his friend's brain: organized yet overflowing with chaos. Wires hung from the ceiling and trailed across the floor like a nest of snakes. A stack of research books blocked the one small window and a huge blackboard covered the back wall. It was full of Theo's undecipherable handwriting that future inventors and academics would struggle to understand.

"What was that all about?"

Alice flinched at Mathilde's question. "What do you mean?"

"The way you spoke to that man." Mathilde picked at the loose threads of her shirt. "It was rude."

Alice sighed and set her cake box down. Theo immediately opened it and the scent of vanilla and cinnamon wafted through the workshop. "If you knew Georges then you'd know that he doesn't deserve an inch of kindness from me," Alice said.

"Why?" Bastien took a slice of the soft sponge cake and bit into it. Maybe Alice knew something that would further his own suspicions about the new bookseller.

"He's been missing so much work. And when he does turn up, he's late and in a bad mood. He's so secretive, but incredibly nosy too. There's something off with him." She bit angrily into her own slice. "Anyway, enough of that. You all look like you have something to tell me. I can smell a most excellent plan brewing."

Bastien unrolled the map and laid it across the least messy table, pushing Georges out of his mind for now. "We're going to break into a house. And not just any house. It used to belong to Olivier's grandfather and we're certain it's where Olivier is staying now."

Alice's expression flittered between clarity and confusion as the boys and Mathilde ran her through the new plan.

"And this is the best plan you can think of?" Alice asked, clearly hesitant. She had always been the most sensible one. "Sneaking into Olivier's grandfather's old house and hoping we'll find evidence." She turned to Bastien. "What if one of us gets caught?"

"We won't," Mathilde interrupted.

"You can't promise that." Alice folded her arms.

"I can." Mathilde pirouetted across the workshop floor, dodging rolled-up balls of curtain fabric, and jumped onto a worktable. "I'm light on my feet, which makes me the perfect person to go in first. I can creep across hallways and landings without making a sound. I can check the coast is clear."

"She has a point," Bastien said. "We can use Mathilde's skills to our advantage."

Alice rolled her eyes, but he persisted.

"Trust me. This is the only way. We can't wait around for Madame Gentille and her friends to help us. We have to act quickly because Olivier is gaining support by the day. And we can't trust the police. Not when we don't know who could be corrupt and on the side of the Red Ink Society."

"But the note and what Olivier sent you…" Alice made a whimpering sound. She squeezed Bastien's hand in her own. "He said that the end is coming. I can't lose you. *We* can't lose you."

Bastien wrapped her in a hug. "I know it's risky, but I'm not going to wait around and do nothing until Olivier comes for me. I'm taking a stand. We have to find evidence and get people to listen to us. Nothing bad will happen if we do it as a team and look after each other. Promise."

Alice sniffed loudly. "I'll hold you to that, Bastien Bonlivre."

It was a nice moment until Mathilde and Theo bundled on top of them, squashing Bastien and Alice in their arms.

Mathilde whistled. "We're all in this together!"

"We thought it was a group-hug moment," Theo added.

"Get off me, will you?" Alice broke away and brushed down her blouse. "Where's this house then?"

Bastien plucked a pencil from behind Theo's ear and scratched a small *X* on the map. "Right here. On Rue des Princes."

"And how are we getting inside? Or finding any evidence, for that matter?" Alice fired question after question. "Do you even know what you're looking for?"

Theo rubbed his hands together. "Your many questions will be answered, but this is where I come in. Mathilde, could you give me a hand?" He pointed at a large wooden crate, which they heaved onto the table.

"First up, my eight-legged lock pick." Theo pulled what looked like a mechanical spider from the crate. "If there is evidence in Olivier's grandfather's safe, then this will help us. The safe could have a combination or a different mechanism altogether."

"How will a metal octopus help us?"

If looks could kill, Alice had just said her last words. Theo's glare was long and intense. "I researched the most commonly-used safes in the late 1800s and welded together different metals to make the perfect-sized pick for each of them. If Olivier is still using the safe, one of these should work."

"That's impressive, actually." Alice picked up the spider-octopus lock pick and gave Theo her best apologetic face.

"What else have you got?" Bastien asked.

Theo threw a satin parcel at him. Bastien unwrapped the parcel quickly to reveal a pair of black ballet slippers.

"Mathilde's dancing inspired me." Theo kicked off his battered lace-up boots and worn socks and tied a pair of slippers to his feet. "We can sneak about wearing these." He hopped from one foot to the other, silently gliding across the floor. "Honestly, every robber should have a pair of ballet slippers."

Mathilde clapped her hands in delight. "I will teach you all how to *glissade* and move as though you were a cloud in the sky."

"I have always wanted to learn ballet." Alice admired the slippers.

"I can't believe you've made all of this in less than a day," Bastien said. He examined a small brown satchel that contained dozens of secret pouches and compartments.

"There's one more thing." Theo cleared his throat. "And it's my favourite." He pulled out a black cardboard box from the bottom of the crate. There was a large hole on one side, surrounded by smaller ones, and a strap across the top.

"What is it?" Bastien asked.

"A box camera!" Theo straightened his shoulders and rotated the box in his hand. "There's a lens in one end. All you need to do is set the shutter, click this button and it takes a photograph." He held it up to his face to demonstrate. "You just need to wind more film at the back to take another one. I've been saving these parts for a while now. I was planning to give it to Timothée for his actor headshots, but I think we need it more."

"You've outdone yourself." Bastien grinned. "We can take photographs of any evidence we find that proves Olivier's guilt!" It was a smart idea, one so technical that only Theo could have thought of it.

"Yemma always said that working fast makes you a better inventor," Theo replied. "You trust your instinct with less time to think."

"Have you got any film?" It was an innocent question from Mathilde, but one that sent an arrow straight through their bubble of happiness.

Theo scratched his head. "Would you think me stupid if I admit I didn't even think about film? I was so concentrated on getting it made."

"Normally I would," Alice said, "but you've done an excellent job, so I'll be nice. I know where to get film. Abdou runs a small photography studio at the back of his printing shop to make some extra money."

"But wasn't his shop destroyed?" Bastien asked, recalling how Jules had run to help his neighbour with buckets of water.

Alice shook her head. "Thankfully, only the front of

the shop. It's still going to take a while to repair, but the fire didn't reach his studio. I'll ask him later."

"You are my hero," Theo said.

"I know."

"When are we doing this?" Mathilde asked.

"Tomorrow evening?" Bastien suggested. "Olivier is holding another protest at the Place de la République at half past six. That should give us plenty of time to get into the house and look through each room, especially the office, uninterrupted. We're looking for things that could link Olivier to the fires or the prison break. Think a set of keys, a journal, a map, a letter. Anything like that."

The others nodded in agreement and Bastien couldn't help but wonder what his parents would think of this plan. Would they be angry for putting himself in danger? Disappointed that he hadn't been able to find out the notebook secret and so had to resort to a daring break-in?

Or would they know that it no longer paid to be sensible? At least not in a world where Olivier Odieux existed, and justice meant nothing. His parents had understood that there were times when you had to be a little bit reckless. After all, they had shown him what it was like to live a full life with so much joy. They wouldn't want him to live a sort of half-life, constantly looking over his shoulder, too afraid to allow himself to create happy new memories.

He didn't want that either. He wanted to live, even if that came with a risk.

"I was saving this for a special occasion." Theo rummaged in a desk drawer and pulled out a green bottle. "But I think this counts."

Bastien's attention snapped back to Theo. "Is that wine?" He sniffed the open bottle.

"Obviously not." Theo laughed. "It's sparkling apple juice. I traded a pair of moss earplugs with a market seller at Les Halles. His wife snores like a gorilla." Theo found four chipped mugs in the workshop and filled them to the brim.

Bastien raised his mug, the bubbles sparkling just like his insides. "Let's do this!"

Georges hoped the creaky cellar stairs wouldn't betray him. He couldn't hear the children's conversation over the noise from inside the workshop. There were no windows looking in, only one solid door. What were they doing? And why were they acting in such a secretive, suspicious manner? He hadn't recognized the strange-looking girl in the ballet slippers either. She hadn't come to the bookshop with Alice or Bastien before. Questions pecked at him, but he would not find the answers here.

He needed to return to his main task. Do what his father had asked of him. Find the notebook. Destroy it. Show his worth and become an official member of the Red Ink Society.

Crossing back through the hallway and up the staircase, he sneaked into the dormitory and rooted through the nearest trunk. Which one belonged to Bastien? Where did he keep his notebook? He had one chance to get this right and he had to use all of his cunning and cleverness to do so.

But the thing about people who call themselves cunning and clever is that they are usually neither. And they don't often account for small, inquisitive boys.

"What are you doing in here?"

A quiet voice stopped Georges in his tracks. A small boy with glasses, clutching a ragdoll to his chest, stood in the doorway.

"I—" Georges started. "I got lost."

"You shouldn't be up here," the boy said. "I'm going to get Camille."

Georges knew his paper-thin excuses wouldn't work with the chef and so he fled, running past the boy and downstairs, across the hallway and out into the courtyard. He only stopped once he reached the Métro station, certain he'd put enough space between him and the orphanage.

Alice and her friends were up to something. Did they suspect him? He'd been so careful to be nice, but Alice clearly didn't like him and Bastien seemed suspicious too. Had Georges asked one too many questions?

He slapped his forehead, cursing himself for running from the dormitory. He had been told not to underestimate the Bonlivre boy or his friends, but they were just kids! Georges was a young man, on the cusp of something greater. He wouldn't be defeated.

He pushed past a group of teenagers and snuck under the station turnstile. If the children didn't trust him, then Georges would have to make them fear him instead to complete his task. Just like the train rattling through the tunnel, an idea gathered speed in his head. It was time to cause pain and suffering to those who Bastien loved the most.

Because playing nice only got you so far.

Admittedly, Bastien had expected that sneaking out of the orphanage and travelling to the other side of the city, all in the name of breaking into a house, would be a challenge. After telling Madame Gentille the truth (three quarters of it, to be precise) about the threats from Olivier and his plans with the Red Ink Society, Bastien thought that the director would watch him and Theo like an extremely attentive hawk.

As it turned out, the Petit Montrouge Protection had been a great hit with local residents and the daily patrols were keeping the director busier than ever. After all, there were still criminals on the loose in Paris.

But the director hadn't forgotten her promise to help

Bastien. Once Thursday breakfast had finished in the dining hall, Madame Gentille had beckoned him over. "I've spoken with my friends and they want to help." The director's eyes had widened. "They're going to come here in a few days' time and we're going to organize our own protest against Olivier and *La Seule Voix* at the Exposition Universelle. So sit tight."

A protest of their own was smart, but Bastien couldn't wait any longer. Fearing his mouth would betray him if he spoke, he'd simply nodded and watched Madame Gentille hurry away to answer her office telephone.

As afternoon seeped into evening, everyone in the orphanage, apart from Bastien, Theo and Mathilde, was tying up their shoelaces and getting ready to leave.

"Are you not coming with us?" Pascal pulled a black cap over his head. "Madame Gentille is letting us join the patrol!"

Bastien looked up from the open book on his bed. "Not tonight, no."

"What about you?" Robin tugged on Theo's arm. "We can pretend to be actual police officers!"

"I'm too tired." Theo faked a yawn. "But you enjoy!"

"Mathilde?" Clément called out from the dormitory door.

Mathilde tore her gaze away from the window, where she sat perched on its sill. "It's kind of you to offer, but I think I'll stay in and practise my *pas de chat*. Be safe."

The heat from Clément's blushing felt powerful enough to keep the dormitory warm until next winter. Bastien held in his laugh until they were alone, and heard the slamming of the front door.

"I think he likes you," Bastien teased. He retrieved the satchel that Theo had altered and filled it with their tools for the night ahead: the neighbourhood map, the box camera and the satin ballet slippers.

Mathilde sighed and pulled on a long black cape; Theo had made one for each of them from old scraps of curtain fabric. The capes would help them blend into the night. "I'm not interested in boys. Or anyone for that matter. Now, let's get going! It's six o'clock."

Guilt turned Bastien's footsteps heavy as they snuck downstairs, past the kitchen and out into the early evening. Madame Gentille had told him to sit tight and here he was leading his friends into the belly of the very worst type of beast. He was responsible for what would happen tonight, but he'd make sure they had enough time to get back to the orphanage before the director returned from the patrol.

The pull of the Odieux family home and the answers it held within its four walls made Bastien run faster than he ever had in his life. He sped ahead of Mathilde and Theo, leading them through the city, cutting across neighbourhoods. Bastien noticed the boarded-up windows of damaged shops and the ashy remains of wooden carts and trolleys that had once belonged to market sellers. Were there families going hungry because of the fires? Because of Olivier's lies? The city felt on edge, not ready for the thousands of people who would soon arrive for the Exposition Universelle.

As expected, Alice was waiting for them by the Pont Mirabeau. She wore a baggy black shirt that belonged to Jules, dark pinstripe trousers, and the black ballet slippers.

"Nice capes." Alice smiled.

"Did Georges walk you here?" Bastien asked as they fell into long, eager strides across the bridge.

"I've not seen him since yesterday. He didn't go back to work after walking me to the orphanage." Alice shrugged. "Papa says he has no choice but to let him go. They need someone they can rely on."

"Did you have to sneak away tonight then?" Theo asked.

"They're honestly too busy to notice." Alice shook her head, sweeping her fringe from her eyes. "I said I was going to visit you, and Maman just told me to be back before night falls. She barely steps out of the kitchen. They're both working so much because our landlord put our rent up after the fires."

Bastien frowned.

"Aren't they worried about all of the…you know… criminals on the loose?"

Alice ignored Mathilde's question and walked faster now that they had reached the quay on the other side of the water. "We should focus on what we're about to do."

Theo jogged ahead, his hand hovering over his jacket pocket that contained the spider-octopus lock pick. "Let's go break into a house!"

"Theo!" Bastien sighed as they passed a horde of Belgian tourists. Thankfully, they were too busy arguing about where to go for dinner to notice a boy shouting about criminal activity.

If breaking into a house that was home to villains

and secret societies didn't get them killed, Bastien was almost sure that Theo's mouth would seal their fate.

The house that had once belonged to Olivier's grandfather, 7 Rue des Princes, had seen better days. Bastien peered through the gaps in the railings and looked at the crumbling façade of Victor Odieux's mansion. The windows were cracked and broken, their art nouveau glass illustrations faded, and the front door had a narrow split down its middle. Was the only thing holding this house together the growing ivy that had wrapped itself around the walls?

The worry that always ebbed and flowed inside Bastien now tightened his throat. His breaths turned short and sharp and he couldn't hide his panic.

Theo patted him on the back. "It's going to be alright. If anything, the state of this place might make it easier to get inside. Besides, we've—"

"Survived worse." Bastien smiled wryly.

"*Cachez-vous!*" Alice flew at him and pushed him into a nearby bush.

Mathilde grabbed Theo and dived behind a cherry blossom tree. "The front door is opening!"

Four figures in red cloaks emerged from the house. They glided across the front garden and opened the gates, which groaned loudly. The figures spoke in hushed tones, and as much as Bastien strained to listen, their conversation was out of reach.

Although their hoods were up, Bastien's gut told him Olivier was amongst the figures. He and the others watched the hoods hurry down the street until they disappeared.

Bastien counted to sixty, just to be sure they were gone, then pulled himself out of the bush. "That was close." He removed a twig from under his armpit.

"Too close." Mathilde tapped the top of her thigh to still her shaking leg. "I thought they would have already left for the protest. It's just gone seven o'clock."

"Did you get a look at who was there?" Alice asked.

"*Non*," Bastien said. "But one of them was Olivier. I felt it in my bones. Xavier was probably with him too."

"Which hopefully means that no one else will be inside." Alice pushed the gate open, wincing as it creaked. She looked behind and stopped in her tracks. "Where's Theo?"

Mathilde's head snapped around. "He was just here."

Terror twisted Bastien's insides, his eyes darting from

223

the house to the street. Had another mysterious red-cloaked figure taken Theo? Was their break-in plan over before it had even begun?

"Theo!"

This wasn't happening. This could *not* happen.

"Calm yourself down!" Theo had reappeared on the other side of the gate.

"Where did you go?" Bastien asked.

"I found our way in."

"But the front door is right there," Alice interrupted.

"You have much to learn. The most obvious way is never the best way." Theo parted the leaves of a wilted rose bush that revealed a narrow alleyway. "Follow me!"

Bastien squeezed through the bush and shuffled forward. He spotted shadows in the windows of the house next door and crouched even lower; they couldn't be spotted now.

"Where are we going?" he whispered.

Theo stopped and pointed to a gap at the bottom of the fence. "This is our way in. Through the garden." Then he disappeared.

Pulling his stomach in, Bastien dropped to his knees and shimmied under the fence, dragging his satchel beside him. He stood up, brushed himself down, and looked around.

Before him was a jungle masquerading as a city garden. The grass almost came up to Bastien's shoulders as he waded across what had been a lawn, narrowly avoiding a pond covered in thick algae. Once-perfectly-pruned hedges now sprouted at awkward angles and the concrete tiles had been reclaimed by moss, with the furry, green sprouts covering the floor.

"What a dump." He held his nose as he walked around a broken greenhouse. Inside looked like a sad fruit and vegetable stall, worms slithering in around shrunken courgettes and rotting tomatoes.

Bastien joined Theo, Alice and Mathilde at the back of the house and quickly counted the number of windows, doors and balconies. Bastien had learned from their mistakes when he, Theo and Sami had snuck into Olivier's former house in Montmartre and ran into a dead end in the cellar. This time, he would know all the escape routes so they could all get out.

"I can't believe Olivier lives here." Alice shook a mouldy leaf from her slipper. "Quite the difference from his last house."

"It won't be long before he buys another statue of

himself." Bastien thought of the monstrosity in Olivier's old house; he was glad the flames had turned the garish monument to liquid.

"Any money that man now has belongs to me and Maman." Mathilde gestured to her pockets. "I'm not leaving without it."

Bastien peered through the largest ground-floor window. He spied a long reddish-brown table bearing a tall silver candelabra, fresh wax dripping down its sides. Had Olivier and Xavier just finished dining together? Bastien bristled at the thought of the awful brothers discussing their vile plans over a sumptuous feast.

The bottom of the window was completely shattered, leaving a hole just big enough for the smallest of adults to fit through. Or four children with varying levels of flexibility.

"Through here!" Bastien lifted his leg towards the hole, but Mathilde pulled it back down.

"I'll go in first, remember? I can check that the coast is clear. I'll be quicker." She grinned. "No offence."

Keeping her body balanced, Mathilde lifted her right leg through the hole. She crouched down and twisted her top half to follow, her left leg pointed and as still as stone.

Bastien winced. One wrong move and her skin would scrape against the glass.

But Mathilde pulled herself through in one swift movement and landed inside the house. "I'll be back in a minute."

As Bastien waited, excited nerves pulsed through him. Olivier and Xavier believed they had the upper hand, but Bastien knew the true faces of the terrible Odieux brothers and tonight he would find the proof he needed to expose them.

A couple of minutes later, Mathilde reappeared at the broken window. "All clear." She held out her hand and helped Bastien crawl through the hole, graciously ignoring how he resembled a worm.

Finally, his feet touched the floor. He was inside the Odieux family home, where the Red Ink Society had been created so many years ago.

There wasn't a single second to waste.

The house creaked and moaned, aware of eight new feet tiptoeing across the dining room. The faded interior looked like it had once been grand and tacky, the preferred Odieux style. The walls were covered with gilded wood panelling, much of which was rotten and had turned a vile green colour. The room smelled musky, with a mixture of cheap cologne and sweat.

Bastien kicked a box of matches across the floor and pulled open the double oak doors, revealing a long hallway. To the left were two doors and a spiralling staircase. On the right he counted three more doors, all flanked by full-size model soldiers in silver armour.

"We should split up," he said. "This place is big and

we need to check every room for evidence of Olivier's involvement in the fire and prison break."

Theo saluted. "*Oui*, boss. Shall Alice and I go upstairs?"

"Good plan. Mathilde and I will look down here. Meet back here in forty-five minutes?" Bastien pointed to the grandfather clock to their right, which was surprisingly ticking away. "That will be eight o'clock on the dot."

"Come on, Theo," Alice called, already halfway up the staircase. "Time is of the essence!"

Bastien and Mathilde walked through the door closest to them and into an unloved living room. A broken shutter hung at an awkward angle across the bay window and underneath it sat two ripped armchairs. A lopsided billiards table was pushed up against one corner of the room.

The two friends worked quickly and quietly; Bastien checked down the side of each armchair, turning the cushions one by one, while Mathilde crawled on her knees, checking the underneath of the billiards table.

"Nothing so far," Mathilde said.

Bastien thought back to when he, Theo and Sami had searched Xavier's old office for proof of the kidnapped writers. They'd looked in the obvious places first – locked desk drawers and trunks, but it had been by accident that he'd stumbled across the secret entrance to the catacombs. What was the least likely place to look in this room?

He hurried over to the walls and ran his hands along the cracked plaster and peeling wallpaper; could there be a secret compartment built into the wall? But, still, he came up empty.

"I don't think there's anything hidden in this room," Bastien said. "Let's move on."

The kitchen was next. From the cobwebs that hung off every cupboard door, it was clear that Olivier wasn't much of a chef. Dirty cups and cutlery were stacked high in the sink and thick yellow smudges were smeared across the countertop, like someone had spilled an entire pot of mustard.

Mathilde pinched her nose as she opened the pantry door with her free hand. "It smells awful."

Bastien reached for a cupboard door, which almost fell apart in his hands. "All the more reason to be as quick as we can." He carefully rooted through drawers and shelves, only finding empty old tins and a few mice who were fighting over crumbs that had turned as hard as concrete. He ground his teeth as he searched through the rest of the kitchen. He knew there was something hidden within these four walls that would help them, but time was running out.

Bastien thought about what his parents would do. He pictured their faces in his mind and, as he did, it came to him. He had to pay attention to the little details.

Just like writing a story, Bastien needed to focus on the smaller details in the Odieux house. He was good at details; as a writer, he noticed the things that others didn't. And even though Olivier's new plan was smarter than his previous one, details were not his strength. It was why Olivier couldn't write and why his last plan had failed.

Finding the details had helped Bastien to stop Olivier once. Now, he hoped, it would work a second time.

At the far end of the kitchen, the oven caught Bastien's eye. It was made of cast iron and looked like an angry metal mouth, but it was somehow different to everything else in the room. Bastien kneeled for a closer look and realized that there was no dust on the oven door handle. It was cleaner than anything he'd seen in the house so far. Someone had opened it recently! And judging from the lack of fresh food in the cupboards, it hadn't been to cook.

"Mathilde!"

She hurried over. "What is it?"

"There's no dust on this handle."

"Great eye! I've looked through all the cupboards and there isn't a single bit of actual food in this kitchen."

"Exactly," Bastien replied. "So I think Olivier has put something else in here."

With great effort, they wrenched the oven door open. A bitter smell like burnt fat hit Bastien. With one hand shielding his face, he reached inside, only for his fingers to wrap around something hard, yet soft. He pulled the object out and let the oven door close again.

"What have you found?" Mathilde asked.

In Bastien's hand was a bundle of red cloaks, stained with ash and soot. The something hard, in the middle of the cloaks, was a silver case.

"It's a lighter." Mathilde grabbed it and flicked open the top. "And probably last used for something awful, like starting a load of fires!"

Bastien unravelled one of the red cloaks and an uneasy stillness came over him as he saw the symbol of the Red Ink Society. "And judging from the number of cloaks, he had plenty of help too." He stuffed a cloak into his satchel as Mathilde pocketed the lighter. "We can't take all of it, just in case Olivier notices."

"Do you think this evidence will be enough?"

Bastien pursed his lips. "It's good, but we need to build a full picture of Olivier's plan. We only get one shot at making people listen to us. If we want anyone to take us seriously, we'll need more."

They hurried back to the hallway, checking the grandfather clock as they headed towards the remaining rooms. There were twenty minutes left until they had to leave to get back to the orphanage. They sped up their search through more rooms, all unsuccessful, until a final door on the left remained.

Bastien stepped first into a dark, cavernous room. No light streamed in through the windows here.

"Wait a moment." He ran back to the dining room and grabbed the candelabra and a box of matches. His fingers fumbled as he lit the wick, but after several attempts and a few burnt fingertips, the small flames finally illuminated the room.

"This is it," Bastien said, a spark of victory in his voice. "This is the office. I bet the safe is in here!"

The office was grand and cluttered, with a large writing desk and armchair pushed up against the back wall. The windows had been completely covered with newspaper, as though to block out both light and prying eyes. Stacks of paper covered the desk and floor and a green sofa sat in the middle of the room. Bastien tried to count the number of bookcases, but lost his place each time.

Mathilde skipped over to the far corner of the room, where a black door was slightly ajar. She peeped her head inside. "There's just a toilet in here. I'll start looking through the bookshelves on this side."

Bastien nodded. "And I'll go through the desk."

The minutes ticked by in silence, the pair of them focused on their tasks. They had to be careful to make sure Olivier wouldn't find anything amiss when he returned. Bastien pulled out papers and objects from the desk drawers, hoping he could remember the correct order to put them back.

From the hallway, the grandfather clock struck the eighth hour. Time was up. They had to meet Alice and Theo, get out of the house, and return to the orphanage before anyone noticed they were missing. Bastien kicked the desk leg in frustration. Olivier and Xavier could be back from the protest at any moment and he still didn't have enough evidence to prove their dastardly plan.

"Have you found any more evidence? The safe? Any money?"

Mathilde looked so hopeful, and it pained Bastien to shake his head. "I can't find the safe. I'm so sorry. I thought it would be in here like Louis's letter said. I think the lighter and the burnt cloaks are as much as we'll find. Maybe Theo and Alice found something!"

Mathilde's moan transformed into something darker; a blood-curdling wail. She turned and grabbed the first book her hands could find and threw it across the office.

"I'm sorry, Mathilde," Bastien whispered, "but we have to go."

The office door creaked open and Bastien froze. But the familiar faces of Theo and Alice peeped round the frame, and they hurried inside. Theo carried a thick brown envelope in his hands.

"Have you found—"

"They're back!" Theo cut across Bastien's question. "Olivier and Xavier are at the gate."

A rattling sound, of a key in a lock, echoed down the corridor.

"They must've come back early from the protest!" Alice carefully closed the door behind her.

Bastien dashed over to the window, but the newspaper stuck on the glass was too thick. There wasn't enough time to tear it all down to get to the window lock.

"They're getting closer." Theo's ear was pressed up to the door. "What are we going to do?"

"Through here!" Mathilde ran towards the black door. "It's a toilet, but it's the only place to hide."

They followed her inside. Theo and Alice huddled under the crumbling sink. Mathilde pressed herself flat against the wall behind the door. The expression on her face worried Bastien. She looked scared, but furious. He knew she wanted revenge for how Olivier had treated her mother, but now wasn't the time.

"Don't move," he mouthed. Then Bastien snuffed out the flames and held the candelabra close to his chest. It was heavy, a weapon he could use if he needed to. He pulled the door shut, leaving a small crack. Just enough to see.

The door to the office flew open and heavy footsteps marched into the room.

Bastien tried to slow his breathing. To him, it sounded as loud as a wild boar's. He couldn't give them away now.

The footsteps stopped and a voice emerged.

"I'd say that was even more successful than our first protest, wouldn't you agree? It's always best to leave the crowd wanting more. They were eating up every word I said!"

The voice of Olivier Odieux was unmistakeable. As rough as the bark of an old dog, it never failed to send a shiver down Bastien's spine. He told his brain to stay calm, but being trapped in a toilet with no escape, when the most dangerous man in the whole of France was on the other side of the door, was a step too far for even the bravest of humans.

And so Bastien gasped. It was only small, but it felt like a scream in the silence.

"What was that?" Olivier's voice turned into a hiss, and his footsteps grew louder.

Bastien clutched his hands to his mouth and scrunched his eyes.

The end had arrived, and it was all his fault.

23

THE ANCIENT ROYAL DECREE

All of a sudden, the office flooded with light, and Bastien shrank back into the darkness of the toilet.

"Did you hear that too?" Olivier's voice sounded less sure of itself now.

"This house is creaking at the seams," Xavier Odieux replied. Bastien dug his nails into his skin as the former orphanage director screeched with laughter. "Don't be so paranoid. We are quite alone. Maybe apart from the ghost of our grandfather."

"Don't mock me, *petit frère*, or it will be straight back to La Santé for you. I've worked too hard to let this all fall to pieces now."

The heavy footsteps retreated and Bastien waited

238

a minute more before daring to peek through the crack in the door. Olivier sat in the black armchair, wearing a crimson suit, a pile of red cloaks laid at his feet. This close, Bastien noted how different he looked from when they had come face-to-face the previous winter. Olivier looked tired, with large dark circles under his eyes. Were his plans for power taking a toll?

"Of course not," Xavier said. "Still, I wish you had let me out earlier." He perched on the edge of the green sofa and it took a moment for Bastien to recognize him. Long gone was his greasy black hair; now, his head was shaved and his once wild eyebrows were plucked to perfection. Gone were his tattered black leather boots and general scruffiness. Xavier wore a maroon herringbone jacket and looked almost respectable, like the sort of person you might see strolling through the gardens of Versailles on a Sunday afternoon.

But Bastien knew that no matter what Xavier wore or looked like, he still had the same hollow core inside his rotten body.

"You knew the timeline." Olivier pursed his lips. "I couldn't rush the plan. You're here now for its triumphant conclusion. This will cement all our work so far and you are crucial to its success."

Xavier's face contorted into a smile. It looked like it had been stitched on, such was the unnaturalness of it. "I cannot wait for the Exposition Universelle. It's always a great time when the world fair comes to our city, but I think this will be my favourite one yet."

Bastien slowly turned to his friends, wondering if they all felt the same growing sense of unease. The opening ceremony of the world fair was mere days away now; what were the Odieux brothers planning?

Olivier stood and walked over to the desk. "Indeed. It truly is the perfect backdrop for our final act. After the recent hardships this city has gone through, the fires and the prison break…"

"Both tragedies, I might add," Xavier said.

"Quite so." Olivier laughed so hard he coughed. "The citizens are growing angrier. The nation needs strong leadership to guide them through this difficult time. And I will take it from President Millefois."

Bastien crept forward again, his legs numb from crouching. He knew that in three days' time, the opening ceremony of the Exposition Universelle would welcome every Parisian, as well as thousands of others from France and beyond, to explore the greatest new technologies and future innovations. But Olivier

Odieux and the Red Ink Society and their ancient ideas and beliefs didn't belong in any future. So, what exactly did their "final act" involve? Bastien was frightened for what he was about to hear, but he hoped that the knowledge would give him his own power: the power to stop them.

"President Millefois is due to give his welcome speech at the fair's opening ceremony." Olivier riffled through a desk drawer, producing a blueprint. Bastien hadn't seen that when searching the desk; what was it for?

"The stage will be closely guarded, but I need to get on at any cost," Olivier continued. "Which means I will need you to come up with a way of getting past the President's security."

"I have a few ideas." Xavier's face lit up. "Each one full of pain."

"I don't doubt it." Olivier smiled, sourly. "Once I have invaded the stage, I will humiliate Millefois. Tie him up, stuff his mouth shut, maybe even rough him up a bit. I haven't yet decided, but then I will declare my use of the Ancient Royal Decree. I will explain to the crowd that I have the legal right to rule and that I shall restore order. By now, most of the citizens respect and adore me. They will rejoice."

Xavier clapped his hands, gleefully. "And Millefois will be defeated. What a moment that will be!"

"It is my moment – *our moment*, indeed." Olivier rolled up the blueprint and waved it in the air. "Everything we talked about during our days in that jail cell was leading up to this."

Bastien slowly turned to his friends. Did they know what the Ancient Royal Decree was and what it meant? From the confused look on their faces, they clearly didn't.

Bastien knew that a decree was an official order or rule that could be enforced by law, but he'd never heard of the Ancient Royal Decree. Whatever it was, this decree would surely only help Olivier cement his power.

"It is a stroke of genius," Xavier said. "I am surprised I don't remember *Grand-père* telling me about the decree."

"You were too young to join the society meetings." Olivier ignored the hurt look on Xavier's face. "But I have never forgotten what he told me. If the capital should ever find itself in a state of emergency, only a royal descendant can successfully demand power to govern the entire country. After everything, I'd say we are living through an emergency, wouldn't you?"

Bastien's mind flooded with dark and dangerous thoughts. Now he truly understood why Olivier had created so much chaos: the fires, the prison break and the protests. Everything he'd done was to create the right conditions to use the Ancient Royal Decree and it would work because Pierre Niney, Head Judge and fellow member of the Red Ink Society, would make sure that the law would pass so Olivier could become king.

"Of course." Xavier's face turned bitter, as though he'd swallowed a mouthful of vinegar. "But what of Bastien? You worried about the notebook for so long. It still holds the truth about our family. If that gets out…"

Bastien watched, barely daring to breathe.

"The Bonlivre boy isn't as perceptive as his parents were," Olivier said. "I was tormented by the notebook for so long, but my obsession held me back. If he hasn't figured it out by now, he never will. Our family secret is still safe. In any case, Charles has assured me that Georges is keeping an eye on the boy and his friends. He has been working at that drab old bookshop to get close to them and ensure the notebook is destroyed. Perhaps Charles's son will do a better job of it than you."

The name Olivier had mentioned struck Bastien like a hammer. Georges, the new bookseller at Le Chat

Curieux, was the son of Charles Fitzmagnat! His eyes stayed fixed on the bad brothers, but Bastien felt Alice's fury behind him. Georges had always avoided questions about his own past and it was because he was a Fitzmagnat, a member of the Red Ink Society. All the personal questions he'd asked Bastien too wasn't to be friendly, but to find out where his notebook was.

Bastien bit the inside of his cheek in frustration; he would make them all pay.

"Anyway, all this talk of power is making me ravenous." Olivier stuffed the rolled-up blueprint in his cloak pocket. "Now that I've got this, we'd better get to Le Malheur. Charles is waiting."

The jealous look on Xavier's face fell away and he licked his lips. "I've been dreaming of one of their steaks for months."

The conversation grew quieter until Bastien could no longer hear the brothers. Footsteps retreated from the room and the light dimmed. The office door slammed shut and then another, somewhere else in the house.

Theo edged forward from under the sink, but Bastien shot him a look that said, *Wait!* They waited for another minute and then the anger came spilling out.

"Traitor!" Alice hissed. "I knew Georges was hiding something!" There was a loud *thunk* and a whimper.

Bastien relit the candelabra and the bathroom brightened to a gentle glow. Alice sat against the side of the toilet, clutching her left foot.

"*Ça va?*" Mathilde asked.

Alice ground her jaw. "I kicked the toilet."

While Mathilde checked Alice's foot – she had plenty of experience, nursing Maman's over-danced feet back to life – Bastien properly looked around the room they were in. There were posters and framed newspaper clippings on the wall and above the toilet was a flag showing a pen dipped in a red inkpot, the symbol of the Red Ink Society.

Below the flag, sitting just above the porcelain toilet, was a sign that read, in crown-gold lettering: *ASCEND THE THRONE.*

"What a bizarre room." Bastien stared at a painting. It had to be Victor Odieux. He wore a Society symbol on his suit lapel and his crooked grin was identical to Olivier's. "It's a personal shrine."

"But in a toilet," Theo added.

What they had overheard about the Exposition Universelle was Olivier's most dangerous plot yet and along with Georges's betrayal, Bastien felt more determined than ever to stop them.

"We can't let him get away with this," he said. "We have to find a way to stop this from happening." He looked over at Theo, remembering the brown envelope in his hands. "Before Olivier and Xavier came back, you'd found something, hadn't you?"

"We found this in Olivier's bedroom, at the back of the wardrobe." Theo handed the envelope to Mathilde. "I think you should do the honours."

Mathilde grabbed the envelope and tore it open. Inside was a thick wad of banknotes.

"Reckon that's enough for a new life for you and your maman?" Bastien smiled at Mathilde, although he felt a pang of disappointment. He'd hoped that Theo and Alice would've found more evidence. Right now, with only the lighter and burnt red cloaks to tie Olivier to the fires, who would believe Bastien? It wouldn't be enough to convince the people.

"I'd say this would get us our house by the sea." Mathilde's grin ran off the side of her face. She pirouetted and squeezed Bastien like he was a lemon.

He laughed, feeling her delight as though it was his own. She had found what she needed to make a new life with her mother. Finally, she had taken back what Olivier had stolen from her.

"I'm happy for you, Mathilde," Alice said. She was still sitting on the floor. "But could someone give me a hand? I think my foot's okay to stand on now."

Bastien walked over to Alice and placed the candelabra on the toilet seat. That was when he noticed something strange about the toilet, another small detail that could easily be overlooked. The cistern, the porcelain tank that held the water supply, was at a strange angle as though it had been recently moved. Bastien had concentrated on the strange paintings and Red Ink Society posters on the walls, so he hadn't thought to properly look at the normal details of a bathroom. Like the toilet.

"Someone has moved this recently!" Bastien pointed at the cistern. "It might be hiding something! Help me move it."

With the help of Theo and Mathilde, Bastien slid the lid from the top. They placed it on the floor, careful not to make too much noise, and turned back to the toilet to peer inside.

"Anything in there?" Theo stood on his tiptoes, peering over his best friend's shoulder to look.

Bastien's heart skittered up to his throat and his hands shook with anticipation, for at the very bottom of the cistern, covered in flecks of rust and mould, was a red box.

SECRETS OF THE THRONE

24

Bastien didn't usually go round sticking his arm into toilets, but excitement came over him and he plunged his arm inside, trying not to breathe in the foul mildew smell, as his hands enclosed around the red box.

Hope rose in him. Could this box hold more evidence that would help them stop Olivier?

"This is as disgusting as it is fascinating." Alice held the candelabra closer as Bastien pulled the box from the cistern and brushed flakes of rust from his arms. Turning the box around revealed a golden clasp and padlock: the final hurdle for them to overcome.

"Work your magic." Bastien handed the box to Theo, who placed it on the floor and removed the eight-legged lock pick from his pocket. He spun the lock pick round, testing each leg as he went, until he found the perfect fit for the lock. He guided it into the oval keyhole and began to twist and turn it, as though he was taking part in a fencing match, this old golden padlock his opponent.

"Why would Olivier hide something in a toilet?" Mathilde asked.

"It's the last place you'd think to look," Bastien said. "But let's hope that this is the closest Olivier will come to sitting on the throne."

Mathilde smiled weakly. "Olivier is truly an awful man, isn't he? I wish he wasn't my father." Bastien opened his mouth, but she cut across him. "I wasn't looking for sympathy. I guess you can't choose your family."

"But you can." Bastien glanced at Alice and Theo; she was holding the candlelight close to the padlock while Theo worked. "And you can have more than one. Family, I mean. It's not a word reserved for the people related to you. Family is anyone who makes you feel like home."

"It's only been a few days, but the orphanage already feels like home."

"We're all glad to be part of your extended family." Bastien smiled. "The family that you chose."

"I'm in!" Theo yelped. The lid of the box creaked open, and the four friends gathered around it, kneeling on the wooden floor.

Bastien leaned forward. A sour, rotten smell wafted up from the box.

"Smells like curdled milk." Alice covered her mouth with her sleeve.

Carefully, Bastien pulled out each object from inside the box. There was a metallic badge, displaying the familiar symbol of the Red Ink Society, a heavy clump of waterlogged papers and a chain of keys, all different sizes and shapes. He quickly counted thirteen.

Disappointment filled Bastien from head to toe. He had been so sure this would hold the evidence they needed, but each key was old, with jumbled letters engraved on one side that gave no indication of where they had come from. The papers were unreadable from the water damage, merely black and blue smudges.

"Hang on!" Theo's excited voice filled the room. He held the red box in one hand and a thin sheet of metal in the other. "There was a concealed compartment at the bottom."

"You genius!" Bastien punched the air in delight.

"Let's see what it was hiding," Mathilde urged.

Underneath the fake metal bottom was a pocket map of Paris, the type that could be found in the tourist office. It took Bastien a minute to make out the first tiny pencil mark. It didn't look like much on its own, but as he found more all over the map, he realized that the marks weren't random. They formed a pattern.

His eyes darted to a larger mark over the Place Saint-Michel, a stone's throw from Le Chat Curieux. Suddenly, it all made sense. "This shows where Olivier started the fires! And he made a note of every neighbourhood he wanted to target. This is evidence that Olivier planned the fires!"

Bastien restrained himself from jumping on the toilet seat to dance. Just how he always trusted a story to work out its plot, he'd trusted his feelings when they had told him that Olivier was linked to the chaos spreading across the city. Although the search had felt like squeezing water from a rock, especially when Bastien hadn't known what he was exactly looking for, he and his friends had finally done it.

"This is going to help take him down," Theo grinned.

Alice stepped closer with the candlelight. "Lay the

map down on the floor so we can take close-up photographs."

Bastien removed the box camera from his satchel and handed it to Theo. He held it up and looked down into the viewfinder.

"Stop your arm shaking," Alice said.

"*Merci*," Theo muttered. "Helpful as ever." A moment later, he pushed the shutter lever and the camera clicked; three rapid noises like the beating of a drum. Then, he did it several more times.

"Take photographs of the walls too," Bastien added. "We need to prove that we were inside the Odieux house. Get the Red Ink Society posters and newspaper clippings. We can tie all of that to what we found in the archives."

"But what about the prison break?" Mathilde asked. "We need all the proof of Olivier's plan to help us convince everyone that he *is* the villain, not the President."

Bastien nodded. The map with the fire targets was a great find, but the more evidence they could find the better.

"Maybe these numbers and letters aren't nonsense." Alice picked up the key chain again. "What if they mean something? Like a pattern?" She spread the keys out neatly on the toilet seat, ensuring the engravings were face up.

Bastien and Mathilde stared at them closely, both whispering what they saw under their breath.

A A T P I O L S N É R S N X I I I

Only the sound of Theo's camera click could be heard, until Bastien sighed. Fog had drawn a curtain around his head; it felt like so much time had passed, and he was still staring at a mess of letters. "It makes no sense."

"Same here," Alice said.

Mathilde huffed. "No clue."

"Sounds like you're all in need of an expert puzzle-cracker." Theo handed the box camera back to Bastien and picked up the keys. "If these are prison keys then there's bound to be an obscure code for safety reasons. Let's take them back to the orphanage and I'll figure it out."

"But Olivier might realize the keys are gone!" Alice's face withered. "We can't make him suspicious."

"It's a risk we'll have to take." Bastien folded the map

and placed it at the bottom of the box, underneath the secret panel, before lowering it back into the toilet cistern. "We need to get back home."

Triple-checking the cistern was secure, the four friends hurried out of the office and back towards the dining room. Bastien glanced at the grandfather clock in the hallway; they had just under forty-five minutes to get back to the orphanage.

"Do you think this will actually help us stop Olivier?" Mathilde asked. "You almost defeated him once before. You were so close. What's different now?"

Alice and Theo were ahead, already climbing out of the window, but Mathilde's question made Bastien stop in his tracks, despite the rush to get home.

"It's about using this evidence to show everyone in this city and beyond who the real Olivier truly is," he said. "It's different now because we know his plan for the Exposition. And we have you." Bastien smiled as Mathilde blushed. "We're going to stop them properly this time. So many lives have already been ruined by their schemes. I refuse to let them hurt anyone else, just like they did to us and our families."

Mathilde's bottom lip quivered. "Olivier was so cruel to Maman. He said she could dip her ballet shoes in invisible ink and dance all over the world, but he'd still find her and make her life a misery."

Bastien saw Mathilde's lips moving, but no longer heard her voice. Suddenly, every thought of the Odieux brothers vanished from his mind. All he could think about were the two words that had just crowbarred open a mystery that had been locked for so long.

Invisible ink.

Was this the answer to his notebook? Had his parents made their secret invisible to the human eye? Bastien had secured proof of Olivier's involvement in the fires, but now there was only one thing on his mind.

"Bastien! What is it?" Mathilde stared at him blankly.

He jolted back into action. "I think you've just cracked open a secret that I've struggled with for such a long time. We need to get back to the orphanage right now."

The friends ran all the way from the Odieux house back towards the river, Bastien leading them as quickly as he could.

"Can we slow down now?" Alice wheezed as they reached Pont Mirabeau. She was still slightly hobbling.

But slowing down wasn't on Bastien's mind. He needed to get back to his notebook and make the invisible visible. "It's invisible ink."

Theo stumbled, not from the uneven bridge cobblestones but excitement. "What do you mean, *invisible ink*?"

"My notebook. The message that my parents left me," Bastien said. "Back at the house, Mathilde mentioned invisible ink and it's triggered something in my brain. Whatever secret is in my notebook, I think... well, I'm *sure*, somehow, that my parents wrote it in such an ink."

"So that's why you've never found anything in the pages!" Theo lightly slapped the side of his head. "I don't know why I never thought of it!"

"Me neither," Bastien replied, breathlessly. "We need to get back to your workshop straight away."

"As much as I don't want to miss this moment, I have to get back to the bookshop." Alice stopped outside the Javel Métro station. "I have to tell my parents about Georges. About who he really is."

The dizzying prospect of finally cracking the notebook secret had made Bastien incapable of thinking about anything else. Until now. With a thud, the discoveries from the night landed in his head once again, weighing down his every thought. Olivier was planning to overthrow the President at the Exposition Universelle by invoking the Ancient Royal Decree. And Georges the spy had deceived them all, pretending to be a bookseller when he'd been sent to keep tabs on Bastien and steal his notebook!

Although the bad news stacked up like cards,

Bastien's notebook was safe in the orphanage library and now, he felt one step closer to cracking its secret.

Bastien turned and hugged Alice. "Don't let Georges in if he comes back to the bookshop. Please be careful."

"Of course. I'll come and see you tomorrow morning with my parents. Ten o'clock. We can figure out what to do next together."

Bastien and Theo held out their hands and Alice laid her palm over theirs to seal the promise made. Then Mathilde curled her left hand over theirs, her right one still holding tightly onto the envelope of money.

Alice nodded and hurried down the station steps, waving over her shoulder. "*Bonne chance!*"

Thankfully, Madame Gentille and the others were still out patrolling by the time Bastien, Theo and Mathilde got back to the orphanage. It was almost quarter to ten and all was still as they tiptoed through the courtyard and the hallway, careful not to disturb Camille from her cooking experiments.

"What do you know about invisible ink?" Bastien asked.

Theo tucked his hair behind his ears, a sure sign he

was deep in thought. "There are many types of invisible ink, and they all have different ways of being activated." A determined glint shone in his eyes. "We've got a lot of work to do."

An unspoken plan formed between them and Bastien rushed towards the staircase. "I'll go and get my notebook and meet you in the workshop." Theo and Mathilde disappeared from sight as he reached the first floor and headed to the east wing. He flew into the library and a small jolt of panic ran through him. What if his notebook wasn't there? Georges had dropped Alice off at the orphanage the other day; what if he'd snuck around?

Knowing that the bookseller was Olivier's spy made Bastien's hands shake as he reached for the top shelf. He grabbed the hollowed-out book and opened it, relief flooding him, to find the red notebook in its place.

Running back to the workshop, Bastien let a strange new feeling rise within him, an anxious sort of joy. Tonight, he would find out the secret his parents uncovered.

In the workshop, Theo had cleared a tabletop and Mathilde's arms were loaded with various jars, candles and small glass vials.

Bastien set down his notebook. "Where do we start?"

"I have a couple of ideas for how we can uncover the writing, but we'll need specific tools."

"What do you need?" Mathilde asked.

"Matches, salt, vinegar and a dash of water," Theo instructed. "And a few other bits." He ran over to a cupboard and came back with all the essentials, plus an old reading light, a paintbrush and a chipped mug.

"Here." He thrust the mug into Mathilde's hands. "Can you fill this with water from the kitchen?"

Mathilde bolted from the cellar and reappeared with a full mug of water in less than thirty seconds. Theo mixed the vinegar and salt in a small glass bowl and poured in the water from the mug.

"I'm going to brush a little of this mixture on the first page. If there's invisible ink, it might react with the acid in the vinegar." Theo dipped the paintbrush and lightly covered the page in a thin layer of vinegary water.

"Smells awful." Bastien pinched his nose.

"This is relatively pleasant-smelling in comparison to the experiments my parents used to do. Have you ever been anywhere near hydrogen sulphide?"

Mathilde laughed. "Does it look like I've ever been *anywhere* near a lab?"

"You're lucky." Theo gagged. "The stench is worse than Felix's bed sheets!"

After five excruciating minutes, the notebook page was the same. The only difference was that the workshop now smelled like a vinegar factory.

"*Dommage.*" Theo scratched his head. "Time for Plan B." He picked up the reading light and lit the candlewick.

Bastien grabbed his arm. "What are you doing? Don't burn the page!"

"Acid is commonly used for invisible ink. It's activated by heat," Theo explained. "Trust me."

Bastien kept his eyes fixed on his notebook as Theo lowered the flame. Tension, as fine and tight as a tightrope, pulsed in Bastien's chest as the page darkened. Just like a chicken roasting, the notebook page began to crackle.

"If you burn my notebook to a crisp, I might never talk to you again."

"*Chut!*" Mathilde cried. "Something is happening!"

Bastien watched the notebook page. The beginning of a letter slowly formed on the paper, a *G*. "Do you see that too?"

Theo nodded and turned to the next page. "You're not dreaming. Your parents really did leave you an invisible message! Looks like there is one letter per page. I wonder what type of acid they used. It's a clever trick."

Bastien searched his mind for a thread to pull. He didn't ever recall bottles of acid or chemicals sitting nonchalantly in the bathroom cabinet. He crawled deeper into his memory, thinking about the last moments he had spent with his parents.

"It feels like a lifetime ago since I was with them. We had dinner together on the balcony the night before they left for Cannes." Instantly, he felt the warm breeze of a summer evening on his skin, heard the sounds of the neighbourhood kids playing below, and felt the sting of the juice from the squeezed lemon that had seeped into a cut on his finger. "Lemon juice! We had crêpes with sugar and lemon juice for dinner that night."

"Lemon-based inks have been used for centuries," Theo said. "People used them to deliver secret messages to towns across the deserts."

He kept the flame close to the next page and another letter formed almost instantly, an O.

Mathilde twirled in delight. "Keeping going, Theo!"

Bastien watched, anticipation tingling from his fingers to his toes, as more letters appeared.

"Write them down in my workbook." Theo nodded towards the brown leather book on top of a stool.

After thirty minutes, they finally reached the last notebook page. Bastien yawned but he pushed against sleep.

Theo blew out the flame of the reading light and swept the used matchsticks from his workbench. "That's it. The whole notebook."

A door slammed above their heads. Madame Gentille and the boys had returned from the evening patrol.

"What does it say?" Mathilde asked.

Bastien looked down at the letters. He started a new line underneath and wrote the letters out again, leaving a space between each word they formed.

Go to the place where stories breathe.

"The place where stories breathe." Theo rested his head on the workbench. "Does that mean anything to you?"

Bastien stared at the sentence. His hope slowly started to dwindle. Where had he heard that before? It felt vaguely familiar, like the name of a song that lingered on the tip of his tongue, but it was just out of reach.

"I know it, I'm sure." He tapped his fingers against his head. "But I can't place it."

His friends had helped him uncover the secret message, but what use was it if he couldn't decode it? Bastien felt like he was running a never-ending race, new hurdles suddenly appearing on the track before him.

"Theo! Bastien! Mathilde!" Madame Gentille's voice rang out above their heads. "Where are you?"

Mathilde opened the workshop door. "Just in the workshop. Be up soon!"

"The patrol lasted longer than I expected," Madame Gentille replied. "Come and join the others. It's way past bedtime!"

Bastien yawned as the grandfather clock in the hallway chimed loudly. "I can't think properly. It's been a long day."

"We'll have another go in the morning." Theo rubbed his eyes. "I'll take a look at the keys we found too."

"You'll figure it out," Mathilde said. "You two have the best brains in Paris."

Bastien smiled. "Will you leave now that you have your money?" That had been Mathilde's plan all along, to get the money and start a new life with her mother, but a part of Bastien selfishly hoped she'd stay a little while longer.

Mathilde twirled a strand of hair in her fingers. "I can't wait to free Maman from the hospital, but after everything we discovered tonight… We can't let Olivier use the Ancient Royal Decree! If he rules this country… Well, that feels like the beginning of the end."

"So does that mean you'll stay and fight?"

"I was born ready to fight. I know Maman would be scared for me, but it's what she'd want. To bring this all to an end." Mathilde put her arm around Bastien, gently guiding him out of the workshop. "But, let's rest now. Maman always says that sleep is the best free medicine. Sometimes, by doing nothing, you figure out everything you need to know."

As tired as Bastien was, his body turned as restless as his mind the moment he slipped under his duvet. He could only think about seven completely normal words. *Go to the place where stories breathe.* What did it mean?

Counting the seconds didn't lull him into a sleep, but only made them longer. Just like a broken clock, time couldn't be trusted, and when the first slither of daybreak filtered through the window, Bastien had barely closed his eyes. The same questions had repeated in his mind all night.

Where did his parents want him to go? Where was the place where stories breathe?

And what would he find when he got there?

26

THE PLACE WHERE STORIES BREATHE

The first one awake in the dormitory the following morning, Bastien headed for the library. Whenever he was stuck, he sought refuge in books, and he currently felt as though his mind was trapped in a boggy marsh. How was this secret message linked to Olivier? What was waiting for Bastien at *the place where stories breathe* that would expose the Odieux secret?

His head as heavy as lead, Bastien sank into his reading chair. He stared blankly at the bookshelves and his eyes landed upon *The Voyage to the Edge of the Sky*, the first book that his parents had written together. He reached out for the book and leafed through the pages. How he wished he could reach into them and pull out his parents!

He'd accomplished so much without them by his side. With the help of his friends, Bastien had broken into the Odieux home and found evidence of the fires that would help him expose Olivier's perilous plan for power.

But Bastien still heard the voice of his parents in every word he read, and so he closed his eyes for a moment, imagining they were together again. This secret was the final nail in Olivier's coffin and he wished he could just talk to his mother and father so they could tell him what the message meant.

Bastien traced his fingers over each page. When he opened his eyes once more, he was on the dedication page. He looked at the single sentence.

To each other, for the love, the support and the long walks through Fontainebleau, where this story found its breath.

"Where stories go to breathe," Bastien muttered. "Where my parents' stories went to breathe!"

An echo of a memory called out to Bastien. He remembered day trips to the Forest of Fontainebleau, where they would venture from the well-trodden paths. His parents always said that if they were ever stuck on an idea, a walk through the forest would clear their heads. They would climb to their favourite spot at the top of the gorge and breathe in the fresh air.

Bastien closed the book and looked at the image on the front cover. Two figures sat atop a gorge looking out onto a forest below and their heads rested against the sky as though they were on top of the world.

The answer had been here all this time, sitting on the bookshelf, waiting for him. His parents wanted him to climb to the top of the Gorges d'Apremont, a place where they had spent so much time together. He thought of the path through the forest, the one that twisted and turned like a corkscrew, scaling up the steep rock face. This was unique knowledge, the type that Olivier could never buy or steal. Knowledge of happier times, full of love and laughter. And a fair bit of teasing too.

Bastien laughed. He wanted to hug his parents and tell them that he'd finally figured it out! But he couldn't and so he did the next best thing. He ran back to the dormitory, his parents' book clutched tightly to his chest, and threw himself on Theo's bed. "Wake up!"

"Are you trying to kill me?" Theo pushed him off. "What is it?"

"I've cracked it! The secret message! I know what it means."

Theo shot up and wiped the sleep from his eyes.

"*Hé!*" A voice interrupted them before Bastien could say anything more. "What are you talking about? What secret message?"

Behind them, Felix stood with his arms crossed over his chest. The other boys were slowly waking too.

The door creaked open and Mathilde tiptoed across the dormitory, her unbrushed hair sticking out at funny angles. "What does it mean?" she asked. "Your parents' message?"

Clément jumped out of bed in a rage, his face as crumpled as his pyjamas. "Wait a minute. How does *she* know what you're talking about? What's going on?"

Mathilde cleared her throat. "*She* has a name."

Hot, uncomfortable guilt crept up Bastien's back as the dormitory descended into chaos. "Don't wake Madame Gentille! You're right. There is something I need to tell you. Everything has happened so quickly, there's been no time to explain before. But I need all of your help for what comes next."

There was a moment of silence in the dormitory, as the others took in his words.

"Olivier freed Xavier from prison, didn't he?" Fred asked.

"How did you know?"

"Call it instinct." Fred shrugged. "It all feels linked. Wickedness follows those brothers like a plague."

Bastien sat next to Mathilde on his bed. "Gather round. I'll tell you everything I know."

The boys hurried over and formed a protective circle around the bed, as Bastien filled them in on the events of last night.

By the time Camille called everyone for breakfast, the boys and Mathilde had been awake for a good hour. Bastien hadn't left a single word spare as he told them everything they had uncovered. He told them about the Red Ink Society and Olivier's calculated plan for leading Paris into a state of emergency. He told them about the other members, how Judge Niney was responsible for Olivier's freedom and that the protests – where citizens came and cheered for Olivier – were all thanks to Charles Fitzmagnat, a powerful newspaper tycoon who had enough money to buy the moon.

And Bastien told them about sneaking into the Odieux house, the pieces of evidence hidden in strange places, and discovering the final part of Olivier's plan: to force President Millefois's resignation at the Exposition Universelle by using an ancient law that would make him ruler instead.

"You see," he had finished, "whatever is waiting for me in the Forest of Fontainebleau is something that Olivier wants to keep hidden. He failed to steal my notebook once and now he's sent Georges after me. But it hasn't worked and neither have his threats to keep my nose out of his business. We can't stop. The evidence we've found so far will help us to expose him, but uncovering the Odieux family secret will deliver the final blow. I know where we need to go, but I need your help. All of you."

At breakfast, Bastien took a swig of orange juice for courage. Nerves jangled around in his belly like a key chain. The Gruyère-and-chive omelette sitting on his plate would go untouched.

He had to get to the Forest of Fontainebleau today, but Madame Gentille had taken a day off from the patrol. There would be no window of opportunity to sneak away.

Bastien had to tell the truth. All of it, even though it meant admitting that he'd gone behind the director's back. Madame Gentille's friends were arriving tomorrow; their help would come just in time for the Exposition Universelle.

"How did the patrol go last night?" Bastien asked.

"It was rather uneventful," the director replied. She opened a pot of strawberry jam. "That's good, of course. What were the three of you up to in Theo's workshop last night?"

"We were experimenting with invisible ink."

Madame Gentille paused. Her baguette end was half-spread with jam. "*Pourquoi?*"

"Because of the secret message in my notebook."

"I thought your notebook contained no such thing." The director put down her knife. "That it was just those bad brothers who believed there was something hidden inside?"

"I was starting to believe I couldn't crack it," Bastien admitted.

"Until last night," Theo chimed in.

"But now we know what my parents wanted to tell me and we need to go to the Forest of Fontainebleau," Bastien said. "Today. All of us."

"It's a treasure hunt!" Robin cried.

Mathilde interrupted. "It's not a treasure hunt."

"It's a quest!" declared Felix.

Timothée held his butter knife in the air. "A quest to find the Holy Grail that will finally stop Olivier!"

"*Arrêtez!*" Madame Gentille rose to her feet. "I can't hear myself think! Timmy, put down that knife before you poke your eye out." She looked at Bastien, her face serious. "What do you expect to find in the forest?"

"Something that will reveal Olivier's family secret," Bastien replied. "I don't know what it is yet, but my parents went to great lengths to keep it hidden. We need to follow this clue to the forest if we actually want to stop him."

"It will strengthen the evidence we found in the Odieux house too," Mathilde added.

"You found *where*?" Madame Gentille gripped the back of her chair to steady herself, her eyes darting between Mathilde, Bastien and Theo. "What did you children do?"

"You said we have to get justice the proper way," Bastien continued, "but there isn't a proper way of doing things, not where Olivier is concerned. I know you're angry, but I just couldn't sit around and let his threats scare me. Right now, he's planning something terrible at the Exposition Universelle that will change everything. If the secret in the forest can help us stop him for good, then it's worth doing. Isn't it?"

Another moment of silence stretched into an eternity.

Then Madame Gentille rose from her chair. "Very well. I don't doubt the trust you have in your parents. We will go to Fontainebleau and do this together, like we should've done from the very beginning. The forest is large, though. Are you sure you know where to go?"

Bastien nodded. He pictured himself lying between his parents at the top of the gorge. It had been a couple of years since he had last visited the forest, but he trusted his instincts to lead the way. "The Gorge d'Apremont was our favourite spot."

"Then let's not waste any more time sitting here. Boys, and girl, find your most battered shoes and meet me in the courtyard as soon as possible."

The dining hall emptied and only Bastien, Theo and Mathilde remained. Madame Gentille sighed. Even though Bastien didn't regret breaking into the Odieux house, he felt guilty for how the director now looked.

"I'm really sorry that we went against your wishes," he said, quietly. "I just had to do something."

Madame Gentille sniffed and wiped her cheeks. "The weight of the world is sometimes too heavy to bear. I only ever wanted to protect you all, but I'm sorry I can't stop this."

"You have nothing to be sorry for," Bastien replied.

"You have made this place our home. But there are some things you can't protect us from and that's okay. You can't fix everything."

Madame Gentille smiled and the lines on her forehead smoothed out. "You children have more heart and hope than anyone I've ever met. You really are remarkable."

The grandfather clock in the hallway chimed half past ten. Suddenly, a cold dread came over Bastien. He'd been so preoccupied with the secret message that he hadn't kept track of the time. "Alice said she would be here at ten with her parents!" He glanced worriedly at Theo. Alice was the sort of person who believed you either arrived on time, or just didn't show up.

"Charlotte said they've been busier than ever," Madame Gentille said. "In uncertain times, people turn to stories and sugar."

"You don't understand," Theo shouted. "Georges, the new bookseller, is Charles Fitzmagnat's son! He's working with Olivier too."

Bastien jumped up from the table, a thousand terrible scenarios crossing his mind. "We need to go now. They might be in trouble!"

"We'll stop at the bookshop on the way to the station." Madame Gentille clapped her hands. "*Vite!*"

Bastien and Theo raced upstairs and pulled on their boots.

"She's going to be fine," Bastien said. Still, Theo's worried face was a mirror image of his own. They ran back down the stairs and through the courtyard, shouting at everyone else to hurry.

Understanding the secret message in his notebook had taken up all the space in his brain and Bastien felt guilty for losing track of time. They had to get to the Forest of Fontainebleau as quickly as possible, but as they half-walked, half-ran down the street, Bastien could only think of Alice, Charlotte and Jules and what would await him at Le Chat Curieux.

27
BETRAYAL AT THE BOOKSHOP

The shutters were still down over the windows of Le Chat Curieux when they arrived and the uneasy feeling inside Bastien grew stronger.

"This isn't normal!" He banged on the door and called out. "They always open at nine o'clock. Something is wrong."

"Alice!" Theo shouted. "Are you here?"

Madame Gentille cupped her face to the window, peering in between the shutters. "There's a light on inside. I think I can see a figure."

"Stand back!" Clément threw himself in front of Mathilde. "I'll protect you all."

Keys jangled on the other side of the door.

"Alice? Can you let us in?" Bastien asked.

The door made a clunking sound as it opened and Bastien rushed inside, Theo and Mathilde close behind him.

His heart broke as he took in the scene that lay before his very eyes. The bookshelves were broken in half, mounds of books – ripped and damaged – covering the entire floor. The till was open; only a few ripped banknotes remained. A quick look to his left, down the corridor, indicated that the café had suffered a similar fate. The glass cabinets were shattered, and the tables and chairs upturned.

At the bottom of the stairs sat a scared-looking Alice. Babette, the cat, had wrapped herself around Alice's neck, sniffling against her pyjamas.

Bastien rushed to her side. "What happened?"

Alice looked at him through red-raw eyes. "Last night I came straight back to the bookshop and found it like this." She gestured at the broken bookshelves and empty cash register.

"Do you know who did it?" Theo asked.

Alice nodded. "Georges turned up just as they were closing the shop. He said that I knew where your notebook was and demanded Papa tell him. Obviously,

Papa didn't say anything and tried to get him to leave. Georges said he was lying and tore this place apart looking for it." Her voice wavered. "Then he said that Olivier had told him to kill Papa and Mama, just like he'd done to the Bonlivres."

Bastien's breath hitched in his throat.

"Maman snuck out through the café entrance to get Abdou and our neighbours to fight him off. When they came back, Georges was gone. They found Papa on the floor."

"Is he okay?" Anger and guilt pricked at Bastien's skin.

Alice wiped her nose on her pyjama sleeve. "He's just woken up if you want to see him."

An army of footsteps headed for the stairs, but Madame Gentille held up her hand. "Let Bastien and Theo go. Too many of you will overwhelm him. We'll tidy down here instead to help."

To the director's surprise, the boys did not object. They scattered around the shop and Mathilde headed through to the café, Robin by her side.

Theo followed Alice upstairs, but Bastien hesitated. "What if he doesn't want to see me? This is all my fault! Georges came here because of me. And now Jules is hurt. It could've been so much worse…"

"Don't think like that." Alice turned back and squeezed his hand. "Papa wants to see you. This is not your fault."

It had been a long time since Bastien had been up to the bookshop's second floor. The attic flat was where Alice lived with her parents and Babette. It was small, but cosy. The staircase opened onto a narrow landing and the bathroom and living room were to the left with the family bedrooms on the other side.

"In here." Alice beckoned them into her parents' room, which was big enough to fit an armoire, a bookcase and a bed. The window was open, the cool spring breeze rippling the curtains.

Jules lay in the middle of the bed, as pale as the bed sheets that were tucked up to his neck. Charlotte sat next to him, holding a flannel to his forehead.

"Come in." She beckoned Bastien and Theo over to the bed as Jules slowly pushed himself up against a cushion.

"How nice to see you both," he said, his smile hiding a wince.

Bastien tried to smile back, but his lips refused; his guilt was too much. "I'm so sorry, Jules. Olivier sent Georges to the bookshop because of me. I dragged

Alice into this mess and look what has happened."

"Listen to me carefully." Jules reached for his hand. "Georges chose his side when he believed Olivier's lies. You didn't ask for all of this. You have nothing to apologize for."

"Besides…" Charlotte looked knowingly at her daughter. "Alice told us everything about the Red Ink Society and what you've uncovered. The corruption, it's awful. We didn't call the police about Georges just in case it got back to Olivier."

Jules coughed. "We can only trust each other."

"Exactly." Charlotte nodded. "And anything you asked of Alice, she agreed to on her own terms. We literally cannot tell her what to do."

"They've tried and failed," Alice smirked, "many times. Now, tell me, did you uncover the secret? Was it in invisible ink? And what about the keys?"

Despite everything, she still managed to smile and Bastien felt an overwhelming surge of love for Alice. He wiped his face and pushed down the guilt and anger. Those feelings would only distract him.

"The message told me to go to the Forest of Fontainebleau. I think my parents hid something there that will reveal Olivier's family secret. It's the last bit of evidence that will stop Olivier from succeeding. I hope."

"And I've got the letter pattern from the keys in here." Theo indicated to his workbook sticking out of his shorts pocket. "I'm going to work it out on the train."

The cuckoo clock on the wall chimed midday. It was time to go.

Bastien turned to Alice, but she shook her head. "I can't come. I need to be with Papa and help clean up the bookshop. Go and finish what your parents started." She hugged them both. "We're with you for whatever comes next."

Theo squirmed and Alice playfully punched him on the arm.

"Are my hugs that bad?"

"Far from it," Theo replied. He fished a roll of camera film from his pocket. "I just remembered this; it'll have the photographs of the map of fire targets. Will Abdou develop them?"

Alice nodded, clutching the film to her chest. "I'll ask him today."

"I feel better already for seeing you both." Jules sank back into bed. "I'm so proud. Standing up for what you believe in and making your voice heard is the bravest thing a person can do."

They said goodbye and Bastien closed the door behind them. He felt overcome, thinking of Alice, Jules and Charlotte and how much they had done to help him. Now, he had to help himself.

"Come on," Bastien said. "We've got a train to catch."

The hands on the clock outside the ticket office were approaching two o'clock as the train pulled into Fontainebleau station. Bastien stared out of the carriage window with his nose pressed up against the glass. He enjoyed people-watching, especially at train stations, where you could find every type of person. It was also another way to distract himself from thinking about Jules and the destroyed bookshop.

Today, the station platform was abuzz. Bastien spied a muscular man carrying a large leather suitcase plastered with stickers from travels around the world, while a group of chocolate-covered children ran up and down, their parents calling after them. At the far end of the platform stood a group of men and women dressed in vests and shorts with bags of bouldering equipment at their feet.

The treetops peeked from behind the station building. The forest path was so close now. The sooner they got off the train, the sooner Bastien could lead them to the gorge and find what his parents had left for him.

The train belched to a halt and he pulled a sleepy Theo from his seat. His best friend had spent most of the journey studying the letter pattern in his workbook, trying to make sense of what the keys were and where they'd come from. Bastien had left Theo to it, knowing how silence helped his brain work. And twenty minutes ago, Theo had finally cried out in success.

"I've figured it out!" He'd pointed to his workbook scribblings. "The space between *O* and *L* confused me, until I realized the patterns *wants* me to start in the gap. But the more I looked at it, I saw that the letter order has been reversed. So, I paired *L* with the very first letter *A*, and then *S* with *A*, *N* with *T*. The *XIII* at the very end are Roman numerals. And look what I got."

A A T P I O   L S N É R S N X I I I
LA SANTÉ PRISON XIII

"They *are* the keys from the prison!" Bastien had squeezed Theo so tightly, unable to contain his joy. "For the thirteen most dangerous cells. Olivier and Xavier released the prisoners on purpose!"

"We have so much evidence now." Theo had smiled, his eyes starting to droop. "We just need the final piece in the forest."

Madame Gentille clapped her hands. "Quickly, boys. This is our stop. Pascal, help me with my bag. It has rations inside for our walk. And helping does not mean eating a chunk of *fromage* to lessen the load."

One by one, they tumbled out of the train and passed through the station, weaving through the crowd at the ticket booth. Exiting onto the street, Bastien looked up at the pale blue sky. Only a couple of clouds, like puffs of cotton, dotted the clear view. It was a good day for finding something lost, he hoped. With only two days left until the Exposition Universelle opening ceremony, time was ticking away.

"So," Madame Gentille said, "what's the way from here?"

Bastien squinted at the signs across the road. "Follow me."

The route from the station to the outskirts of the forest took them into the centre of Fontainebleau and past a parade of shops, all with red-and-white awnings like peppermint sticks.

"Can we stop and get some sweets?" Timothée and Robin lingered in front of the *confiserie*, their eyes fixed on the colourful jars of sweet treats.

"How can you still be hungry? You all ate a very early lunch on the train!" Madame Gentille ushered them down the street. "Maybe on the way back. We're on a quest, remember?"

Bastien led them past the square fountain and towards the edges of the town where brick met dirt. "This way to the forest!" he called over his shoulder. "We should hurry."

The pavement gave way to a dusty path and soon enough they were in the forest. Oak and beech trees towered high above their heads like giants and the sandy soil turned to lush green grass, violet and red orchids blooming.

Bastien breathed in the scent of fresh earth. Mathilde and Theo walked by his side. "It smells so different here."

"Better, you mean?" Mathilde stepped out of the way

of a squirrel. "The air in Paris always feels so thick and heavy. I can't wait to see the sea with Maman. We will buy a little cottage in Deauville, a stone's throw from the beach."

"With a spare bedroom for visitors?" Bastien asked.

"Of course." Mathilde skipped ahead. "I might not be able to fit all of you boys in, but maybe we can sleep on the beach instead!"

Theo picked a twig from a nearby branch and moulded it into a stick-man figure with his hands. "My parents always wanted to leave Paris one day and move back to Yemma's home town of Ath Yenni," he said. "She always preferred the Algerian mountains and sand to the concrete and cobblestones here."

"It must've been hard to wake up to a city when all you've known is open space," Bastien replied, guiding them through rows of pine trees. As much as he loved Paris and could never imagine living elsewhere, he was glad to be here in the forest. His parents were right; a stroll through Fontainebleau helped to clear the mind.

Theo popped the stick man into his shirt pocket. "I'll go to Ath Yenni one day and walk on her mountains."

Bastien grinned at them both. "Adventures await us all!" The ground beneath their feet rose gradually and the landscape opened into a valley, the green forest floor stretching far and wide. He looked to the right, where a line of trees met the valley edge, and felt a pull. "We need to go in that direction. There should be wooden stairs past the pond that will take us to the top of the gorge."

As they walked deeper into the forest, the grass started to squelch. They took a rest when Pascal demanded a snack. Madame Gentille passed around slices of *jambon*, but Bastien soon became impatient and five minutes later they were all back on their feet.

They passed a large pond, covered in algae and lily pads, and then continued past boulders and rock formations. After thirty minutes of walking, Bastien saw the wooden steps in the distance.

"We're here!" He ran towards the stairs and climbed so quickly that his feet barely touched each step. Bastien didn't hear Madame Gentille telling him to slow down, or feel his knees knocking against each other, or the sharp tug of thorns catching on his trousers. He simply climbed and climbed until the last step fell away and he was standing on the top of the world.

29

AT THE TOP OF THE GORGE

He was finally here. Bastien walked towards the edge of the gorge and saw the forest below stretching in every direction. The tops of the trees looked like a cloud canopy, and he imagined walking above the entire forest. It was exactly how he remembered, and he was glad that views didn't change as quickly as life, or people, did.

"Is it safe?" Bastien turned at the sound of Theo's voice. He stood at the top of the steps, clutching his arms around his waist and desperately trying to swallow down his fear of heights. "Is it structurally sound?"

Bastien knew that rocks could sometimes crumble; mountains and gorges could give way, but he thought it best not to remind Theo. "We're safe. Just stay back from the edges. But you will miss this incredible view."

"Come on." Mathilde grabbed Theo's arm. "I'll help you."

They walked across the sandy rock, although Theo's walk was more of a grandfather's shuffle. He reached out and grabbed hold of Bastien's arm too, edging closer and closer, until he finally dared to look down.

"I'll admit it," Theo said. "It's sort of beautiful. I can see why you spent so much time here."

"Well done." Mathilde smiled.

"Well," Theo breathed. "We help each other to be brave when we need it most."

Bastien drank in the view. He saw his parents' faces in the clouds, drawn across the sky, and felt a sense of peace wash over him. This was a place where they had spent so many precious days together. Then, remembering why they were here, he turned back to the platform, taking in the sandy floor and boulders piled like marbles.

Looking over at the grass and shrubs that surrounded the copse of oak trees, he understood that this was no easy task. There were a thousand hiding places and the enormity of it all made him dizzy. He was glad not to be alone.

"I know we're in the right place. I feel it in my bones," he said. "But what if I'm too late? Whatever they left for me to find might've been washed away by rain or winds a long time ago."

"I doubt that." Madame Gentille dropped her bag onto the ground and rested on a boulder. The boys were climbing the last steps up to the gorge behind her. "Your memory has got us this far."

"And we're all here to help," Felix said. "One time, I found a Roman coin in the Seine."

"Shut up, Felix." Fred clapped him round the head. "That was me."

"You can do it." Theo gave Bastien's shoulders a gentle shake. "You just need to breathe and remember."

Bastien closed his eyes. Everything inside him was simmering, just like one of Camille's slow-cooked stews. For so long, he had let every bad feeling – guilt and shame and sadness – bubble beneath his skin. It struck him that he didn't have to let it be that way. "You're right. I forget to, you know, *breathe* sometimes."

Theo smiled. "It is a basic life skill that even the most accomplished of people can forget."

Bastien looked around again and allowed his memories to wash over him. He and his father had spent many hours sitting atop the boulders here. Was something hidden between them, in the cracks? They had watched birds nestled in the bushes near the top of the steps. Was that the hiding place?

"It could be anywhere," he said. "Let's split up and look in different areas."

Theo nodded decisively. "Mathilde, Felix, Fred, Robin. You're with me. Let's look through the bushes and check the boulders."

"The others with me!" Madame Gentille rolled up the sleeves of her blouse. "Let's find branches to use as spades."

Everyone set to work. Bastien walked over towards the trees on the left and tried to think of things the way Theo would: a simple equation that had a clear solution. His parents had left something here for him in one of their favourite places and he would find it.

He walked further into the trees and spotted an old, worn rope dangling from the biggest oak tree; it was all that was left of the makeshift swing his mother had set up five summers ago.

Bastien placed his palm against the rough bark of the tree trunk, where small circles of moss grew outwards in search of sunlight. Did the ageing lines of the tree remember him and the memories he had created with his parents in this very place?

Something rustled in the bushes beyond the trees. Bastien froze. He hoped it wasn't a hungry wild boar. Still, curiosity walked his feet forwards, until a small brown bird hopped out from beneath the leaves and, spotting him, flew away into the treetops. Somewhat relieved, Bastien turned back towards the big oak tree and discovered that its trunk was hollow.

He had always made a beeline for the rope swing, demanding his mother push him high enough for his toes to knock the sun from the sky. He had never ventured any further into the trees before. But looking at the hole in the oak now, it was as inviting as an open door. Bastien felt himself being pulled towards it. He climbed over the base of the trunk and stepped into the hollow. It was wide enough for him to fit inside, and anticipation tingled up and down his arms.

It was the perfect hiding spot. Had his parents thought the same?

He slid down and began to search through a pile of muddy leaves at the bottom of the hole. The afternoon light filtered in through cracks in the bark and illuminated his hands as he dug up layers of undisturbed dirt. A hidden message in invisible ink, following a path through a forest and, finally, a secret buried under roots and earth; it had all the makings of a fairy tale. Except this was no fairy tale.

His parents had gone to great lengths to keep this secret secure, ensuring that Bastien was the only one who could figure out its hiding spot. His hands were muddy and pockmarked with the shape of stones and pebbles, but he forced himself to dig deeper into the cold ground.

A fragment of light suddenly shot through a gap in the tree trunk and a glint of something metallic caught his eye. He crawled forward and plunged his hands further into the ground, grabbing at handfuls of leaves, some crisp, others soggy.

Then his fingers hit something hard. Not a leaf, or a mound of dirt, but something solid and cold. From under a pile of crumbling soil, Bastien retrieved a blue metal tin, the size of both his hands together. He used his sleeve to wipe away a thick layer of dirt and read the engraving underneath: *Bêtises de Cambrai*. The minty, boiled sweets had been his mother's favourite. He remembered her chasing him around the apartment, trying to get him to taste one. To Bastien, they tasted like day-old toothpaste.

He wiped the entire tin clean. On the bottom, scratched so small it would have been easy to miss, were the initials MB.

Margot Bonlivre. His mother's initials.

Bastien stared at the sweet tin in disbelief. Was this it? Was this tin hiding a secret that Olivier had been so desperate to bury? He steadied his shaking hands and stood up, oblivious to the mud that covered his trousers as he stepped out of the hollow.

Dazed and confused, Bastien stumbled out from the trees. He clutched the tin tightly, as though his body would fall apart if he let go. Whatever his parents had wanted him to know was inside this tin. His mind urged him to open it, but his hands disobeyed.

Bastien couldn't open this alone.

He needed the strength of his family.

30

THE ODIEUX FAMILY LIE

Robin was the first one to notice Bastien. He dropped the twig he was using to rake through the sandy ground and clapped his hands in delight. "Have you found it?"

Everyone turned at the sound of Robin's voice. They ran over to Bastien as he fell to his knees. Crowding round, they stared at the small blue tin.

"I found my mother's old sweet tin."

"Are there sweets inside?" Pascal asked, much to the despair of everyone else.

Bastien smiled, weakly. "I'd rather it be useful information."

"Go on then." Theo nudged him. "Open it up."

He slid the lid from the top of the tin with difficulty; some of the mud had dried around it, sealing it tight. Inside was a thick envelope, bursting at its edges.

"That was an anticlimax," Mathilde said.

"My parents always entrusted their most precious secrets to paper." Bastien picked up the envelope and pulled out the first paper stuffed inside. His heart tugged upon seeing the familiar looping scrawl of his mother and the short, staccato stabs of his father. They had written him a letter together.

"What does it say?" Madame Gentille looked over his shoulder. "Will you read it to us?"

Dear Bastien,

Your father and I are sorry for leading you on such a wild goose chase to get to this point. We had to be sure that you, and only you, would know where the hidden message in the notebook would lead. Memories are as unique as footprints, and we knew that the ones we made together would help lead you here.

Well done for figuring it out, our precious son. Does the view from the gorge still look as beautiful as when we first visited? While you and your father passed the hours watching birds, I stole away into the tree hollow, scribbling stories and dreaming. It was the perfect hideaway, as you have just now discovered yourself.

If you are reading this, then it is likely that we are no longer with you. For leaving you, we can never apologize enough. You are our joy – our own heartbeat played back to us – and please know that whatever happened to us, our final thoughts were only of you.

The road I chose to take with your father was a dangerous one, but it was the right path. There is a sickness growing in the city and, slowly, it will spread across the entire country, perhaps even the world, if we do not act. Olivier Odieux is more than just one wicked man, weaving stories for his own amusement. His vision must be extinguished, his plan exposed.

If we cannot do this ourselves, we must tell you what we know so that our fight for a better world can grow.

The letter now changed to his father's hand.

My dear boy, it is time to tell you the truth. Olivier Odieux and I were once friends, a long time ago. I cut ties with him before you entered the world, but over the years, I have kept watch on his movements. I needed to see whether he would continue with the ideas he shared with me when we were once friends. Olivier admired his grandfather, Victor, and swallowed his dangerous beliefs as easy as a pill.

You see, Olivier has always believed that he would one day become a ruler. His grandfather told him that the Odieux family are noble, that they are descended from royalty and that prestige runs through their blood. Victor created the Red Ink Society to gather support from like-minded nobles, who all longed for a return of the king.

But the Odieux name is a lie. It does not belong to Victor or Olivier, but to another family altogether. Your mother's keen eye for research was always the best, and together we have risked so much to uncover the extent of their evil.

Victor stole the Odieux identity, and we have the proof to show that they are not who they say they are and that the Red Ink Society was founded on a bed of lies.

In case anything happens to us, this tin contains everything you need to know, including the final piece of evidence that Olivier is desperate to get his hands on. This piece proves his grandfather's deceit. It is the one thing that can stop Olivier from ever taking power.

We have gone to great lengths to keep this safe, and if anything does happen to us then we ask that you do the same.

We are sorry for the burden that we have left you with, but know that there are good people in the world still, who you can trust. Pay attention to that feeling in your gut. This is not something you should do alone.

With all our love in this world and the ones that follow,

Your parents

The only sound that could be heard were birds chirping sweet melodies above their heads. There was so much information that Bastien needed to absorb, not least the revelation about the lie that had spawned generations of fake Odieuxs. They were not royalty and Olivier had no right to use the Ancient Royal Decree to overthrow President Millefois and take power; it simply didn't belong to him.

Still, one thing stood out from the letter that didn't yet make sense.

"I don't understand. What is the 'final piece' I'm meant to be keeping safe?" Bastien turned the envelope upside down and emptied the contents onto the sandy ground.

Theo picked up a photograph. "Recognize this person?"

Bastien stared at the image of a man in a grey woollen suit, a bowler hat perched on his head. He was tall and youthful, a wisp of a moustache growing above his mouth. "It's Victor Odieux, Olivier's grandfather. He looks much younger, though."

Fred snatched the photograph from Theo's hands and turned it around. "But why does it say Victor Durand on the back?"

Bastien looked at his mother's handwriting on the back of the photograph. There was no denying that the picture was Olivier's grandfather, but why was there a different surname? He picked his parents' letter back up and skimmed through the words. His finger landed on a sentence at the bottom.

"My parents said that Victor stole the Odieux name," he said, understanding turning into excitement. "Durand must have been his real surname."

"So, Olivier is actually Olivier Durand," Mathilde said, her voice quiet.

"Look at this, Bastien!" Timothée thrust a ripped

book page into his hands. "It's from a royal encyclopaedia."

"*Quoi?*"

"An encyclopaedia is a book that holds expert information, in this case all about the royal family," Madame Gentille explained to a confused-looking Robin.

Although his throat was dry, Bastien read aloud the entry.

The Odieuxs are a noble family, descendants of King Henry IV, the founder of the House of Bourbon. Although they were once a large household, time has seen the family's lineage grow smaller and smaller over the years. At the time of writing, 1860, there is only one remaining family member: Victor Odieux. Not much is known about Monsieur Odieux, as he retreated from society after the death of his parents. It was last reported that he lives in the north, on the outskirts of the spa town of Saint-Amand-les-Eaux. It is not believed that he is married or has children.

Bastien slotted the final puzzle piece into place. "Olivier's grandfather stole Victor Odieux's identity!"

A darker thought followed quickly. "What if he killed him? If the real Odieux was a recluse and the last living royal family member, Olivier's grandfather must've known he could easily get rid of the real Victor Odieux and take his place!"

"I can't quite believe it!" Madame Gentille said. "I think your parents uncovered a royal scandal."

Hope came back, kicking and screaming, for Bastien. "This is information we can use, isn't it? We can prove that Olivier isn't who he says he is. That his whole family are imposters!"

Madame Gentille's face had been bright, but her mouth now drooped slightly. "I'm afraid this wouldn't be enough alone to change people's minds about Olivier. We need more, if we want a real chance at stopping him."

Bastien turned back to the envelope and realized there was something stuck to the inside. It was brown and had blended in, so much so that he hadn't noticed it at first. Carefully, he peeled the fragile paper from the envelope.

"What is it?" Theo asked.

He opened it up and immediately understood this, not the photo, was the final piece. "It's a birth certificate for Olivier's grandfather. The Odieux family, as all know them, are definitely the Durands."

ACTE DE NAISSANCE

Born 30 April, 1820
Victor Durand, born in Paris at 7, Rue des Princes
Son of Thibault Durand, landowner, aged 25, and
of Barbeline Durand, aged 22. Married couple
living at aforementioned address.

How had his parents found this birth certificate? However they had managed it, they had risked everything to find this information and keep it safe. Now, Bastien had to do his part.

"Will this help?" He thrust the certificate into Madame Gentille's hands.

The director pursed her lips. "It could well do. Alone, these items might not mean much, but together they prove the last testimony of your parents. Which is also a clear motive for Olivier wanting to silence them."

"How do we use this and the evidence we found at his house to take him down?" Mathilde asked. "We have less than two days to figure it out before he invokes the decree!"

"But he can't use it, can he?" Bastien said. "His family are not royalty. We need to show everyone that Olivier and Xavier are nothing but liars!"

They all cheered and it was a moment where every single one of them felt like a part of something special. They were no longer alone, they had each other, and together they would stop this terrible injustice.

Madame Gentille was the first to break the cheers. "I think we had better get home in that case. We have a lot to do."

Bastien folded the birth certificate back into the crinkled envelope and shut the tin. Once on his feet, he gravitated towards the edge of the gorge for one last look. The others had started making their way back down the wooden steps, but Bastien didn't want to let go of this moment just yet. He wanted to remember this view and the feeling of achieving the impossible and uncovering his parents' secret.

Although he felt smaller than ever here, looking out at a landscape that could swallow him whole, he also felt bigger, the enormity of everything he now knew filling up his mind and heart.

Olivier Odieux wasn't descended from royalty. He was a liar and a cheat, just like his grandfather, and he had fooled everyone around him into believing he was someone special. Well, he had fooled everyone apart from Bastien's parents and now Bastien and his friends. As he turned away from the edge of the gorge, a new resolve came over him.

In two days' time, at the Exposition Universelle, Olivier was going to declare a state of emergency and declare himself as rightful ruler.

Except that he wasn't the rightful ruler and never would be.

And Bastien was determined to be the one to put an end to the villain's plans, in one shark-like bite.

31
NEVER TOO YOUNG TO MAKE A DIFFERENCE

The train journey back to Paris was subdued. Everyone except Bastien and Madame Gentille was snoozing. Thankfully, they were the only passengers in the second-class carriage. Fred and Felix had chosen to lie on the carpeted floor and spread out as they slept; the others were curled up in their seats, their heads bobbing in time with the gentle sway of the train.

Bastien stared out of the window, watching the fields and forest slowly turn into buildings and busy roads. The bright lights of the city prepared themselves for the evening ahead. As much as he loved the forest, Paris was his home. It had given him life and helped him survive.

Now he had to survive what came next. He thought

of Olivier standing onstage at the world fair, imagining how the man's words would seep into the minds of every citizen there and beyond. With everything that Bastien now knew, he had to find a way to stop him.

"You should give your mind a rest." Madame Gentille looked up from the book in her lap. "I can hear it working overtime from here."

"Everything just feels too big to overcome." He slouched further into his seat, his mother's sweet tin stowed safely between his legs.

The director nodded and closed her book. "Whenever anything feels too big, you just break it into as many smaller pieces as you need. Then it doesn't feel so impossible. That is how we survive."

Bastien knew how some adults pretended to understand how you felt, but really, they couldn't ever imagine. Yet right now the director's face was sincere, and he truly believed that she understood the rollercoaster of emotions that passed through him.

"I'm really sorry again for going to the Odieux house behind your back," Bastien said. "But now we have all the evidence we could possibly need to make people see who Olivier truly is. By exposing his plan, we *can* stop him."

Madame Gentille opened the clasp on her bag and pulled out a handful of fudge, offering a piece to Bastien. "I was angry. I *am* angry. I care for you a tremendous amount and would never forgive myself if something happened. But I'd be lying if I said I wouldn't have done the same thing as you. I was just as recklessly courageous when I was younger." The director popped the fudge in her mouth. "As you get older, you change. Still, no one is too young to make a difference. That I believe with all of my heart."

Bastien found himself sitting taller. "You do?"

"Like you, I lived in an orphanage. My mother died when I was nine and my father couldn't afford to raise me. Once I was old enough to leave, I worked many different jobs, and ended up in Brussels as a governess just as the Great War broke out.

"I never really considered myself as someone who paid much attention to the world around me before then, but everything changed. I met my fiancé Michel not long before he went off to fight. So I decided to join the Belgian Red Cross."

Bastien sat, mesmerized, listening to Madame Gentille share her past with him. "Were you a nurse?" He wondered if the friends she had called upon for help now had been her colleagues during the war.

She nodded. "For a short while. Michel was injured while fighting in Antwerp and so I cared for him until he was better, and helped him get across the Dutch border to reunite with his regiment. It was then that I started passing on information about the German army to the British."

Bastien's mouth fell open in disbelief. "You were a spy?"

Madame Gentille laughed. "Don't act so surprised! I told you, I was as reckless as I was brave once."

"What happened?" Bastien leaned forward, wishing he had his notebook to write down Madame Gentille's real-life story.

"I went to London and trained before returning to Brussels. I collected information about the enemy's movements for a couple of years, but I was betrayed and almost paid the ultimate price." The director dug her nails into her wrists.

"I'm glad you're still here," Bastien said quietly.

Dark clumps of make-up were smudged underneath Madame Gentille's eyes, but there was still a kind smile on her face. "I know you would do anything for the ones you love. I would do the same."

"*Merci*."

"Anyway, my friends will arrive in Paris tomorrow morning. Their skills will help us expose Olivier's manipulative lies."

"When you said your friends were from your 'old job', do you mean they were spies too?"

The director nodded. "This is your battle, my brave one, but we will be by your side."

Gratitude spilled out of every pore in Bastien's body. He leaped from his seat and hugged Madame Gentille. His parents' letter in the tin had reminded him that goodness still existed and Madame Gentille had proved them right. It had become so very easy for Bastien to see only darkness in others after everything – he'd been right in his gut feeling about Georges, after all – but the director was good and kind and she was on his side.

The last of the light had almost vanished by the time they returned to Petit-Montrouge. Upon disembarking, Madame Gentille had hurried them out of the train station and past the crowds that had gathered around a lone newspaper seller, who was shouting out the latest news.

"Further protests around the country! Lyon, Toulouse, Marseille. Other cities seeing growing support for the redeemed Olivier Odieux and La Seule Voix! *President Millefois set to address accusations of his incompetence at the Exposition Universelle in two days' time!"*

The words of the newspaper seller repeated in Bastien's mind all the way home. Support for Olivier was spreading throughout the country, but they had an advantage that still gave Bastien hope: the Odieux family secret and evidence to tie Olivier to the fires and prison break. Now, Bastien just had to figure out *how* to use what they had.

Turning onto the orphanage street, he made out a figure standing in front of the gates. Everyone whispered and walked faster,

"Who is it?" Madame Gentille called.

"Someone who is very late to make amends," a voice replied.

The director frowned, but Bastien and Theo looked at each other, realization spreading across their faces.

Bastien broke away from the others, running down the pavement. "You're here!"

The first thing Bastien noticed about Louis Odieux was how much younger he seemed. He was dressed in an emerald-green suit and the lines around his eyes and brows had vanished altogether. Throwing away the baggage of his brothers had given him a new lease of life.

"I didn't think we'd ever make it." Louis wrapped Bastien in a hug. "The journey was awfully bumpy. Philippe is still seasick, *le pauvre*. He's around here somewhere, battling against his insides."

A gurgled murmur that sounded like a hello came from a bush nearby.

Louis placed his hand on Bastien's shoulder. "Anyway, I hope I'm not too late."

Bastien smiled, guiding him through the orphanage gates. "In fact, you're just in time."

32

A LITTLE HELP FROM FRIENDS

The next day, the morning hours passed by in a blur of conversation and endless cups of warm milk and coffee. Bastien and Theo retreated to the library with Louis and told him everything they had uncovered, as well as Olivier and Xavier's plan for the Exposition Universelle.

While Mathilde helped Philippe recover from his continuing travel sickness by bringing endless slices of plain toasted baguette to his bedside, Bastien told Louis the secret of the invisible ink and what his parents had uncovered: the Odieuxs did not descend from royalty. They were not a noble family. It had all been a lie.

After an avalanche of information – all terrible, but

unsurprising to Louis, who knew the depths his bad brothers would sink to in the name of power – he sat back in the reading chair and held his head in his hands.

"*Ça va?*" Bastien shuffled over to Louis from where he'd been sitting on the floor. "We know it's a lot. I didn't mean to overwhelm you."

After a minute, Louis slowly rolled his head back up. "I never felt as though I was an Odieux. Now it finally makes sense." He sighed and pulled himself up. "I can't believe everything you have all been through. It feels as though you children could right the world all by yourselves."

"We could," Theo said.

"We *will*," Bastien added. "We just need an extra few pairs of hands to help us."

Louis rolled up his sleeves. "These hands are old, but they are hard-working. Now, before we talk any more about how to stop that terrible twosome, let's get some breakfast. I've missed croissants so much."

The dining hall was already bustling by the time Bastien and Theo took their seats at the table.

"Madame Gentille said Charlotte called this

morning," Robin said, tugging on Bastien's sleeve. "Jules is out of bed and doing much better."

"*Merci*, little one." Relief brought a smile to Bastien's face.

Louis hurried over to where Mathilde was and sat down next to her.

"My niece!" he exclaimed, his arms out wide. "*Je peux?*"

Mathilde begrudgingly accepted the hug; Bastien could see her squirming from the other end of the table. It wasn't that she disliked Louis – when Bastien had introduced them last night, Mathilde had been thrilled to discover a new family member who wasn't a megalomaniac (and Louis had been equally delighted to discover that another kind heart existed amongst his family). But Mathilde had experienced humanity at its very worst and it would take a little longer for her to let down her final wall. Once she did, Bastien suspected that she and Louis would become the firmest of friends.

"Bastien! If you ignore me one more time, I'm throwing this grapefruit at you and I *won't* be sorry."

He snapped out of his daze to find Clément standing on the dining bench.

"*Désolé*. I was daydreaming. What is it?"

319

"You've spent all morning chatting to Louis in the library and now you're staring into space. What are we going to do about the bad brothers? Do you even have a plan?" Clément tightened his grip on the grapefruit. "You'd better not be leaving us out like last time."

Bastien ignored Clément's temper; he knew that he was just anxious, like everyone else.

"I didn't and I won't," Bastien said. "And, as it goes, I do have a plan."

The words fell from his mouth without thought, but they weren't exactly lies. Something had been slowly forming since the train journey home from the Forest of Fontainebleau. Bastien had been balancing the different pieces of evidence in his mind: the photograph they'd taken at the Odieux house of the pocket map marked with the fire targets; the prison keys; the Red Ink Society manifesto containing the names of the three founding families; and the birth certificate that proved the entire Odieux family were completely *un*royal.

Together, the proof weighed heavy. Now, with just over twenty-four hours until the opening ceremony of the Exposition Universelle, Bastien knew he needed to share it with the rest of the country, even the world. Although Louis and Philippe were here, for his developing plan to work, they would need even more help.

"We're waiting," Pascal said.

"Bastien!" Madame Gentille called from the hallway. "*Viens!*"

"I'll be right back." He stood up. "And then I'll tell you exactly what we're going to do."

Hurrying into the hallway, Bastien saw four figures with great rucksacks standing at the entrance.

"My friends have arrived!" Madame Gentille beckoned him over. "Come and meet them."

He shook the hands of two men with brilliantly blond hair. "This is Alain and Maarten," the director said. "We helped soldiers across the Dutch border together. And Katharine and Edda were medics for the Red Cross, until they started the underground mail service that we used to deliver and share intelligence."

Katharine smiled at Bastien. He tried to hide the shock on his face at her missing front tooth. Unfortunately, hiding emotions had never been one of his strengths.

"Oh, this?" Katharine winked. "Happened when I was delivering a letter in the middle of the night through the Ardennes Forest. Tripped on a tree stump and went flying."

"We've heard all about you and your friends." Edda spoke with a thick Flemish accent. "You are truly remarkable."

"That's kind of you," Bastien said, "but we're just doing what's necessary. There's nothing remarkable about that."

"Indeed there is," Alain said. "Looking the other way is the easier option, but you are all facing what needs to be done. That takes real, remarkable courage."

Madame Gentille clapped her hands, ushering her friends towards the staircase. "Let me show you four to your rooms. We have much to prepare."

Bastien waved and headed back to the dining hall. Madame Gentille's friends seemed just as impressive as the director. Four good people had joined their fight against Olivier, spies who knew how to spread information and share the truth.

Standing in the doorway, he beckoned to the others. They shot up from their seats, the benches scraping against the floor.

"*Tout le monde*, come with me," Bastien said. "This is part one of the plan. We have deliveries to make."

Paris felt like their playground that afternoon as Bastien led the boys and Mathilde all over the city. They made a delivery to Le Chat Curieux, which now looked more like its old self. Gone were the broken bookcases and ripped-up books. Jules was out of bed, sitting next to Alice behind the counter while she served customers. She promised to pass the message onto all of their neighbours and handed Bastien the developed photographs in return. Next, they dropped off a message to Bastien's publisher LeGrand, the archivist Pauline Savoir, and finally headed to the offices of *Le Parisien Quotidien* with an extra special delivery.

And what exactly was being delivered by eight boys and a girl wearing battered ballet slippers? Inside a small envelope, each person found the same message.

Come to the Orphanage for Gentils Garçons at 6 p.m. tonight. It is time to fight back against the lies of Olivier Odieux and La Seule Voix. We want to spread the truth, but we can't do it without your help.
- Bastien Bonlivre

By the middle of the afternoon, the last resistance message had been delivered. As he and his friends made their way back to the orphanage, the soles of Bastien's feet were as weary as his busy mind. Bastien crossed his fingers and wished for the good and honest people in his city to answer their call.

33

MEET THE RESISTANCE

Was it possible to speed up time? As Bastien ran in and out of the dining hall, checking the grandfather clock in the hallway, he desperately wished Theo could invent a switch that would fast-forward them to six o'clock. It was now only ten minutes away, but each second felt double as long.

"*Calme-toi*," Mathilde said as he sat back down for the twentieth time. "People will come."

Bastien knew she was right. Still, a part of his mind always drifted towards doubt.

Tonight, the dining hall was the setting for his first ever resistance-group meeting. He looked over at Alain and Maarten, who were currently showing Clément,

Pascal and Robin how to crawl quickly on their bellies and avoid enemy detection. The others were gathered at the table as Theo proudly displayed his renovated box camera to Edda and Katharine.

Bastien's head snapped around at the sound of a creak in the hallway. Then came muffled whispers. The noise grew louder, and soon enough the sound of shoes clacking on the wooden floor filled the hallway. He jumped to his feet and opened the dining-hall doors, allowing a river of people to flow inside.

Leaning on Charlotte for support, Jules shuffled across the room with Abdou by his side. Pauline Savoir and Gaston LeGrand followed, in deep discussion with a number of journalists from *Le Parisien Quotidien*. Last to arrive was a group of adults and children led by Madame Gentille and Camille. Bastien didn't recognize them, but from the familiarity that the director treated them with, he guessed they were likely members of the Petit-Montrouge Protection, the neighbourhood watch group.

Closing the dining-hall doors behind her, Alice ran over to Bastien. She cradled Babette in her arms as though the cat was a baby.

"You brought Babette with you?" Bastien laughed.

Alice nodded. "She wants to join the resistance. We can't have her feeling left out, can we? Cats are against Olivier too."

Love filled Bastien from head to toe. He knew it was a feeling he should never underestimate, because the love he felt for his friends, old and new, was what set him apart from Olivier and Xavier Odieux. Hate was what had brought the bad brothers to this point in their evil schemes, but it would only get them so far.

"*Écoutez!*" The dining room fell silent at Madame Gentille's command.

Now it was Bastien's turn to speak. His tongue twisted in a knot at the sight of all the expectant faces. "Thank you all for coming," he said. "It means you care."

"Of course we do, dear boy." LeGrand took off his bowler hat. "I'm frightened. I haven't felt like that in a while. Not since the war."

The room murmured in agreement.

"That's why I asked you all here tonight. So I can tell you what I know and how I'm certain it is the truth."

"The truth about what?" Pauline asked.

"The fires and the prison break," Mathilde interrupted. She stood next to Bastien, alongside Theo and Alice too. "The protests here and all over the country, organized by *La Seule Voix* and Olivier Odieux. It's all connected."

"Fitzmagnat's newspaper is a joke," Abdou spat. "If you're telling me he is involved in all of this, I wouldn't be surprised."

Bastien had their attention now. He took a breath and told them everything he knew.

"Olivier Odieux has been planning something for a long time. Even before the author kidnappings last year. It was never just about being the most successful writer. It was a way for him to make money and grow his power by hiding dangerous beliefs in stories, but it didn't work. Now, he is trying to grow his power again with his most manipulative plan yet."

"What do you mean by manipulative?" one of the journalists asked, a pen in their hand and notebook in their lap.

"Olivier has re-established the Red Ink Society, an elite, secret group that his grandfather created. They believe that a king should rule our country and that anyone who is not like them – or does not believe the same things as them – should become second-class citizens. The Fitzmagnats were another founding family of the society, which explains why Charles Fitzmagnat and his son Georges are helping Olivier spread his lies through *La Seule Voix*.

"But we know that Olivier is not the saviour he is pretending to be – in fact he was the one who started the fires and planned the prison break, along with his brother Xavier. Olivier has organized the chaos that has damaged our city!"

Angry voices erupted in the dining hall and, from the corner of his eye, Bastien saw Louis slump against the dining table. Did he still feel partly responsible for his brother's actions?

"So Olivier is criticizing the President for failing to protect people from crimes *he* committed?" LeGrand asked.

Bastien nodded. "We also know that he is planning to interrupt the Exposition Universelle's opening ceremony tomorrow. He will declare President Millefois unfit to rule and will demand power by using the Ancient Royal Decree."

"What is that?" someone from the neighbourhood watch group asked.

"It's an ancient law that allows a royal descendant to take power over the country in a state of emergency,"

Pauline interrupted. "But it hasn't been used for hundreds of years. In fact, I don't even think such an old law would still be accepted."

"But it will." Theo now stood by Bastien's side. "Pierre Niney, the Head Judge at the Palais de Justice, is a member of the Red Ink Society. He is the reason that Olivier walked free. He will be the reason that the Ancient Royal Decree will pass."

The chatter in the dining hall grew even louder. Bastien sensed everyone's anger; all together, it felt just as powerful as his own. But he couldn't let their anger boil over and distract them from what they had to do.

"Olivier wants to choke us with fear, to make us so afraid that we never dare to open our mouths and speak the truth." Bastien's shouts cut across the room. Everyone turned to look back at him, but he found that he did not shrink under their gaze as he had done the night of his book party. In this moment, standing in front of the people who were on his side, his voice only grew louder. "We must shout back at fear and tell it that we will not be silent! We will do what is right. Will you stand with us to stop this?"

Several moments passed before anyone said anything – and then, one by one, a chorus of "*Oui*"s and neck-snapping nods started up like a procession. The once-outraged faces were now determined and resolute, and it was the most glorious thing Bastien had seen in a long time.

"We stand with you!" Louis shouted.

"Whatever it takes!" Philippe added, squeezing Louis's hand in his own.

"For the Bonlivres," Jules said, his eyes smiling at Bastien. "For Margot and Hugo and telling the truth when it most matters!"

Others followed, whistling and stamping their feet, and Bastien blinked back happy tears.

Once the noise had died down, Madame Gentille walked over to Bastien and handed him a pen and paper. "Now how do we prove all this?"

"*Écoutez bien*," Bastien said, ready to divulge the plan that he and his friends had finalized that very afternoon. "This is how we stop those bad brothers."

34

ALL THE WORLD COMES TO PARIS

If Bastien had asked the people of Paris a month ago, they would have said the opening day of the Exposition Universelle was dragging its heels. The citizens had been impatient for thousands of people to visit and watch their city come alive.

But now that day had finally arrived and Paris was far from ready. Despite the brilliant sunshine and clear skies, only cautious excitement rippled from neighbourhood to neighbourhood. Many of the escaped convicts from La Santé had been recaptured, but there were still dangerous criminals at large – in particular, the vile kidnapper and killer, Xavier Odieux.

Cautious excitement rippled across the orphanage

too that morning. Bastien remarked on how everyone was so quiet and focused. Clément hadn't teased Mathilde once and even Theo had only managed one *pain au chocolat* at breakfast instead of his usual three. The plan was all anyone could think of and it played on a loop in Bastien's head.

Members of the resistance group would meet at the fair at eleven o'clock and carry out their assigned tasks. At midday, President Millefois would take to the stage in front of the Eiffel Tower and give his welcome speech. But Bastien knew that was also when Olivier would storm onstage and demand to be crowned King.

They had one hour to stop that from happening, or sixty minutes as Bastien preferred to think of it – every single second of every minute mattered now more than ever.

Walking to the Exposition Universelle took twice as long as the Métro, but Madame Gentille stood firm despite protests. Although different exhibitions were scattered throughout the city, the largest part of the fair was on the Champ de Mars, a large green space between the Eiffel Tower and the École Militaire.

"The Métro will be as packed as a mackerel tin today," the director said, leading them past Montparnasse station. "If we take the train, you will know who ate eggs for breakfast."

She marched up ahead with the rest of the neighbourhood watch group and everyone else fell into line behind, as per Alain and Maarten's orders. The director's old work friends were definitely *much* bossier than her. Bastien looked over at Louis, who walked with Philippe. Louis fiddled with his trouser pocket, as though his hands were searching for something to do. Everyone was nervous, but some were better at hiding it than others.

The streets filled up the further they walked across the city. Bastien hadn't seen Paris look this busy in so long. Drivers tooted their horns at the crowds walking in the middle of the road, their frustration almost drowning out the faint melody that tickled the air.

"Do you hear that?" Theo's eyes glazed over, his fingers automatically clicking to the music. "A jazz band!"

Mathilde skipped down the pavement. "The music has already begun!"

Bastien could hear the melody, but it wasn't loud enough to drown out his own thoughts. He couldn't concentrate on anything but stopping Olivier.

"*Regardez!*" Robin squealed. "We're here!"

The taller buildings fell away and the Exposition Universelle rose up to meet them. Buildings and huge tents covered the Champ de Mars. A Ferris wheel spun slowly and, in the middle of the space, an artificial mountain surrounded by a jungle of palm trees and plants rose up. Paris was no longer just a single city; there were cities within cities, stacked inside one another like Russian nesting dolls.

"It's quite the sight, isn't it?" Madame Gentille said. "Incredible to think that this was all built to be temporary."

Bastien turned to Theo, wanting to know what his best friend made of such engineering wonders, but a sad look on Theo's face stopped him in his tracks. Theo was staring at a *Tricolore*, the French flag, flying high above a white stone minaret. Bastien recognized the minaret as the tall, thin tower that was part of the mosque – an exhibition on one of France's African colonies, Algeria.

"That flag shouldn't be flying," Theo muttered.

Bastien squeezed his best friend's hand. He could

never understand how it made Theo feel, to see his mother's home country displayed as a possession.

They hurried to the end of the entrance queue, which snaked down the boulevard and twisted around the corner.

"There are more people here than I thought," Mathilde whispered. She stood behind Bastien and Theo as the queue moved forward inch by inch and her voice sounded full of nerves. Bastien hadn't heard her sound so unsure before; was she thinking of the moment when she would come face to face with Olivier?

"Maybe people are finding their courage again after the fires and the prison break," Theo said.

"They've just trusted the wrong person to be courageous for," Bastien added, thinking of Olivier's false promises.

Finally, they arrived at the ticket counter and handed over their paper stubs. Emerging on the other side of the gate, Bastien finally understood the enormity of the fair. Everywhere he looked, people were stuck together and the crowds seemed to grow thicker in every single direction. Panic turned his skin itchy. Would the hordes of people slow them down?

He turned to Madame Gentille. "What's the time?"

She rolled up her sleeve to check her wristwatch. "Ten minutes to eleven."

"No time to waste!" Louis clapped.

Bastien nodded. "To the bandstand! The others should be there by now."

"Remember what I said," the director called. "Everyone hold onto the person in front of you. We will move through the crowds as one."

With Theo's hand resting on his shoulder, Bastien stepped into the commotion of the fair. He navigated them around tents and amusements, car displays and food stands, always keeping one eye on the Eiffel Tower in the distance. In front of the tower was the large makeshift stage. President Millefois would give his opening speech from there and Bastien wondered if Olivier and Xavier were already amongst the crowds too. If so, he and Mathilde had even less time to warn the President's security about the bad brothers' plan.

Finally, the green metal roof of the bandstand appeared above a cluster of exotic plants and trees. Bastien crossed his fingers behind his back and quickened his pace. Had everyone from last night come to help them? He knew Alice, Charlotte and Jules wouldn't let him down, but what about the others?

Bastien's worries fell away as he spotted the familiar faces of their resistance group.

Alice was talking with LeGrand, her golden hair pulled back into a tight plait. Jules and Abdou sat on the steps of the bandstand with a large leather bag at their feet, while Charlotte, Pauline and the journalists from *Le Parisien Quotidien* waved at them.

"You're all here!" Bastien sprinted the last remaining steps and skidded to a halt next to Alice.

"Where else would we be?" She grinned and gave him a hug. Bastien noticed a rolling pin sticking out of her skirt pocket. "It's for protection," she said.

"Everyone gather round!" Louis shouted. "*Non*. Not around me. Around Bastien!"

The group huddled in the middle of the bandstand and Bastien picked up the leather bag that Abdou had brought for him. It was heavy, but he lifted it with surprising ease.

"*Merci* for the help."

"It took me the whole night," Abdou said. "But I used up every last bit of paper in my shop."

"Inside this bag are the leaflets that Abdou created for us to distribute – us being our resistance group, The Paris Patrol."

Everyone cheered.

"Excellent name choice," Mathilde said.

"We sound tough." Clément grinned.

"The leaflets contain the truth about Olivier Odieux and his family," Bastien explained. "I've also written about the Red Ink Society and how Olivier and Charles Fitzmagnat are working together." Words were their best weapon against the Odieuxs' poison and Bastien hoped, with every fibre in his being, that his own would be strong enough to plant a seed of doubt into people's minds about who Olivier truly was. Because once there was a seed, it could only grow.

"Take as many leaflets as you can and distribute them as quickly as possible. We need everyone in the crowd to read this before midday." He turned to the journalists from *Le Parisien Quotidien*. "Do you have everything you need?"

The journalist at the front – a small man with bushy sideburns – nodded. "Our colleagues are on their way now with our freshly-printed special edition showing the photographs of the map with the fire targets. We will set up at this bandstand. It's the perfect location as everyone has to walk past to get to the stage."

Bastien's heart beat in time with the vibrating

thumps of the nearby sabar drums. Everything was in place. Looking at the people all around him, enjoying their beautiful city, he felt a renewed desire to protect them from Olivier. He had to do more than just make his voice heard. He had to make people *listen* to not just what he and his friends had uncovered, but also what his parents had known about the Odieux family. It fell to him and Bastien wouldn't fail now.

He opened the bag and everyone queued up in front, taking a stack of leaflets before disappearing into the crowd. "Stay safe and let's meet back here once it's – hopefully – over," he called.

Madame Gentille kissed Bastien, Theo and Mathilde on the cheek. "You stay safe, too, precious ones." She nodded at Alain, Maarten, Katharine and Edda and the five former spies walked into the crowd together to get into position.

Charlotte and Jules hugged Alice tight before leading the other boys into the crowd. Louis kissed the top of Mathilde's forehead. This time, she didn't squirm at all.

Only the four friends remained.

"Let's get into position." Alice tugged on Theo's arm. "We need to factor in at least five minutes for your meltdown about climbing."

Bastien looked towards the metal giant of the Eiffel Tower, where his two best friends were headed. Theo had spent all evening stitching a banner and, together, he and Alice would hang it from the first-floor platform where the whole crowd would clearly see its message.

Bastien stepped towards Theo with open arms.

"Don't hug me." He backed away, smiling. "It feels too final. We'll see you soon."

At the same time, Mathilde pulled Bastien away from the bandstand. "We need to get to the stage."

With a final glance, they headed off in different directions. To anyone else, the four friends would have looked like children enjoying a much-deserved day out, splitting up to visit different exhibitions and amusements. Little did the crowds know that the four friends were here to save them all.

THE FACE OF DISTRACTION

35

The closer Bastien and Mathilde got to the stage, the thicker the crowd grew. It forced Bastien to crawl under legs and squeeze through gaps between the various market stalls and tents. After battling their way through a particularly rowdy group of people dancing and singing, Bastien stopped for a moment to catch his breath. He doubled over, leaning against a flagpole.

Mathilde shimmied up the pole for a better view ahead of them. "There are stairs to the left of the stage. We can climb those and get round the back. It's not far now. Come on!"

Buoyed by her energy, Bastien pulled himself to his feet – his heart rate slower and lungs nicely replenished

– and almost fell over at the sight before him. Two figures in red cloaks had suddenly appeared in a small clearing in the crowd. Instinct took over and Bastien headed towards them.

"Where are you going?" Mathilde shouted. She lowered herself back down to the ground and ran after him, but Bastien's eyes remained fixed on the red cloaks. The figures moved strangely, stopping and starting and changing direction at a moment's notice.

Then one of the red cloaks turned sharply and the hood fell away slightly. He only saw a flicker of a face, but Bastien would have recognized Xavier Odieux's cruel smirk anywhere. He had been on the receiving end of it many times before.

"Bastien!" Mathilde pulled on his shoulder. "What are you doing? We can't get distracted. Not now!"

"It's Xavier! I don't know who the other red cloak is. It's too small to be Olivier. But we need to follow them. We can't let Xavier hurt anyone!" Bastien thought of the conversation he'd overheard at the Odieux house; how Xavier had plenty of painful methods to get past the President's security.

The red cloaks moved off again and the two friends followed, closing the gap between them.

"I'm not sure about this," Mathilde whispered. "We're wasting time. We need to warn the President about Olivier!"

"Trust me," Bastien said. "We need to know where they're going."

People in the crowd turned to look at the red cloaks, mistaking them for performers' outfits, their pleas for a show ignored completely. Only Bastien knew what evil lurked under the deep hoods.

Finally, the two red cloaks stopped outside a large circus tent nestled between two honey locust trees. Their heads turned towards each other and then they disappeared inside. A clock hanging above the tent entrance read half past eleven.

"What do we do now?" Mathilde asked. "We've only got thirty minutes!"

Instinct gave way to indecision. Bastien looked at the tent and then to the right of him, where he could see the long, golden drapes framing each side of the stage. Behind the stage the Eiffel Tower stood proudly, and Bastien squinted, as though he might see Theo and Alice climbing the tower if he looked hard enough. They were doing their part of the plan and he was supposed to be doing his, but right now all he could think about

344

was preventing Xavier from seriously hurting anyone. He'd killed Bastien's parents to stop their family secret from getting out; would Xavier do the same to anyone who stood in his and Olivier's way today?

Bastien turned to Mathilde. "We need to go inside that tent. We need to stop Xavier. Somehow."

In the short time that he had known her, Mathilde had proven herself to be fearless. She wasn't scared of much and he didn't think he could go inside the tent without her. After a moment's pause, she sighed and rolled up her sleeves. "Let's make this quick."

As they hurried towards the tent, Bastien's head told him it was the right decision.

Except, as it turned out, it was most definitely not.

36

TWO AGAINST TWO

As soon as the entrance closed behind them, Bastien felt trapped. It was only a piece of fabric separating him and Mathilde from the thousands of people outside, but there was something distinctively eerie about the place they'd just walked into. The red tent was empty apart from large wooden crates stacked in each corner.

Only it wasn't. Xavier had to be in here somewhere, along with the other red-cloaked figure. Where had they gone?

"I followed you in here." Bastien's voice echoed around the tent. "So why don't you just come out?"

Silence answered and Bastien kicked the nearest crate in anger.

"Maybe there's a secret exit they left through?" Mathilde suggested.

But Bastien was no longer listening; something on top of the crate had caught his eye. "Look at this!" He pointed to the familiar emblem of the Red Ink Society on the wooden lid. Curiosity gripped him in a chokehold, and he opened the crate to find stacks of fireworks and long thin cylinders with tubes and wires hanging out of the end.

"Are these fireworks part of the opening ceremony?" Mathilde asked.

"They can't be," Bastien said, dread turning him cold. "Why would the Red Ink Society logo be on them? Maybe Olivier is planning some sort of distraction. Whatever they're for, it can't be good."

A slow clap echoed around the tent. Bastien spun on his heels, Mathilde standing behind him, as the two red-cloaked figures emerged from the shadows.

"*Bravo,* Bastien." The taller figure lowered his hood and the beady black eyes of Xavier Odieux stared hungrily at him. "You've figured us out once again, you interfering pest. The fireworks are to celebrate our soon-to-be King Olivier. We'll set a few off in the crowd too. A little bit of mayhem never hurt anyone – much."

It took all of Bastien's courage for him not to fall to his knees. That and the fact that Mathilde had placed her hand on the small of his back to keep him steady. "You can't do that!" he shouted. "You might kill people!"

"I've been dreaming of seeing you again." Xavier ignored Bastien and took a step forward, beckoning the other figure to follow. "So many days alone in my cell, imagining the thousand different ways in which I would make you pay for ruining my life."

"Ruining *your* life?" Bastien choked down a hollow laugh. "You have no idea what it's like to have your life knocked down and destroyed each time you try to build it back up."

"Spare me the poetic prose," Xavier spat. He pulled down the hood of the figure standing next to him to reveal Georges.

"And you!" Bastien pointed at the disgraced bookseller. "How could you hurt Jules? Destroy the bookshop and Charlotte's café?"

But Georges simply shrugged, not an inch of remorse on his face. "Orders are made to be followed."

"You're pathetic," Bastien said. "You and your father deserve what's coming to you just as much as Xavier and Olivier."

"And what might that be?" Xavier crept closer and Mathilde pulled Bastien back behind the open crate.

"I know who you truly are," Bastien said. "I know the secret of the notebook. You have no royal blood flowing through your veins – you're a Durand, not an Odieux. Your whole life is a stolen identity! You and Olivier planned the fires and the prison break and we have the evidence to prove it. This ends today. There will be no King Olivier. I won't let it happen."

Bastien's words hung in the air like a never-ending note. Xavier stood silently, his face twisting with different emotions – none of them good.

"I don't know what you are talking about," Xavier said finally. "I *am* an Odieux. Always have been, always will be. And any 'evidence' you claim to have found is too little, too late. The people of this city and country are on my brother's side."

"It's never too late!" Mathilde finally stepped out from behind Bastien. Fierceness radiated from her in great waves.

Xavier cocked his head, his eyes slowly widening in recognition. "How sweet that the two of you found each other! I must admit, I thought you'd be locked up with

349

your mother in an asylum for the insane, too. Why you're the spit of her, aren't you?" He grinned and stretched out his arms. "Come and give your *cher oncle* a hug."

But Mathilde didn't even flinch. "You are no uncle of mine. You helped Olivier destroy my mother. And now, *we* will destroy *you*."

Xavier wheezed with laughter. "I doubt that! If you are as weak as your mother, then you don't stand a chance. Although Bastien, surprisingly, has more fight in him than I thought. Give us your best shot."

Georges sneered, balling his hands into neat fists. "This is the end for you both."

"You're wrong," Bastien replied calmly. He squeezed Mathilde's hand and an unspoken agreement passed through them. "Only we get to decide how our story ends."

Mathilde jumped into the crate, letting out a scream that belonged only in nightmares as she grabbed a handful of fireworks. Bastien ran head first at Xavier and Georges. He dropped to his stomach and slid under George's long cloak, rolling out behind him.

"Get them!" Xavier roared. "Don't let him escape!"

Mathilde threw the fireworks across the tent.

Although unlit, they were heavy and one hit Georges squarely on the back of the head. Xavier dodged them effortlessly, his eyes focused only on Bastien.

Bastien scrambled to his feet and climbed a stack of crates, hoping to put as much distance between himself and Xavier as possible. He climbed to the very top until his head touched the tent fabric. "Stay away from me!"

Daring to look below, Bastien saw Xavier dragging himself up each crate, like an injured spider. "There's no catacomb trap to save you now," Xavier cackled. "Or your silly little friends for backup! I'm finally ending this. I have to. For Olivier."

There was nowhere else to go for Bastien. He couldn't jump from this height. If he scrambled back down the crates, Xavier would be able to grab him. He racked his brains, thinking of how to keep Xavier at bay. What was the former orphanage director's weakness? And then it came to Bastien.

"Just how long have you done everything Olivier asks of you without question?" Bastien shouted. "Can't you think for yourself?"

Xavier paused mid-climb, his head snapping up. "Don't speak such nonsense."

"You're the one risking everything for his plan." Words flew from Bastien's mouth like a steady stream of darts. He could see Mathilde standing her ground against Georges on the other side of the tent. "You've always risked so much more. Olivier left you in a prison cell for months. Think about it. Would he ever do the same for you? Would he put his life on hold just to see you soar?"

Bastien watched his questions hit Xavier in the face like a string of punches. His expression twisted and contorted as he tried to deal with his thoughts.

Angry, desperate screams sounded in the distance somewhere.

"Olivier is the chosen ruler," Xavier said flatly. "That is the way. That has always been the way."

"It doesn't have to be," Bastien said. "It could be you."

More screams bounced through the tent, but they weren't coming from him or Mathilde. It was the same sound as before, but this time it was even closer.

"What's going on?" Xavier turned quickly. He lost his footing and slipped slightly.

The flap of the tent entrance was ripped open and in burst The Paris Patrol. Clément ran head first at

Georges, an angry Robin bouncing on top of his shoulders. Charlotte and Jules stood side by side with rolling pins in their hands. The rest of the boys followed with a flagpole that was now a battering device, and Louis and Philippe hurried behind, carrying thick coils of rope.

Bastien watched in stunned disbelief as the tent descended into chaos. Sensing his chance, he scrambled back down the crates as Louis whipped the rope in Xavier's direction.

"Louis," Xavier hissed. He batted away the rope with one hand, the other desperately trying to cling onto the side of the crate. "If you ever considered yourself a loyal Odieux, you will leave at once."

"But we're not Odieuxs, are we?" Louis shrugged. "Family traditions have never really been my thing and now I know why. So, no. I'm not running away this time. I'm staying to fight."

Bastien ran over to Charlotte and crushed her in a hug. "How did you know where to find us?"

But Jules pulled him away and towards the tent entrance before she could answer. "The President's speech will start soon! You need to get to the stage!"

Bastien didn't need to be told twice. He nodded and

sprinted from the tent, Mathilde by his side, his eyes fixed on the stage surrounded by thousands of people.

He had been given a second chance to stop Olivier Odieux and he wasn't going to waste it.

37

THE PRESIDENT'S SPEECH

A gargantuan crowd had gathered for the opening ceremony. Other tents and exhibitions had emptied and every visitor at the Exposition Universelle now walked towards the stage. The throng stretched in every direction and the sound of thousands of voices chanting, singing and heckling was unlike any noise Bastien had heard before. He tried to squeeze under legs and sneak past people, but each time he was pushed back even further than before.

"This is impossible." He turned to Mathilde. "We're never going to get to the stage in time."

The music stopped and an announcement boomed across the fair as the drapes were drawn back.

"Introducing President Millefois!"

There were some cheers and whistles from the crowd, but also loud boos and shouts of protest that somehow seemed louder than any of the support. The President walked onto the stage, but from here he was only a distant blurred figure.

"We've not come this far to give up now." Mathilde grabbed Bastien's hand and pulled him through the crowd, elbowing those who dared to stand in their path. A group of loud teenagers jostled with each other, making it difficult to pass, but Mathilde simply tapped one of them on the shoulder.

"You will move out of our way or face the consequences." Her voice was calm, but to Bastien it sounded as though she could lead an entire army.

And at her command, the group parted.

She shot vicious looks at those who tutted or moaned, and as she pulled Bastien closer to the stage, he marvelled at her strength. Mathilde possessed strength in many different ways, but the most powerful one, he thought, was that she simply didn't care what others thought about her.

Finally, they arrived at the front of the crowd. A small barrier stood between them and the stage, surrounded by security guards dressed in navy-blue uniforms. A guard spotted them and marched over, his big hand shooing them away.

"Get back!" he barked. "You're not allowed here."

Before either of them could reply, another security guard appeared beside Bastien and Theo. The guard wore a large, rounded hat that covered most of their face.

"Let them through!" the guard said, their voice hard like granite. "Special orders from the President himself!"

"*Quoi?*" The first guard scrunched up his nose at Bastien and Mathilde. "I haven't heard anything about this."

"Orders are on a need-to-know basis and you're a lower rank." The guard prodded the badge on the other guard's uniform. "Now, I won't ask again. Please stand aside."

After sighing for what felt like an eternity, the first guard crossed his arms and stepped back, clearing the path to the barrier. "I don't get told anything round here," he muttered.

The other security guard lifted their hat and Bastien spotted a smile that was missing a front tooth. "*Merci,* Katharine," he whispered.

Madame Gentille's friend winked before disappearing back into the crowd.

Bastien followed Mathilde as she jumped over the barrier and headed to the stairs at the side of the stage.

"Can you see Olivier?" Mathilde whispered.

Bastien shook his head. "Not yet. I——"

"Good afternoon, *tout le monde!*" The voice of President Millefois cut across the entire fair. "Welcome to this year's Exposition Universelle, which we are honoured to be hosting here in Paris. It is a great sadness that this incredible celebration has been tainted by the recent events in our capital and across the rest of the country."

"We need to get closer!" Bastien jumped up the next steps. He couldn't see any sign of Olivier just yet, but he had to be lurking somewhere. If Xavier and Georges were held up in the tent, was he now on his own? Or was Charles Fitzmagnat nearby?

"There are people who wish to divide us," President Millefois continued. "People like Olivier Odieux and *La Seule Voix* newspaper, who have published nothing short of propaganda this last week."

This time, the response was strangely quiet and Bastien turned back to scan the crowd. There were angry faces, some confused and worried. As he squinted to see better, Bastien saw that many people were holding something in their hands. Had they read The Paris Patrol's leaflet? And what about the new edition of *Le Parisien Quotidien*? Were people beginning to doubt everything that Olivier had told them over the last few days?

President Millefois wrung his hands together and continued his speech. "This very morning, I was made aware of widespread corruption within my government. Good people of France and beyond, you have been told that I am a weak President, who has done nothing but sit by and watch great tragedies unfold! But that is simply not true." He looked down for a moment, before returning to the microphone. "I have been working hard behind closed doors and into the early hours of every morning, all in the name of protecting every single one of you. Now I can share with you my plan for a better future. And that starts with putting a stop to O—"

A screeching sound cut through the fair. Bastien cupped his hands over his ears. The sound lasted only for a second, but when Bastien looked up again, he saw, finally, what he had been waiting for. Olivier Odieux had emerged from behind the stage drapes, his face as vicious as the sword in his hands as he held off the security guards on either side.

From the look on his face, Olivier Odieux thought he'd outsmarted them all. But in fact, he was exactly where Bastien wanted him.

38

BASTIEN REWRITES THE ENDING

Bastien ran to the top of the stairs, watching Olivier swipe the sword erratically through the air. Olivier was no longer the inspiring, calm leader he had pretended to be in his newspaper articles and at the protests. Finally, he was showing his true self: filled with chaos, the kind that fed on lies and suffering.

Mathilde pulled Bastien towards the edge of the stage. "It's a ceremonial sword, do you see? The tip isn't actually sharp at all. He's brought it to be sworn in as King."

"That's not going to happen today," Bastien said through gritted teeth. "Or any other day for that matter." He looked back at the Eiffel Tower, where he saw the figures of Theo and Alice on the first platform, preparing to drop the banner.

"*Bienvenue!*" Olivier waved to the crowd. "Many of you will recognize me, but for those guests who have joined us from afar, let me introduce myself. I am Olivier Odieux."

Cheers erupted across the crowd, but they weren't as loud as Bastien remembered at the last protest. Had the tide started to turn against Olivier?

President Millefois backed away. "How did you get up here so easily?" He looked at his security, but they were kept back with the swipes of the sword. "Leave this stage at once. You have already done enough damage."

"It is surprising that President Millefois has decided to show up." Olivier walked over to the microphone behind the podium. "Where has he been this last week when you needed him most? How many of you have counted on *La Seule Voix* to give you the answers your President cannot provide?"

Again, the crowd reaction was different: a mixture of applause, heckles and chants.

"President Millefois is unfit to protect our country." Olivier produced a scroll from his jacket pocket. "And so Pierre Niney, Head Judge at the Palais de Justice, has approved use of the Ancient Royal Decree. I wish to invoke this decree, which grants me the right to assume power during a state of emergency. This decree can only be used by a royal descendant like myself."

"That's not possible!" President Millefois replied. "You have no right." Despite the tremble in his voice, he stood strong at the front of the stage. Olivier walked closer.

"You can all feel safe and secure in the knowledge that I will rule with a strong hand," Olivier continued. "You can trust me as though a member of your own family. I will restore our beloved country to its former glory."

The crowd looked up, their eyes no longer focused on Olivier, but over the top of his head. Bastien followed their gaze up to the Eiffel Tower. Theo and Alice had released the banner from the platform.

OLIVIER ODIEUX IS LYING TO YOU!
READ OUR LEAFLET FOR THE TRUTH!
THE PARIS PATROL

"People are distracted by the banner." Mathilde nudged Bastien. "This is the moment. Go and make your voice heard! We need everyone to listen to *us*, not Olivier."

Looking out at the crowd, Bastien felt his throat start to close. He fought against the panic with everything he had. Now was not the time to let his nerves control him.

"Doesn't your new leader deserve a round of applause?" Olivier called out.

Unlike the protests over the last few weeks, the crowd was no longer roaring in agreement and hanging onto Olivier's every word. Now was the time for Bastien to speak up and put an end to the bad brothers' plan for good. Olivier thought he had the upper hand, but in fact, up there on the stage alone, Bastien was going to trap him.

Bastien took a deep breath and walked onto the stage. Olivier was turned away from him, but President Millefois watched Bastien approach, confusion in his eyes.

"Olivier doesn't care about anyone but himself!" Bastien shouted as loud as he could, hoping the breeze would carry his voice across the crowd. "He has lied to you at every step. He started the fires! He released the criminals from La Santé prison! Read our leaflet and *Le Parisien Quotidien* today. Discover the truth."

Olivier slowly turned around. "You!" He pointed the sword in Bastien's direction, anger and hate radiating from him in great waves. "Always turning up when I'm on the cusp of greatness. I thought I told you to stay away."

"You are not capable of greatness, only evil." Bastien stood his ground. "I'm not frightened. I knew you were coming here today to do this and I'm one step ahead of you."

"How?" Olivier snorted. "I'm on this stage, about to become King? Doesn't seem like you have the advantage."

"That's where you're wrong!" Bastien whistled and the security guards onstage dropped their hats to reveal familiar faces. Madame Gentille stood with her friends, Alain, Maarten and Edda. Gaston LeGrand was shoulder to shoulder with Pauline Savoir. "You are surrounded by people who know the *real* you."

Olivier flinched and arched his back. "Please excuse these childish antics." He turned back to the crowd. "No one cares what this boy has to say."

"We do!" one voice called out.

"Isn't that the Bonlivre boy?" another voice shouted.

The crowd erupted into cheers and, this time, it didn't sound all in support for Olivier.

"I am Bastien Bonlivre. And your story ends here…
Olivier Durand." Bastien squared his shoulders and
looked directly at Olivier. He wanted to see the moment
when Olivier realized his plan could never truly
succeed. The villain's face crumpled; he moved his
mouth, but no words came.

Seizing the moment, Bastien faced the crowd. He
felt braver than he'd ever imagined he could be and he
sensed his parents by his side, giving their strength to
him, as the buzz of the crowd surged through his entire
body.

Where Bastien had once hidden away and made
himself small in front of others, he now stood in front of
his city and the rest of the world. He would not step
down. He would not let his shaking knees or the wild
look on Olivier's face stop him from telling the truth.

"Olivier Odieux could never be a king," he continued,
projecting his voice loud across the crowd. "His name is
Olivier Durand and he is no nobleman. His grandfather
stole someone else's identity and pretended to be royal
his entire life. Olivier decided to continue that lie, but
my parents discovered the truth and he…" Bastien
pointed to Olivier. "He killed them for it! All because
he cares about his own desires more than he cares about

anyone else's life. But I am here to finish what my parents started. Olivier doesn't care about you and he will never be our leader."

A wail, wolfish and wild, sent a shiver up Bastien's spine. Slowly, Olivier was revealing his true self. And when a plan wasn't going Olivier's way, his anger would only get worse.

"You dare besmirch my name on this stage!" Olivier roared.

"It's not your name!"

Before he could say anything else, Olivier lunged towards him. Bastien went to move, but before Madame Gentille or any other adult could get to him, a whirling figure flew past and pushed him from harm's way.

"Stay away from Bastien!" Mathilde had twirled with such speed that Olivier didn't realize the sword was no longer in his hands; she had disarmed him in one swift movement and thrown the sword over the edge of the stage.

The immediate fury on Olivier's face softened, replaced with something like tenderness. "You look like someone I used to know."

Bastien saw how he studied Mathilde, trying to place her familiar features.

"Lucienne," Olivier said, finally. "Are you my…?"

"I'm not your anything." Mathilde bared her teeth. "And don't you *ever* speak her name again."

Olivier stared down at his hands. It was a second of hesitation, but Bastien knew the moment had arrived. He took a large breath, summoning all of the noise in the world.

"Get him!"

At the sound of Bastien's rallying cry, Madame Gentille sprang into action. Along with her friends, they surrounded Olivier. LeGrand and Pauline blocked the stage exit and President Millefois ran towards, not away, from the man who had just tried to topple him. The President was standing strong, showing that he wouldn't back down.

"Get off!" Olivier howled, his voice strangled with desperation. "People of this city! I've protected you. Now it's your turn to protect me!"

A single, piercing cry sounded from somewhere in the middle of the crowd. And another. Then the front of the crowd surged forward and they climbed over the barrier and onto the stage.

But they had not come to help save Olivier. In fact, the people of Paris had come to trap him.

"*Crook! Liar!*" The crowd mobbed him and Bastien saw Olivier sink to his knees.

"Get away from me!" Olivier screamed. "Xavier! Charles! Georges! Where are you?"

"Xavier and your new friends aren't coming to help you," Bastien said. He slowly backed away, as the crowd closed in. "It seems as though you are all alone in your hour of need. Looks like you teamed up with the wrong people."

"You should fear a man who has nothing left to lose," Olivier snarled. He was the portrait of a desperate man; his face dripped with sweat and his breath was short and sharp, like the panting of a stray dog who hadn't eaten in weeks.

Yet it surprised Bastien that he no longer felt afraid. Looking at the man who had taken his parents away and caused so much pain and heartache, he only felt pity.

"Actually, you should fear a boy who has his whole life left to live." Bastien held his hand out to Mathilde and, together, they turned their back on Olivier Odieux for good and walked away from the crowd.

It would take much more than an attempted overthrowing of the President and a stage invasion to stop the Exposition Universelle. Despite the restless energy of the crowd, the official announcement was that the fair would go on. In fact, President Millefois had insisted upon it, shortly after personally placing Olivier Odieux in handcuffs.

Bastien and Mathilde had been ushered off the stage and asked to wait under the iron legs of the Eiffel Tower. It had been more of a demand, in fact, from a burly man with a bald head who'd introduced himself as President Millefois's private bodyguard. A few minutes later, the President arrived, flanked by even more security than before.

"I cannot thank you enough for what you uncovered and how you moved so quickly to share the truth." The security officers stepped aside and President Millefois shook their hands. "You must come to the Élysée Palace. Such bravery deserves recognition."

"What will happen to Olivier?" Mathilde asked.

"He will be placed under house arrest along with his brother and Pierre Niney until my corruption investigation is complete. I cannot trust our courts and prisons after what you have all uncovered. My team are looking for Charles Fitzmagnat, as his son Georges refuses to talk." President Millefois shuddered despite the warm spring day. "I can't trust anyone but those closest to me. What you've found out about the Red Ink Society could just be the tip of the iceberg."

"But they'll never be free again, will they?" Bastien stepped towards the President, who commanded his security to step aside. "Olivier and Xavier Odieux are too dangerous."

"Not if I have anything to do with it." President Millefois cupped Bastien's hands in his. "You have my word that, for as long as I live, those brothers will never be able to hurt anyone ever again."

Bastien hoped that the President truly meant what he'd just said.

"I must be getting on, but you'll be hearing from me soon." President Millefois bowed and his security hurried him away.

Bastien turned to Mathilde. "That happened so quickly I think I must've heard wrong. Did the President just invite us to his house?"

"I think so." Mathilde looked just as bemused. "What does someone wear to the President's house?"

Bastien shrugged. "No idea."

There was a chorus of shouts and Bastien turned around to see Alice and Theo running towards them, waving their arms.

"You were incredible!" Alice threw herself at him. "I could hear you so clearly on the platform. Your voice was so powerful. I've never heard you like that before."

"The wind helped carry it, obviously." Theo grinned, nudging his best friend. "Bravo, Bastien. That was your biggest audience yet and they hung on your every word."

"You played your part perfectly too." Mathilde smiled. "The banner was a brilliant distraction."

"One of many!" Alice replied. "But what happened to Xavier and Georges?"

"Let's go to the bandstand." Bastien turned back to the hub of the fair. "I think the others will be able to answer your question better than I can."

The walk to the bandstand took twice as long as before. People stopped Bastien at every step, asking him to sign copies of The Paris Patrol leaflet, while Theo and Alice posed for photographs as "The Heroes on the Tower". Young children tugged at Mathilde's legs, asking her to teach them how to glide through the air like she'd done onstage.

When the bandstand came into view, Bastien ran towards the huddle of people standing inside.

"Here they are!" Madame Gentille clapped rather enthusiastically, and the other members of The Paris Patrol followed. The orphanage boys rushed towards the four friends and bundled on top of them.

"We did it!" Fred and Felix shouted.

"We are heroes!" Timothée punched the air.

Once he'd escaped from the bundle, Bastien looked around at all the tired but happy faces. Charlotte and Jules, LeGrand and Pauline Savoir, Madame Gentille and her friends. His family had grown even larger today and together they'd succeeded in their most impossible mission yet.

Overcome with emotion, Bastien forgot the question that had just been on the tip of his tongue. Thankfully, as all best friends possessed the magic ability to read minds, Theo had not.

"What did you do with Xavier and Georges?"

Louis, who was sitting on Philippe's knee, looked incredibly sheepish. "We may or may not have packed them both up in a crate."

"You did what?" Bastien spluttered.

Louis sighed, a devious smile pulling at his lips. "I would have loved nothing better than to put my youngest brother on the next cargo ship leaving Le Havre port."

"I'm afraid I spoiled Louis's fun." Madame Gentille raised her eyebrow. "But it's true we did pack them up until I was able to locate one of the President's security officers."

"There was no chance Xavier was escaping on our watch," Clément said.

"I drew a moustache on his face while he was tied up," Robin boasted proudly.

The last of the worry and tension that had dug its

claws into Bastien ebbed away and he burst out laughing. He scooped Robin up into a hug as the others fell about laughing too. The atmosphere crackled with energy and reminded Bastien that, after everything, they all deserved to have some fun of their own.

"We've still got the rest of the afternoon," he said. "Can we stay a little while longer?"

The boys all looked pleadingly at Madame Gentille.

"You don't need my permission." The director smiled. "After what you've done today, you can eat a hundred ice creams for all I care!"

"*Génial!*" Fred and Felix patted their stomachs.

"Could we go on the Ferris wheel?" Mathilde asked. "I've always wanted to go on one."

Bastien turned to Theo, not sure how his best friend would react to the idea of battling his fear of heights for the second time that day.

"You know what, I think I'd actually quite like that." Theo looked over at Alice, who was having a rolling-pin duel with Charlotte. "Being up high doesn't terrify me as much any more. It's not so bad when you have good company."

The young girl selling the tickets for the Ferris wheel ushered them through to the front of the queue.

"No payment necessary." She smiled.

The pods of the Ferris wheel swung ever so slightly in the breeze and as Bastien stepped inside, he held out his hand to help Theo steady himself. Alice and Mathilde sat down and squeezed in next to them.

"Keep your hands and body inside the pod!" the girl called.

"She doesn't need to tell me that," Theo muttered. He rested his head on Alice's shoulder as the wheel lurched into action.

"If you can conquer the Eiffel Tower then I think this will be easy," Alice teased.

Slowly, their pod climbed its way into the sky and the crowds of the fair soon looked like colourful specks against the green grass. The buildings and tents reminded Bastien of miniature models; the world beneath his feet didn't feel real any more. None of what he had been through felt real, but it had all happened and he had survived.

"It's incredible, isn't it?" Mathilde said, gazing out at the city.

"If you squint really hard," Bastien said, "I reckon

you could see the sea from here."

"I'll see it close up soon enough." Mathilde smiled. "I don't think Maman will quite believe it when I tell her about what happened today."

"You were incredible! You weren't afraid of Olivier."

"I didn't feel anything towards him at all," Mathilde said. "All I could think of was Maman and how she deserved so much more."

Bastien shuffled closer to Mathilde and placed an arm around her shoulders.

The wheel came to a stop when the pod was at the highest point in the sky. Bastien looked up at the clouds that felt just within his reach and laughed to himself; here he was at the edge of the sky, and he had finally done what his parents had hoped he would. Olivier was gone, his secret exposed, and the Odieux brothers would never be able to hurt Bastien or anyone he cared about ever again.

It felt like more than just a great weight lifting from Bastien's shoulders. It was a fog disappearing from his mind. It was a hole in his heart slowly stitching itself together again.

And above all, it was the start of a new chapter.

A month later…

Bastien woke up and felt an immediate flash of panic. Where was he? And why couldn't he see anything? He patted his face and quickly calmed, glad that no one else was there to tease him.

He'd fallen asleep with a book on his face. His favourite reading spot, the chaise longue at Le Chat Curieux, had proved too tempting and Bastien had drifted off, dreaming of the wonderful weekend they'd just spent with Mathilde and her maman. Madame Gentille had taken the boys and Alice on the train to Deauville and they'd passed the days throwing themselves into the cold grip of the clear, blue water, relaxing on the sand in their bathing suits, and eating as much ice cream as humanly possible. Mathilde and Lucienne Méchante had shown them around their brand-new house: a timber-framed cottage that sat just back from the sea. It was everything they'd ever dreamed of.

While Madame Gentille and Lucienne spent the evenings chatting at the kitchen table, the others camped out on the large front balcony. They'd stayed up talking and playing games all night and had demolished fifteen apple pies across Friday and Saturday. By the end of the weekend, their hearts were as full as their stomachs.

Mathilde had walked them to the train station on Sunday to say goodbye. "Come back soon," she'd said, hugging each one of them tightly. "You have to stay for summer."

Bastien had grinned. "Just try and stop us."

As the train had pulled out of the station, he'd watched Mathilde walk away from the platform, hand in hand with her maman. In that moment, Bastien had known that it would only be a matter of time until people from all over the country paid good money to watch the great Lucienne Méchante and her daughter Mathilde dance together.

The curtains of the chaise longue nook flew open and a purple cushion hit Bastien square in the face.

"*Lève-toi!*" Theo said. "We've got work to do."

"But it's so cosy." Bastien yawned, stretching his arms. "I don't want to get up."

Theo's hands fiddled behind his back. "What if I told you I have a letter from Sami?"

Bastien moved faster than he ever had in his life. "What does it say?"

"I haven't opened it yet." Theo passed him the envelope. "Read it aloud, would you?"

Dear Bastien and Theo,

I can see that you have all been busy! I had hoped that your dangerous-adventure days were over, Bastien, but it seems as though you cannot stay away from trouble. Or perhaps, trouble cannot stay away from you?

Theo – was that really you who climbed the Eiffel Tower? You've come a long way from the boy I knew who was afraid of the orphanage staircase.

"That's not true!" Theo interrupted. "I only said they were surprisingly steep."

"*Chut!* Let me finish."

I would love to be a part of The Paris Patrol, even though I am an ocean apart from you. What you're doing is bigger than just Paris. Every city in every country has problems. There is good and bad everywhere and we must shine a light on them both, in order to figure out what sort of people we should be and how we can make the world a better place.

There are many injustices happening in Morocco, most of them at the hands of France, and I want our voice to be heard too. There is much work to do, so I will write again soon.

Tell Madame Gentille, the boys and Alice that I said hello. I hope you'll come and visit me in Mogador one day, although I warn you that once you come you might never leave.

Sami

"He's joining The Paris Patrol!" Bastien grinned.

Theo beckoned him to follow. "All the more reason we should get to work now."

They stopped off in Charlotte's café to pick up a bag of chocolate truffles before walking down the street to Abdou's printing shop. Abdou had offered to turn his shop's back room into the official headquarters of The Paris Patrol. He had an old printing press that the children could use.

After the Exposition Universelle opening ceremony, Bastien, Theo, Alice and the rest of the boys had decided to continue The Paris Patrol, but instead of just being a resistance group, they would be reporters of truth. Together, they'd investigate dangerous and strange goings-on in the city as well as giving a voice to others, just like them, who wanted a chance to tell their own stories.

"Hello, boys!" Abdou looked up from his desk as they entered the printing shop. "Go on through."

Opening the door to the back room never failed to bring a smile to Bastien's face. The whir of the printing press was loud, but everyone was busy with their own tasks, unbothered by the groaning old machine. Fred, Felix and Clément sat next to each other at the long wooden table, polishing a pile of typewriters; Robin was stretched out on the purple rug, working on his illustrations for a comic strip; Timothée and Pascal were fiddling with the box camera, and Theo quickly excused himself to stop them from breaking one of his most cherished inventions.

Bastien sat down next to Alice on the sofa that LeGrand had kindly donated. The brown leather seats were slightly cracked, but they'd covered them with soft blankets and cushions that they'd found at Saint-Pierre market.

"What are you doing?"

Alice held up a piece of lined paper. "Writing our schedule. Our first newspaper will be ready to print next week, which gives us three weeks to get a start on the second."

Bastien shuddered. "Your level of organization genuinely frightens me."

"Someone has to keep you lot focused." Alice poked out her tongue.

From the pockets of his shorts, Bastien pulled out a pen and his burgundy notebook. He hadn't written in his parents' notebook since last winter, but it finally felt like the right time to put pen to this paper. He was safe, his notebook was safe and the threat of the bad brothers was finally behind him. Bastien remembered the peace he'd felt at the top of the gorge and closed his eyes, allowing it to surge through him once again.

Words were weapons when used for dangerous ideas and beliefs, just like Olivier had always done. But words didn't deserve such a bad reputation. Bastien saw them as beacons of hope that could inspire and change things for the better.

And the thing about words, he knew, was that they lasted for ever.

Bastien opened his eyes and started to write.

FIN

THE PARIS PATROL

MARDI, 15 MAI 1923

A note from the editor, Bastien Bonlivre

Welcome to the first edition of THE PARIS PATROL, a newspaper solely run by the children of this city and beyond. It is our hope that you will count on us as a trusted source of information. We promise to never lie. We will report the news, good and bad, so we can all better understand the world we live in.

Get to know us. We're here to stay.

We are recruiting new members to join, but if you are an adult you need not apply. We only need bright young minds who are looking for an opportunity to be part of something special.

If this is you, please come to Le Chat Curieux bookshop next Saturday at midday.

We look forward to meeting you.

Bastien's Glossary

A born and raised Parisian, Bastien's native language is French. For those readers curious to discover the meaning behind the French words and phrases used throughout this book, here is a useful guide.

Arrêtez ! – Stop!

Attends ! – Wait!

Bienvenue – Welcome

Cachez-vous ! – Hide!

Comment? – How?

Confiserie – Sweet shop

Dépêchez-vous – Hurry up

Dommage – Shame

Dors bien – Sleep well

Écoutez bien – Listen carefully

Félicitations – Congratulations

Fraisier – A génoise sponge cake made with cream and strawberries

Génial – Great

Goûter – Snack

Incroyable – Incredible

J'arrive ! – I'm coming!

Je ne sais pas – I don't know

Je peux ? – May I?

Le pauvre – The poor thing

Lève-toi ! – Get up

Mebruk! – Congratulations in Kabyle, Theo's mother's native language

Ma poulette – My little chicken (a term of endearment…)

Mon livre – My book

Mon petit chou – My little cabbage (another term of endearment. Yes, really!)

Oncle – Uncle

Pain perdu – Literally translated as "lost bread", this sweet treat was historically a way to reuse stale bread

Pourquoi ? – Why?

Poulet rôti – Roast chicken

Quelle bonne idée ! – What a good idea!

Qui ? – Who?

Regardez ! – Look!

Suivez-moi – Follow me

Tout le monde – Everyone

Venez manger – Come and eat

Voici – Here

Author's Note

Dear reader,

If you made it all the way to this page (*bravo et merci!*), then allow me to tell you a little more of some of my inspirations behind writing Bastien's second adventure!

I have always been interested in history, and the way in which we can learn from the past to change the future. I set *The Unexpected Tale of Bastien Bonlivre* in the 1920s and I explore more of this decade in my second story, *The Unexpected Tale of the Bad Brothers*, as well as digging further into the past... I'd love to share with you a little of what I found out during my research and how I incorporated these real-life elements into Bastien's adventures.

La Santé, where Xavier is imprisoned, is one of the most infamous prisons in France, and there have been a number of attempted escapes. In 1927, Léon Daudet, a journalist, successfully escaped when his colleague called the prison, pretending to be a government official, and ordered his release!

Madame Gentille is inspired by a real-life legend, a Belgian woman called Gabrielle Petit. Gabrielle spied for the British Secret Service during the First World War and helped to distribute a secret underground newspaper called *La Libre Belgique* while Belgium was occupied by Germany. The newspaper was an act of resistance, much like The Paris Patrol in this book.

Unfortunately, Gabrielle was betrayed. Refusing to reveal the identity of other secret agents, she paid the price with her life on 1st April 1916. A statue of Gabrielle Petit was built in 1923 and she still stands defiantly today in the Place Saint-Jean, Brussels. It is the first monument to a working-class woman in European history.

The final showdown between Bastien and Olivier takes place at the Exposition Universelle. "Exposition Universelle" means "Universal Exhibition" in English, but it is often translated as "World's fair" – and that's just what it was! It usually took place over three to six months, and was a way for many countries to, basically, show off. Countries from all over the world came together to display new technology, science and innovation.

I have taken some artistic license for my story, as there wasn't an Exposition Universelle in Paris in 1923. In fact, the most well-known fairs that took place in the

French capital were in 1889 and 1900. The Eiffel Tower was built specifically for the 1889 fair, an incredible architectural achievement. However, there was a darker side to the fair. France, along with many other Western countries, used these fairs to show their superiority and justify their behaviour towards the countries that they had colonized. Theo gets angry when he sees the French flag flying high above the Algerian pavilion, because his mother's country is being treated as a possession.

The Exposition Universelle, in all its light and darkness, made an interesting backdrop for Olivier Odieux's biggest plan yet. Olivier manipulates everything and everyone around him and, unfortunately, people like him also exist today. We live in a world where we receive lots of different information from lots of different people and places all the time, and it can be hard to know what to believe. Like Bastien, Theo, Alice and Mathilde, it is important to ask questions and challenge something if it doesn't feel right to you.

Sometimes, it can feel as though the world hasn't learned much from its previous mistakes. But in this story, I wanted to show that there is always hope and the possibility of a different future. And in the fight against bullies like Olivier Odieux, you, like Bastien and his friends, already possess the most powerful weapon: your voice. Don't be afraid to use it! Don't be afraid to get loud!

Clare Povey, May 2022

Acknowledgements

I have joined the Difficult Second Book club! It was a completely new experience writing Bastien's second adventure, while still working full-time and moving across the country. I'm incredibly grateful to everyone who supported me, so the *grandest merci* to the following people:

My brilliant agent Kirsty McLachlan for all her support. My editors Rebecca and Becky for teaching me so much about writing. I love working with both of you; here's to many more adventures.

The whole Usborne family: Sarah Stewart, Alice Moloney, Katharine Millichope, Sarah Cronin, Hannah Reardon-Steward, Kat Jovanovic (you are missed!), Christian Herisson, Arfana Islam, Lauren Robertson, Laura Lawrence, Jess Feichtlbauer, and everyone else. I feel so lucky to be one of your authors. Extra special thanks to my wonderful publicist Liz Scott who is an absolute powerhouse.

Héloïse Mab's incredible artwork has brought the world of my story to life once more. I'd also like to thank Ouissal Harize for her continued advice and support regarding Theo's Algerian Kabylie heritage.

I had the incredible fortune to visit a number of Waterstones in September 2021, when Bastien was selected as Children's Book of the Month. I met booksellers all over and even persuaded my partner to drive me from Leeds to Liverpool one Saturday, stopping at eleven Waterstones on the way! It was also his 30th birthday weekend so I owe him a cracking 31st present…

A huge thank you to brilliant booksellers: Fiona at Durham, Rachel at Warrington (thanks for the cakes!), Rhiannon at HSK, Tsam and Bronagh at Newcastle, Jo and Catherine at Derby, Claire at Deansgate, Richard at Meadowhall, LJ at Finchley Road, Melissa at Gower Street, Paul and Alicia at Doncaster, Dani at Harrogate, Dave at Bury, Alice at Preston, Terry and Hannah at Ormskirk, Elaine at Liverpool and so many more. This list is by no means exhaustive and I will never forget the kindness of every book champion I met on my travels.

The children's book blogging and author community is one of the most supportive groups of people you could ever hope to meet. Thank you to Kate Heap, Amy – Golden Books Girl, Karen, Jo Clarke, Jacqui Sydney, KC, and every other blogger, librarian or teacher who reached out to me through Twitter. Thank you to the wonderful authors who were supportive of my book from the start: Thomas Taylor, L.D. Lapinski, Jenny Pearson, Peter Bunzl, Judith Eagle, Rashmi Sirdeshpande and Christopher Edge.

The Usborne Community Partners are a friendly book army who do so much good for their community. Your support for my books and school visit skills have been so helpful to a novice author like myself!

My family and friends. For every book purchase, review, spreading the word about Bastien to anyone and everyone: thank you. I love you all.

Adam McKie is the Corinthian column that holds me up. To fall in love with your teenage crush and have it reciprocated (admittedly, a fair few years later on...) is a romcom dream that I never thought would happen in real life. But it's real. It really is.

Finally, thank you to every single reader who took the time to read my book when there is such an incredible wealth of brilliant children's books out there. Whether this is your first Bastien adventure, or you are following on from the first, I hope you enjoyed this story. As long as you keep reading, I will keep writing as quickly as my fingers allow!

Discover where Bastien's adventures
began in...

"A charming and bookish tale of friendship,
villainy and the power of stories."
Thomas Taylor, author of *Malamander*

THE UNEXPECTED TALE
of
BASTIEN
BON LIVRE

CLARE POVEY

BASTIEN BONLIVRE is a boy with a big imagination, determined to finish the story his parents started, left to him in a red notebook.

On the other side of Paris, bestselling author OLIVIER ODIEUX is struggling to complete his latest novel. Along with his villainous brothers, he is masterminding his greatest plot yet...one that will spread fear throughout the city and beyond.

What connects these two stories is a dangerous secret, a hidden mystery and an unexpected race across Paris for the truth. Can Bastien and his friends Alice, Theo and Sami be brave enough to stop Olivier stealing the ending they deserve?

"A charming and bookish tale of friendship, villainy and the power of stories."
Thomas Taylor, author of *Malamander*

Share your story of reading

THE UNEXPECTED TALE
OF THE BAD BROTHERS

 @Usborne

#BastienBonlivre